Type and Cross

Type and Cross

J. L. Delozier

WiDō Publishing
Salt Lake City • Houston

WiDō Publishing
Salt Lake City, Utah
www.widopublishing.com

This book is a work of fiction. Names, characters, places, organizations and incidents are either products of the author's imagination or are used fictitiously. Any resemblance to actual persons, living or dead, events or organizations is entirely coincidental.

Cover Design by Steven Novak
Book design by Marny K. Parkin

ISBN: 978-1-937178-74-1
Library of Congress Control Number available on request

Printed in the United States of America

For my grandfather, Anthony Portanova,
who never learned to "talk"
yet taught me everything good about this world

Chapter One

The Terrorist

August 1st, 2016
Brooklyn, New York

Three weeks into the plague, and I can smell who is going to die. Baine passed them by as he walked down his city street, watching them scurry about like mice in an urban cage. They did their outdoor business as quickly as they could, wearing surgical masks over their mouths in a futile and ignorant attempt to ward off an infection they knew nothing about.

Plague. Such an old-fashioned word. "Pandemic" was the preferred term these days, but he found it too cold a word. Plague resonated better. It instilled immediate fear, as if people could somehow remember, in the dark recesses of their subconscious minds, the Black Death of medieval Europe. *Yersinia pestis.* The bubonic plague. Two hundred million people dead. *I can do better, much better. I'm an overachiever.* The thought amused him, and he smiled, his unmasked face frightening the woman walking by him. She ducked her head and quickened her pace.

The car at the red light had its windows up, of course, but its radio blared through the thin glass. *Goodbye to youuu,* the pop star wailed. The unintentional irony of the words amused him further, and he paused to watch the brightly colored notes bounce off the windshield and onto the ground, where they swirled into psychedelic puddles that caused him a twinge of vertiginous nausea.

"Blink hard and swallow." He heard his father's voice instructing him. His father understood, because he had to blink hard too. They shared many things, but primary among them was this genetic fusion of the senses, this uncomfortable over-stimulation by the normal rhythms of life.

Baine could still taste the music as he unlocked the door to his apartment, his sanctuary. The blank grey walls were a welcome relief after the frenzy of Shanghai and the squalor of the Mumbai slums. He dropped his luggage on the floor and felt his shoulders relax. His job was done, and things were going exactly as planned. He never doubted they would.

Chapter Two

The Psychologist

August 15th, 2016
Atlanta, Georgia

Seph waited, hands folded and resting in her lap, while the new director of the Centers for Disease Control's Special Pathogens Unit reviewed her file. It was amusing, really, that in the midst of an international crisis he was taking the time to read her references and peruse her sample profiles. After all, they'd both been vetted by the federal government at one point—albeit by very different agencies.

Seph had resigned her job as a psychologist for the Department of Veterans Affairs many years ago now; but judging from the thickness of her file, it appeared the government had chosen to record everything from her DNA sequence to how well done she preferred her steak. The bulk of the information was likely gathered more recently, though, when she first applied for her current position as an independent contractor for the FBI. She helped the agency solve their most difficult and unusual cases, the ones their own criminal psychologists could not. She had exchanged her personal privacy for a top level security clearance about ten years ago, and she had yet to regret that decision. Someday, perhaps, she would.

The director flipped through her file page by page, exhibiting a complete lack of facial expression other than the occasional furrowing of his brow or adjustment of his tortoise-rimmed reading glasses. Seph fidgeted in her chair. At least he was being thorough. She felt a little sorry for him, actually. The Ebola debacle had cost the last director his job and now "Director Samuel Blanchard," as his gold name plate read, was under an enormous amount of pressure to mop up the mess. First that, now this. No wonder he was proceeding with such caution.

"Dr. Seph Smith—is that a typo on your resume? Shouldn't it be Steph?" His voice was silky smooth but rippled with condescending undertones, as if he were pointing out a humorous mistake to a simple child.

"Seph is correct. It's short for 'Persephone.' My mother was a big fan of Greek and Roman mythology. She also thought it counteracted the banality of 'Smith.'" The director returned her smile with a bemused stare. He either didn't know the story of Persephone, or he had no idea what "banality" meant. Seph opened her mouth to give a brief synopsis of the myth but thought better of it and shut it again. He clearly didn't give a rat's ass anyway. The sympathy she had felt for him earlier was fading fast.

The director turned his attention back to her file. Seph surveyed his office while she waited and, more out of habit than any actual interest, started forming his profile in her mind. Her eyes roamed over the *objets d'art* perched just so on cherry bookshelves, the high-grade leather sofa pushed against the wall, the awards and commendations situated in conspicuous locations around the room, and the pictures of him shaking hands with various famous and important people hanging on the walls. A smattering of family photographs—a too young, blinged-out trophy wife, a perfect toddler clad head to toe in Baby Gap—had been thrown into the mix to add just the right touch of humility. The furniture smelled new, but the prevailing stench was that of old money.

Seph closed her eyes to let the pieces of his profile come together and reopened them when a clear image emerged. He was an asshole, for sure. The type to go home, slug down a gin and tonic, smack his wife, kick the custom bred Cavalier poodle and spend his evening watching Internet porn. She was in for a fun ride; she could feel it already.

Director Blanchard pulled one paper out of the stack for closer inspection. "Says here under 'special qualifications' that you exhibit 'enhanced empathy.'" He looked up and raised an eyebrow. "Care to explain?"

"I have the ability to sense exactly what others are feeling, sometimes even feel what they feel, and I use that ability to solve past crimes and predict future actions. I know who and what they are on a profound level." *Asshole.*

"Sounds like a bunch of psycho-bullshit to me." His affect remained smooth despite the confrontational nature of his words.

"Maybe." Seph shrugged. She'd experienced that same response a million times before, starting in her early teens. "But it sure helps with the job."

They stared each other down. The director blinked first. He picked up her file and shuffled through the remaining stack of papers, as if he were bored with the whole affair. He paused when he reached her grad school psychology thesis.

Ancient history at this point, but he appeared to find it interesting. Or confusing. She couldn't tell which. He had that blank-stare thing down pat, probably from attending too many boring meetings. The ability to fake intellectual interest was a critical skill for government bureaucrats, and those who lasted learned it posthaste. Seph suspected he could be quite suave when the situation required him to be. Today was not that day.

He started to read aloud. "'How do you probe the depths of another's soul? Some people just seem to know, to have a gift that reveals to them the exquisite nuances of another's character. They take delight in the scarce number of individuals whose complex souls have beautiful colors and hidden shadows in the murkiness of their depths, while despairing over the vast majority who are as one dimensional as the flat TV screens in front of which they decay. But while entertaining to the profiler, those complex souls labor under one universal, defining characteristic. On some level, they all suffer.'"

The blank stare was gone. He pushed himself back in his chair and all but rolled his eyes. Seph could hardly blame him. She had been far too full of herself in her early academic years, before her work in the field alongside many a plain-spoken detective cured her of her verbosity and replaced it with a simpler, much more colorful patois.

"Look, let's just cut the crap," he said, tossing her file onto his cluttered desk. "We've got the start of a man-made pandemic with catastrophic potential on our hands. My people are doing everything they can to figure out what the hell is going on. Right now, we don't even know whether we have a snowball's chance in hell of containing it, much less of shutting it down completely. Meanwhile, the woo-woos in Washington are sending me people like you . . . to do what, exactly? Dazzle me with your academic bullshit and nab us a terrorist by cozying up to his 'complex soul'?"

The director leaned forward in his chair for emphasis. "You serve no purpose here. As far as I'm concerned, the manhunt should be left to Homeland Security. My people here at the CDC are scientists, not law enforcement." He jabbed a finger in her direction. "I don't have time to babysit you. Am I making myself clear?"

The gloves were off. Seph always found it particularly gratifying when one of her profiles was proven to be on target so quickly. "Why do you assume the terrorist is a male?" she replied.

He blinked in surprise. "Aren't they usually? Either way, that's not my problem. My job is to limit the damage." The director stood and rounded the corner of his desk to hover over Seph. "If you want to tag along and see what you can discover, I'll take you to command central. You'll have access to our files and the research team. The rest is up to you. You will not have any specific resources allocated from my department."

That's government-speak for "stay the hell out of my way." Seph rose to follow the director out of his office. Fine. It's not like she hadn't been in this position before, although she had to admit, the potential body count in this case was exponentially higher.

Chapter Three

The Team

Command Central turned out to be an outdated basement conference room that reeked of stale coffee and magic markers. There were roughly twenty people in the room when Seph walked in: some in white lab coats, a few in buttoned-up suits and ties, and still others sporting the rumpled khaki look that suggested that they hadn't slept for days. She liked the rumpled khaki types best. They tended to be the hardest workers, the ones to make things happen instead of pontificating endlessly like the suits.

The team didn't seem to notice as she and the director entered the room. They were all hunched over a conference phone with papers scattered around it, and the tension was palpable.

"What's the latest?" Director Blanchard asked with a scowl as he and Seph approached the table. Twenty heads shot up nearly in unison, but no one said a word. The humming from the overhead fluorescent lights grew oppressively loud in the otherwise silent room. Finally, one of the pasty white coats stepped forward, cleared his throat and began to speak.

"We've identified that the contagion is definitely a virus. And we believe it's spread via blood as opposed to respiratory secretions, although we're not one hundred percent certain of that. We have yet to figure out the vector. And," he added with a nervous twitch of his face, "Washington wants hourly updates." More silence. Another twitch. One of the suits shuffled his feet. The white coat next to him tortured a paper clip, contorting it into abstract shapes, which she then used to gouge at her manicure, scraping the polish into bright red slivers that floated to the floor.

"So what you're really telling me is that you don't know jack shit," the director said.

One of the rumpled khakis smoothly intervened, much to the relief of the martyred scientist, who took several steps backward in an attempt to blend in with his white-coated colleagues.

"Let's recap what we do know—for the new members. Hi, I'm Eric Dietz, the epidemiologist and biostatistician of this cheery little coffee klatch," the rumpled khaki scientist said, extending one hand toward Seph and brushing an errant lock of curly greying hair off his forehead with the other. "We heard you were joining us. Welcome aboard."

"Thank you," said Seph. She was grateful for his welcoming smile—the first she'd received all day. Eric appeared to be a calm and studious sort and just old enough to be a steadying influence. He was precisely what this team needed. Seph mentally placed him on her list of "go-to" people for this investigation before adding, "I'm ready for that recap. I only know what the FBI told me when they gave me this assignment."

Seph pulled a file out of her briefcase and skimmed through her notes. "The world's most populous city has been attacked by a biological weapon, which is not exactly my area of expertise. I was asked to get involved because the FBI believes the perpetrator is an individual as opposed to one of the terrorist cells known to possess such weapons. The causative agent appears to be self-replicating, meaning it's spreading on its own . . ." Seph paused and looked up at the group of scientists. "I guess you didn't need me to explain that to you," she said with a wry grin. "Anyway, the agency is concerned about the illness hitting American soil. They want me to help find the individual behind the attack and determine his motives."

Eric nodded. "I don't believe the person behind it is a run-of-the mill bioterrorist, if any such thing exists. Most attacks use known biological agents—anthrax, for example. This guy created his own, which takes brilliance, arrogance and an ability to think outside the box. It's a 'designer virus,' for lack of a better term: very specifically and technically built, gene by gene, to create the situation we are now facing."

Eric put on his reading glasses, grabbed a marker and prepared to jot pertinent details on the dry-erase board as he spoke. Next to it was a bulletin board upon which brightly colored graphs, scribbled notes and some rather graphic pictures of the dead and dying were posted. Seph stepped closer to inspect the details.

Most of the people in the pictures were Asian and all appeared to have hemorrhaged to death, some of them from multiple body orifices. Huge purple blotches covered the visible skin, and their noses and mouths were crusted with blood. Even their eyes were red. Some of the photos captured the victims frozen in a stiff arch, as if they had died during the throes of a massive seizure.

Luckily, Seph was hard to shake. She flashed back to older photos taken during another horrific outbreak situation years before, while she was still working for the Department of Veterans Affairs as a medical psychologist. That outbreak had been a much more contained situation and located solely within a single federal medical shelter during a devastating hurricane; but it had been a bloody mess, and she was lucky to have survived. Her assignment then had been to provide emotional and psychological support to the evacuees despite the chaos swirling around them. Now Seph's job description was very different, but that prior traumatic experience had helped to not only strip her of her religion but harden her into the criminal psychologist she was today.

She was aware of both the director and Eric surreptitiously watching her face, so she remained carefully neutral, blasé even, until they appeared satisfied. She'd passed their test. Eric resumed speaking.

"We know the illness started in Shanghai three weeks ago and spread rapidly throughout the city. The victims die within seventy-two hours of falling ill, and thus far the pathogen has had a one hundred percent mortality rate. If you catch the virus, you die. The fact that the victims die so quickly suggests, at least in theory, that they should have only a narrow window of time in which to spread the disease. Therefore, the outbreak should be contained within their local area. However, the illness started showing up all over China, and, within a seven-day time span, new cases popped up in the slums of Mumbai, three thousand miles away." Eric paused to see if Seph was still following him. She gave him a slight nod, and he continued on.

"Up to that point we hadn't realized what we were seeing was a novel virus, much less an act of terrorism. We assumed it was a variant of one of the known respiratory or hemorrhagic viruses such as SARS or Ebola. But—and this was the key to realizing that this thing is man-made—it doesn't follow the standard rules for transmission, especially with close contacts. Sometimes family members get sick, and sometimes they don't." Seph struggled to understand the significance of that last detail. Her confusion must have shown on her face, because Eric clarified further.

"How the virus chooses its victims seems somewhat random. Also, there have been no sick domestic animals. Typically, chickens or pigs are the vector—the source for spreading the infection. They get sick first and then spread it to their human caretakers."

"Like in the swine or avian flu," Seph said. She interjected mostly to slow Eric down so her brain would have time to catch up to the fountain of facts spewing from his mouth.

"Exactly. What typically occurs in situations that progress beyond a localized region is the virus mutates and learns to spread from human to human, usually via respiratory droplets from coughs and sneezes. That's the basic formula for an epidemic. But this illness acts more like the reaction a patient would get from a mismatched blood transfusion, with a massive activation of the immune and blood clotting systems resulting in shock, circulatory collapse, and finally death. Cough is a minor symptom and when it does occur it's late, when the victim's lungs fill up with blood. The victims essentially drown in their own blood, if they don't bleed to death first."

The director coughed and fiddled with his gold watch. One of the white coats dropped into a chair and began shredding his empty cup into thin rings of coffee-scented Styrofoam. Eric ignored the impact of his words on his boss and colleagues and plowed forward, keeping his tone as matter-of-fact as possible.

"Health organizations around the world started to take notice when the disease appeared in India—simultaneous outbreaks of the same illness in two widely separated geographic areas like that is unusual. The last time I recall something even remotely similar happening was in 2002, when I investigated a simultaneous outbreak of the same strain of SARS in Hong Kong and Toronto. As it turned out, that situation was caused by a single infected person who'd traveled back and forth between the two cities for a wedding. So when this showed up in India a week after appearing in Shanghai, alarms started sounding that perhaps we had a disease which wasn't spreading naturally. Then . . ." Eric paused for only the second time in the last several minutes. ". . . then we got the letter."

"The letter" was a thirteen-page outline of the author's murderous intent. Although it stopped short of revealing the entire plan, it contained enough explicit scientific detail that its authenticity was all but assured. This message was the primary reason Seph had been asked to lend her expertise.

"Have you seen the actual document yet?" he asked. Seph shook her head no. "Then you'll need to read it yourself, obviously, and dissect it using whatever system it is that allows you to work your profiling magic," Eric said with a faint smile. "But just to give you a taste, I have a copy right here." He pulled a file off the conference table, removed a neatly stapled stack of papers and flipped through until he found a section to his liking. He read the passage aloud.

"'In time, the world will come to know me as its savior, the one who culled the human herd to sustainable levels, who rebalanced the earth and advanced the human genome. China and India are just the beginning. Soon the City of Angels will meet my masterful creation, and from there, the bloat will be further reduced by half. Chaos and pestilence lie ahead, but those who survive will experience a brilliant new world built in my image.'"

Eric grimaced as he returned the letter to its folder. "You get the point. Nice guy and only a wee bit full of himself. What I don't understand is, why bother sharing details? Why give us the heads up, the chance to catch him and the opportunity to contain or even cure the virus before he achieves his goal of offing half the world's population? What's his angle? The whole setup doesn't make sense. He'd have a lot better chance of success if he'd kept his mouth shut."

Seph suspected these last few questions were the reason Eric hadn't slept in a couple of days. Even though he was surrounded by pictures of the pathogen's horrific effect on the human body, it wasn't the virus that was bothering him. It was the master plan. She agreed. She'd studied enough antisocial, narcissistic psychopaths to know that they always have a master plan, and it was usually an unpleasant one. These images were just the harbingers of something much larger and uglier to come.

Director Blanchard was still standing next to the conference table, listening to Eric's summary with a scowl on his face and his arms crossed over his chest. "So that's what you want me to tell Washington? 'Good news! We've identified the virus. We might even name it after you, Mr. President. The bad news is that it's going to kill three billion people before we figure out what we're supposed to do about it.' I need something more than that, people. You're supposed to be the best in your fields. Start producing like it." He barreled out of the room in a huff, presumably to transform back into some semblance of a blank-faced bureaucrat before talking to the President and the press.

"Well, we do know more than we did before the letter," said a white coat whom Seph had not yet met. He was young and fresh, probably interning under one of the more established researchers. Cute, too. Seph beamed him what she hoped was a sophisticated yet mysterious smile. Now was hardly the time to notice such things, but, hey, even self-possessed psychologists suffered from hormones. And "Dr. Daniel Laird, Department of Immunovirology," as his name tag read, was certainly attractive, albeit in a nerdy sort of way. Seph hoped he wouldn't ruin her immediate impression of him when he opened his mouth. Most men did.

Dr. Laird continued trying to inject some life into what was now a deflated room of people. "We know his basic intent. We know the virus can't spread well on its own, because he said he personally released it into at least three cities. If it were highly contagious, he wouldn't have had to— it would have spread all by itself. This implies whatever vector he is using doesn't travel far or fast, which argues against birds, and it definitely rules out human-to-human transmission. It also means he has to have created a vaccine or a cure at the same time he made the virus, because he doesn't appear concerned about catching his own creation even though he's spreading the pathogen himself. That's a crucial point, because it means if we catch the creator, we catch the cure, too. I think that's a good place to start."

Seph found the latter point most interesting. Surely there couldn't be more than a few dozen people in the world possessing the in-depth knowledge required to engineer and disseminate this kind of designer virus. The inner circles of such scientists were as cliquish as a group of high school cheerleaders. Someone in that clique must have a suspicion about one of his peers that he'd be willing to share.

"I'd like to have a copy of the letter, Eric, if I could," she said, "and I agree with you, Dr. Laird. We know a lot more than we did. Do you think you could get me a list of contacts at the major research centers capable of producing novel viruses? I'd like to start making some calls."

"Absolutely," he replied. "And please, call me Dan. We're all working toward the same goal here, so I think egos and titles should get parked at the door."

Dan was definitely on her go-to list.

"One more thing," said a thin, frail voice from the far back of the conference room. An elderly Asian male in a white lab coat with the words "Department of Hematology" embroidered on the front pocket shuffled forward and bowed slightly at Seph.

"Yes, Dr. Lee?" said Eric.

"I need to respectfully correct one thing, Dr. Dietz. You stated there have been no reports of any sick animals. As many of you know, I am from China, and I still have family there. My nephew is a zoologist at the Shanghai Zoo. He emailed me this morning to report that many of the zoo's chimpanzees and gorillas are sick, and some have died. However, the zoologists haven't found any dead or ill wild primates. That is unusual, because most new viruses start in wild primates first and then jump to humans from there. The captive gorillas are dying in the exact same way as the human victims, yet there has been no evidence of an infected human having been involved in their care. Something else appears to be transmitting the infection, something capable of getting through the bars and into the cages. Our vector is obviously quite small. I thought this information might be important."

Eric had a thoughtful look on his face, as if he were taking puzzle pieces and rotating them around in his mind. "I think it might be, Dr. Lee. We could be dealing with an insect vector, like the mosquitoes that carry malaria, although this still wouldn't explain why only very specific people—or individual gorillas, for that matter—are falling ill while other are not. Primates and humans share certain infectious diseases. HIV is the classic example. There may be others, but I'm certainly no expert on apes. We need to involve someone who is—someone who can help us determine if a biologic connection exists. I know just the right scientist. Dr. Paulson's a rock star in the world of primatology, and if I can reach her, I'm sure she'll be able to connect the dots and get us moving in the proper direction. We'll meet back here at two o'clock for an update."

Chapter Four

The Type

By two o'clock, Eric had not only contacted the country's preeminent primatologist but scheduled a video conference with her as well. The high definition VTel equipment took up one whole wall of the conference room and floated like a black, ultra-modern sculpture against the bland, beige wallpaper.

At precisely 2:15 p.m. Dr. Hannah Paulson's face appeared on the giant screen, her friendly smile and motherly countenance injecting some much-needed warmth into the sterile room. She was not the diva Seph was expecting from Eric's description. In fact, Paulson seemed as pleased as a cat in a patch of catnip to be asked to join such a prestigious group of scientists as an expert consultant.

"Thank you for joining us on such short notice, Dr. Paulson," Eric said. "I know you've been briefed about the dying apes in China and how it may relate to the human deaths across the globe. What we need from you is some input about the commonalities between the two species with specific regard to infectious diseases. Biologically, what do the apes and humans have in common?"

"A lot," said Dr. Paulson. "After all, we are essentially their evolutionary children. We're similar neurologically, psychosocially and, particularly, hematologically. The virus seems to be attacking the apes' blood cells, as opposed to targeting a particular organ. The red blood cells are actually disintegrating, or hemolyzing, to use the proper scientific term. The apes bleed to death internally, which, from what I've heard, is also what's occurring in the human victims."

Dr. Paulson continued her verbal dissertation, moving to a discussion of the neurologic similarities, but Eric had stopped listening. He stood motionless, head bent, staring at the conference table as if it were the most fascinating object in the universe.

"They share our hematologic system." He murmured to himself. It wasn't a query, but Dr. Paulson responded anyway.

"Yes. As a matter of fact, they even have the same blood types we do. They are the only animal that does."

Eric's head jerked up. Seph's skin prickled as an electric current ran through the room. Everyone—Seph, the white coats and the rumpled khakis alike—registered the same thought at the exact same moment. It was the blood type. Of course it was. The truth seemed so evident now. The virus targeted the blood type.

Dr. Lee asked the obvious question. "Dr. Paulson, do you know what the dead animals' ABO blood types were?"

"Um, yes, I have it here somewhere." She rifled through her papers. "O. That's odd. They were all type O. All thirteen of them."

"Forty-five percent of the world's seven billion people are type O," Eric said. He didn't have to explain the non sequitur. Everyone in the room knew exactly what he meant.

✛

The next several days were a blur of activity. Seph studied the letter, looking for clues as to the author's identity and whereabouts. Eric's job, as the team's epidemiologist, was to confirm that all the human victims had indeed been type O. Dan, Dr. Lee, and the other scientists had the more difficult task of attempting to identify the exact mechanism by which the virus recognized and attached to the type O blood cells, thus triggering the hemolysis. Once that mechanism was determined, a vaccine, or at least a treatment, could be developed. In theory.

Despite the director's best efforts, it didn't take long for the information regarding the connection between the infection and a person's blood type to filter to the media, and from there, into the public sector. A worried phone call here, an errant text there, and the leak soon became a torrential flood. The web spewed reports out of Asia and the Far East as panicked type O's, certain of their imminent demise, took their own lives instead of waiting for the virus to do it for them. The suicide rate exploded. People squandered pensions and quit jobs. In the absence of long-term ramifications, deferred gratification gave way to criminal indulgence. Every whim was fair game.

The Western hemisphere watched and waited, clinging tightly to its faith in the scientific method. Seph and her team did their part, burying themselves in their research, gathering together several times a day for briefings and doing their best to ignore the blaring media. With type O's making up nearly half of the population, every family had someone to potentially mourn, and their team was not exempt. Despite their attempts to pretend otherwise, they knew no one would escape unscathed. If they weren't type O themselves, someone at home most probably was.

Seph's suffering was compounded twenty-fold as she absorbed their fears and added them to her own. Through snippets of conversation, she learned who was at risk—Dr. Lee's wife, Eric's son—and their images lurked in the back of her brain, stabbing at her as she tried to concentrate on her work. Trying to save millions of nameless, faceless people was one thing; but trying to focus with that familiar face, that known entity, smack dab in her line of vision was nearly impossible.

For Seph, the face was that of her sister.

She and Grace were only a year apart and had always been close. Seph knew she and their father had type A blood, while Grace and their deceased mother had type O. Seph was grateful her mother wasn't around to live through this. Her mom, ever the stoic, wouldn't have given a crap about her own type O status, but worrying about Grace would've killed her outright.

As for their father, Seph hadn't thought much about him over the years. He'd run off shortly after she was born, leaving her mother to fend for herself and her two infant daughters. Ironically, Seph now knew she and her father had one very important thing in common, something she could thank him for. They were both going to survive this plague, whereas Grace might not.

Her phone vibrated, indicating a text from one of the team members. She picked it up and grimaced. She had a picture of Grace and her nieces as her smartphone's screen saver and background wallpaper, and the constant reminder was not helping her ability to concentrate. She should just call her and get it over with.

Seph started to dial her sister's number, but paused midway through, trying to imagine how the conversation might sound.

"Have you seen the news lately?"

"What—you think I live under a rock, or somethin'?"

"Well, I know you're busy with the farm and the girls and such. Um, about the girls. Do you happen to know their blood types?"

"Seph, give me a break, okay? Just tell me what you've got."

And *that* was the crux of the problem. Seph wanted to have something encouraging, maybe even reassuring, to say. She had nothing.

Even though she was the younger of the two, Seph had always been the "fixer" in her family, the one to smooth over the bumps, soothe the ruffled feathers and generally enable the family to churn along despite how little they had to work with—not poor, but "disadvantaged," as her mother used to say. Grace would be looking to her to fix this, and Seph couldn't bear to tell her that this time she might not be able to work her usual magic. Right now, in the face of global devastation, Seph's usual "Don't worry, Sis. I'll take care of it" would sound a little thin. Grace would see right through it. Seph, the empath, could read anyone, but only Grace could read Seph. She'd been doing an expert job of it since they were in diapers.

Seph cancelled the call and adjusted the settings on her phone, removing Grace's picture from her screen. The virus hadn't reached the East Coast yet. She still had some time. She would call Grace once she was done analyzing the letter and contacting the names on the list that Dan had given her. Maybe she would have something better to say at that point. She had to.

Chapter Five

The Letter

Seph buried her thoughts in the letter, dissecting each word and teasing out every nuance she could find. A picture was emerging, but the image was still unfocused, and the blurriness caused her head to ache. She was stuck in a tiny, windowless basement office in the same ancient research building that housed command central. The old HVAC system was clearly not capable of keeping up with the oppressive late August Atlanta heat and humidity, and the room's closeness contributed to her pounding headache.

When she couldn't stand to read another sentence of the perpetrator's egomaniacal blathering, she'd call one of the contacts on the list Dan had given her. She had already reviewed their profiles and was satisfied that the terrorist was not among them. So far, nothing. Not a single lead. No one reported any unsavory characters, and there had been no noted suspicious activities. It didn't sound like anyone so much as farted out of turn in the white coats' prissy little corner of the world.

Seph winced at her own snarkiness. It was excessive, even for her, but she was so frustrated. She hated to admit it, but she felt as if she had to prove herself to her team, especially the hard core research scientists. In past experiences, she had found that many of them considered psychology to be a "soft science," not worthy of the long white coat or the prestige of the letters "PhD." She also knew that in any other circumstance, where the stakes weren't so high, the director would love to see her fail—and fail spectacularly, at that.

As a profiler with almost ten years under her belt, Seph had faced these biases before, and they'd never bothered her. In fact, they'd often yielded moments of great pleasure. First she'd solve a seemingly impossible case, much to the chagrin of the assigned detective. Then she'd tell said detective to shove his soft science rhetoric completely up his ass. It might not have earned her any friends, but it sure felt good, and it hadn't stopped the referrals from rolling in.

With this situation, however, there was no pleasure involved. She felt the pressure too acutely—"performance anxiety" they would label it in the psychology literature. She sighed in self-disgust. There was no time to feel sorry for herself. She had to keep plugging along. Seph tugged at the back of her damp shirt, separating it from the sweat rolling down her spine and picked up the phone to call the next name on her list—Dr. Chauncey Eggert at Harvard. She rolled her eyes and launched into the same spiel she'd given a dozen other times in the last four hours. Only this time, she got a hit.

Dr. Egghead turned out to have some interesting things to say about one of his former lab fellows, a man by the name of Bill Baine. Not that he really wanted to. By the time he got done hemming and hawing around the point, Seph firmly believed in the existence of a Mafia-type code of silence within the scientific community. Luckily, she was trained to hear what he was trying so hard not to say.

"Not that I'm saying he was evil or a criminal or anything like that. He was just, you know . . . odd. Very arrogant for a fellow. Always staring off into space like he could see things that weren't there, things I sure couldn't see. Weird. He practically lived in the lab. Didn't seem to have any friends or social life. Something was just not quite right about him."

If she had a dollar for every time she'd heard *that* before, she'd be retired and lounging in a hammock on some tropical island that sold umbrella drinks around every grass-thatched corner. Still, Seph felt she was truly on to something. At least this was a lead, the first real one she'd had.

She'd learned through the years to tune into the phrase "something's just not right about him/her." It never boded well, and she didn't understand why people didn't pay more attention to these oddities within their communities. Sure, there is odd as in harmless, but then there is "cannibalize grandma" odd, such as in a recent case she'd had in Vermont. In that situation, the locals were quick to point out how polite the twenty-something-year-old killer was when they ran into him at the post office, but they'd glossed over his permanently pulled window shades, lack of employment, and the fact that he liked to volunteer tons of hours at the local senior center. Not to mention the very apparent and undeniably funky smell emanating from his garage.

These red flags on his profile had been so obvious to her that she found it hard to believe no one else had noticed anything amiss. Her peers insisted it was her empathic "gift" which allowed her to somehow see such things others could not. But Seph rejected the uncomfortable notion that she was in any way unique. She didn't want to be different.

Instead, she preferred to believe that attention to detail was a learned skill open to anyone willing to make the effort. Instinct, on the other hand, was inherent, ubiquitous, and totally ignored by most people, for reasons she would never understand. This flagrant disregard usually came back to bite them in the ass, like when it was *their* grandmother who ended up being lunch.

She stood and stretched, then turned her attention away from the letter and the phone calls to focus instead on conducting an Internet search from her laptop. With the information she'd extracted from Dr. Egghead, it didn't take her long to find Dr. William Baine online. Thanks to an apparent lack of interest in any form of social media, his personal life remained obscure, but he had been published in enough scientific magazines that she was able to cobble together some basic details about his educational and professional history to share with the team. A degree in genetics from University of North Carolina at Chapel Hill. A PhD in virology from Harvard by the tender age of twenty-five. One journal article posted a brief bio with a small, black and white picture, which Seph studied with interest. Crossed arms and haughty countenance? Check. Supercilious smirk? Check. As far as Seph was concerned, the picture was a mug shot. For the first time in a while, she was looking forward to the next briefing.

Chapter Six

The Vector

Command central was abuzz with activity when she walked in. Eric and Dan were staring at some new photographs posted on the bulletin board. Dan turned and smiled as Seph approached. "New cases, I'm afraid. They're popping up in different cities, too. So far, we've got confirmed cases in Vegas, Denver and Des Moines. They're following an obvious pattern of eastward migration."

"Not just eastward," said Eric as he pulled out a map of the US. "Interstate Route 80 eastward. All the cities are off Route 80, which means that he's driving from Los Angeles and somehow directly inoculating those cities with the virus. What's also interesting is that most of the initial victims are of lower socioeconomic status—homeless or in shelters—the poor, the unemployed. There doesn't seem to be an age or sex predilection, but the income factor is clearly present."

"So what's the significance of that?" Dan asked. He sounded peeved, and Seph suspected it was because he hadn't figured out the Route 80 detail on his own.

"I'm not sure," Eric said. Something appeared to catch his eye, and he leaned forward to more closely examine the graphic photographs on the wall. He began rocking side to side and muttering in a singsong fashion under his breath.

Finally, he started to sing. "Ring around the rosy, pocket full of posies, ashes, ashes, we all fall down."

Seph glanced at Dan, and Dan raised one eyebrow in response. "Okay, Eric," said Dan, now more befuddled than irritated. "You lost me. Do you mind sharing?"

The latest photos from India were distinctly different from the first set out of China. In those, the victims were photographed in their homes or in the hospital wards at the time of death. They were fully clothed, with just their faces and extremities visible to the lens. In these more recent photographs, the victims were at autopsy, lying naked on stainless steel slabs with their pestilence hanging out for the world to see. Most were covered from head to toe with a purpuric circular rash, made from blood collecting under the skin and in the lymphatic system. It colored them various shades of red, purple and black, obscuring any semblance of normal human skin. Some had grotesquely swollen lymph glands in their neck and groin areas. All of them had blood crusted mouths and red eyes.

"There's a theory that the children's nursery rhyme is actually about the bubonic plague. The word 'bubo' refers to swollen, pus-filled glands like the ones you see in our victims' groins. Some believe that the phrase 'pocket full of posies' refers to these buboes, although others think it was in reference to the medicinal herbs they used to try to cure the disease. The 'ring around the rosy' part, well, that's pretty self-explanatory when you look at what's left of their skin." Eric ceased talking and returned his laser-like focus to the photos, contemplating them silently for a few more moments, oblivious to anything else except the line of reasoning he was chasing in his head. "The Black Death would have killed more if not for the Great Fire of London in 1666," he said, to no one in particular.

"How would a fire stop a plague?" Seph asked. She was confused now, too. Not that this wasn't interesting, but they really didn't have time for a history lesson right now.

"By killing the rats. The rats that carried the fleas that carried the disease." Eric's speech was increasing in rate and volume, and Dan's face lit up as he jumped on Eric's train of thought. "Back then," Eric went on, "the rats spread from country to country by stowing away on boats, which is why the rate of spread was so slow. The fleas spread from the rats or from person-to-person in infested clothing. A bacterium caused the bubonic plague, but if you substitute a virus and use modern air travel to spread the fleas . . ."

"I believe we've got ourselves a vector," said Dan.

Chapter Seven

The Myth

September 5th, 2016, 1400 hours
New York City

Seph started itching from phantom fleas the moment they were determined to be the vector. That, plus the fact their team was apparently chasing a mass-murdering virologist-hematologist with a minor in medieval history was enough to make anyone cranky. It didn't help that she was sitting in the back of a rank NYPD cruiser with a couple of testosterone poisoned police officers, one of whose attempts at flirting was nothing short of disastrous. *You should try not to speak.* Despite her attempts at telepathic guidance, the officer yammered on.

Seph remained silent in an attempt to avoid perpetuating any sort of conversation. She stared out the rear window at the sunlight reflecting off the mica in the concrete buildings, froze a blank smile on her face and tuned his chatter into a background *blah, blah, blah.* Director Blanchard wasn't the only one who could fake interest.

She'd been in contact with the Department of Homeland Security, which had pulled the alleged terrorist's passport records. The fact that he had traveled from New York

City to China, China to India and India to Los Angeles was enough for them to want to meet her at his apartment for the initial contact. The city, for a holiday weekend, was dead. Even though the virus had not yet been reported on the East Coast, the mayor had cancelled the Labor Day parade. The minimal traffic would have been a welcome change in Gotham's norm had it not represented a city in anticipatory mourning. Officer Blah Blah told her the apartment had been put under surveillance twenty-four hours ago with no activity noted. *Maybe he's not back from his little road trip yet.* There were a whole bunch of cities along Route 80 that he could still be inoculating.

As the city blocks flew by, Seph's mind wandered back to her prior conversation with Grace. When fleas were definitively identified as the culprit, Seph had finally made that phone call to her sister, but she worried she'd done more harm than good. Grace talked a good talk, but she was nowhere near as mentally tough as she pretended to be.

"Hey. How are things up north?"

"If by that you're asking if we're all still alive, then things are good."

Seph laughed at her sister's tart, but accurate reply to Seph's indirect question. She should have known better. "Yeah, I guess that's what I meant."

"Any new info?"

"That's why I called. We now know the infection is spread by fleas, so make sure Duncan's been treated, and maybe the horses, too, if that's even possible. Hell, I'd just flea bomb the whole damn place if I were you." Duncan, Grace's Irish Setter, was in and out of the woods so often he was bound to have fleas.

"I'll take that under consideration. What about you? How are you protecting yourself?"

"I don't need to. Wrong blood type." Seph paused. "How are people holding up? In town, I mean?"

The conversation went downhill from there.

Seph had seen disturbing reports out of L.A. where, in some neighborhoods, the type O's had become the walking dead—reviled, feared or pitied by those around them. Fringe religious leaders cast blame and sin upon them for carrying the plague, conjuring up obscure apocalyptic Bible passages to support their castigations. Overly eager politicians exploited terrified voters for the sake of grabbing headlines by proposing outrageous interventions, like the forcible detention of all the type O's into vast "leprosy" camps in order to contain the infection. The fact that such allegations and interventions held not a shred of scientific basis didn't matter, nor did it deter the gluttonous media from feeding on the frenzy. Seph had mental images of a posse of torch-wielding town folk storming the farm to drag her type O sister away.

"Well, you know how New Englanders are," Grace was saying. "Pretty stoic bunch. The school year's been delayed, and the banks had a run on withdrawals, but it hasn't been too bad. Ellie had an ear infection, and I couldn't get her seen. That was the worst thing. The doctor's office was closed, and the hospital had a mob of people out front all wanting their blood types checked. I can't imagine what it's going to be like when the virus actually hits here."

"I can." For a moment, Seph closed her eyes and channeled the fear she had seen in the faces from the horrendous pictures out of Mumbai. If the reports from India were true, three thousand years of human progress had taken a sharp downward turn, as fragile societies splintered along not racial, religious or ethnic, but biologic lines. In India, Type O's were the new lowest caste.

"You don't really think it's going to go that far, do you?" Grace picked up on her sister's ominous tone.

Seph opened her eyes and scrambled to undo the anxiety she'd created. Just because Seph could feel what was coming didn't mean Grace needed to.

"No. I hope not. I mean, we're on it. Our team's amazing, particularly this one young scientist named Dan. He's cute, too, I might add. He's all over this. I have complete faith."

Grace played along. "Dan, huh?"

"Yep. Hopefully I'll have more to tell you about him later. For now, just stay on the farm, okay? You've got everything you need there—your own well, food, a generator. You're all set. Ride this thing out, and I'll come join you when I can."

Seph had hung up before Grace could ask any more questions. She felt somewhat guilty for her gloss job, but there was no way a little thing like a plague was going to change a lifetime of overprotective behavior. For the first time in a decade, Seph felt like she should say a prayer, not for herself, but for Grace. But the words would not come, and the moment passed. If she knew her sister, Grace was already praying enough for both of them.

The cruiser slammed on its brakes at a red light, yanking Seph back to the present and scattering the file she'd had sitting on her lap into a flurry of papers all over the back seat floor. Officer Blah Blah grinned at her in the rear view mirror. "Sorry about that!" She glared in return and bent to gather her notes.

She'd spent the last few days making phone calls and sending emails to anyone and everyone who might be able to give her useful information on her potential lead. From high school teachers to coworkers in Baine's research lab, Seph had talked to them all. She'd mostly received the same answers over and over again: Baine was smart, distant and otherwise unmemorable. A coworker recalled a "minor" mistreatment of lab animals. One particularly perky high school instructor was pleased to divulge that Baine had been an "active participant in chess club." Another professor remembered an appearance so bland, "he could have been your neighbor, your office mate, or your least-favorite uncle." Every nugget of information, no matter how mundane, went into Seph's file.

She had received one interesting response, a profile written by the psychologist at Baine's high school. Seph winced as she read it. She sounded like that once, back in the day.

I find no evidence of a formal thought disorder. William's personality features and interpersonal style, to include a preference for solitary activities, minimal interactions with others, comfort with routine and concurrent anxiety with change in such routine, interest in science fiction and fantasy, and additional information obtained from this evaluation, would strongly suggest the presence of a developmentally-based Asperger's Disorder. Although I also considered schizoid personality disorder as a diagnosis, the preference for routine is more characteristic of Asperger's.

Seph disagreed, not just with the verbose style with which the profile was written but with the content. Schizoid?

Maybe. Asperger's? Definitely not. Everything she had gathered so far implied that Baine was at least a sociopath—antisocial with decreased empathy and no conscience. Whether he was also a psychopath remained to be seen.

She'd finished his initial profile on the flight from Atlanta to New York, but the report was simplistic at best. Seph was sure she would glean additional information from his apartment—details with which she could flesh out the profile. The cruiser slowed as it approached 2400 Jay Street, stopping short to avoid unwanted attention. Seph felt a quiver of something—she wasn't sure if it was anxiety, excitement or a little bit of both—bubbling up from within. *Keep it together, Persephone. Remember your myth.*

In times of stress, particularly when on a case, Seph liked to recite the myth of Persephone to herself. It was her way of refocusing—a visualization technique, to use the proper psychology terminology. She put her hand on the handle, but before she opened the car door, Seph closed her eyes and pictured her namesake.

Persephone was the daughter of Demeter, the goddess of nature and the harvest. One day, while picking flowers in a Sicilian field, Persephone was kidnapped by Hades, the God of the Underworld, and taken underground to be his reluctant wife and queen. Demeter searched in vain for her daughter, and while she wept, the earth wilted from neglect.

When Demeter finally found Persephone being held captive deep underground, she appealed to Zeus for intervention. After intense negotiations, Persephone was allowed to return to the surface for nine months out of each year. The other three she spent in Hell with her captor, and while her mother mourned, the earth suffered through three months of wintry desolation.

Her mother could never have foreseen Seph's occupation when choosing her name. Still, the uncanny way in which the myth paralleled Seph's life disquieted her to no end. In her line of work, she had met many a sadomasochistic Hades and had been dragged to the Underworld more times than she cared to remember, but she always returned to the surface to be reborn with the next new case. *This time will be no different. Let's just get it done.*

She stepped out of the cruiser and into the glare. She squinted, taking in her surroundings. They were at the rendezvous point on a nondescript street about a block from the suspect's apartment building in a working class neighborhood in Brooklyn. Two suits approached. She could tell by their practical shoes they were the Homeland Security agents.

"Dr. Smith. Officers," the older of the two said with a brisk nod in each of their directions. He was tall and physically fit despite the fact that he looked to be pushing retirement age. His sharply erect posture and the crisp military-type cadence to his speech suggested he'd been around the block a time or two, probably while carrying an M-16. "I'm Special Agent Paul Marin, and this is my partner, Special Agent Craig Patterson. We have the search warrant. Anything in particular that you feel we should be looking for, Doc, before we go in?"

Seph was flattered and a little surprised that Agent Marin had asked for her input before the raid. Rarely was she afforded such professional courtesy outside of her own field, especially from someone whom she had never met. "Well, obviously, we're hoping Baine is in there so we can interview him directly," she replied.

Officer Blah Blah looked amused. "You mean, inter-rogate, right? He's not a fucking movie star; at least, that's not what *my* report says." He pretended to flip through his pocket notebook.

Seph shot him the coldest glare she could muster, but he just grinned back in response. "But if he's not home," she continued, "then we need to watch for traps, particularly IEDs. He's very clever and obviously not at all concerned about human life, so keep your eyes open for trip wires, motion sensors or anything else that could trigger a bomb."

Officer Blah Blah was no longer smiling, especially after Agent Marin nodded at him and said, "Okay, Officer, you've got point. We'll follow you in. Doc, you're in the rear. Don't come in until we give the all clear, okay?"

Seph nodded and took a deep breath. Time to see if her profile was on target.

Chapter Eight

The Apartment

2400 Jay Street, 1405 hours

The chase was starting to heat up, at least according to the headlines. Baine allowed himself to be ever-so-slightly impressed by the CDC investigators. They'd made a lot of progress in a relatively short period of time, considering how many years he'd spent working on his overall plan and the development of the virus. Of course, he had been gracious enough to help them along with his letter, so he wasn't going to give them too much credit. He threw the newspaper in the garbage and headed downstairs.

Time to start erasing history. Baine had already purged his home and work computers. He was keeping all the key scientific data on a book-sized external hard drive. Easy to transport, easy to hide. There were just a few more things to be rid of before he left the city forever—some personal artifacts and papers, items that might give the investigators insight into what made him tick. He hated profilers—a bunch of pseudo-science mind-hackers who thought they were rock stars if they got one detail right out of the thousands that constituted a person's psyche. He scanned the papers as he fed them, one at a time, into the incinerator in the basement of his apartment building. He paused to read one that caught his eye—a letter from his high school psychologist to his parents.

Baine remembered that evaluation well. His mother, who had requested the testing, was crushed by the results. His father, however, knew better. They shared a secret— a "family curse," as his father called it. His father had even helped him develop the code.

The code was unique, undecipherable to anyone unlike his father and him. Of that, Baine was certain. He used it in his journal to encrypt his most sensitive information and tweaked it compulsively, playing with it the way others would an Internet game or a musical composition. In some strange way he could not define, his code gave him solace. It would outlive him, of that he was sure. It would be his legacy to the new world. Those surviving would talk about it long after these days had passed. They would talk about his code, his virus and him.

2400 Jay Street, 1415 hours

Seph stood across the street and waited while the others entered the building. The apartment was on the second floor. She pictured them stealthily climbing the stairs, and she held her breath at the moment when she imagined they would be opening the door. She closed her eyes and waited for an explosion that, thankfully, did not come. She exhaled when her phone rang with the "all clear." Then she crossed the street to join them in apartment 2B.

The apartment wasn't at all what she'd imagined. It was almost a blank canvas, muted shades of grey that blended into nothingness. But the interior was more than just a designer's attempt at minimalist modern décor. It appeared to be intentionally scrubbed of all color and pattern. Black-out curtains covered the windows and muted the sound from the streets below. There were no pictures on the walls; the few pieces of furniture present were upholstered in ash-grey microsuede. Even book covers had been torn off.

"It's like a cave in here," said Agent Marin.

"I was thinking more along the lines of a sensory deprivation chamber," Seph replied. She wandered the tiny space, notebook in hand, prepared to document anything that might require her to modify her profile. There was little to see, almost nothing to give a hint about the person living there. The kitchen cupboards held one plate and one set of utensils. The refrigerator was bare, as were the counters. In the living room, built-in shelves held a smattering of books: mostly historical novels, medical school neurology, and neuropsychology textbooks. The only fiction present was by Nabokov.

Nabokov's autobiography, *Speak, Memory*, still had its original cover, while the others' had been removed. Seph pulled the book off the shelf for closer inspection. The pages were worn and tattered, indicating it had been particularly well-read. She slid it back into place and moved to the next shelf over, where she thumbed through the few jazz and classical CDs on display. The doctor was especially fond of Duke Ellington, Franz Liszt and Olivier Messiaen.

The only other item on the shelves was an ornate wooden box that appeared very out of place in the utilitarian environment. Its top was inlaid with pieces of exotic and burled woods, and it was quite heavy. Seph opened it and was hit by the strong odor of Spanish cedar and tobacco. A humidor. It contained just two cigars, and since the sterile apartment did not smell, she presumed him to be a casual smoker at best.

Seph placed the box back on the shelf and did one final pass through the apartment. Even with the bare bones décor, she had no doubt that someone was actively living there. The bed was unmade, and the garbage held both today's paper and a smattering of recently discarded take-out containers. However, all in all, Seph found the apartment to be a disappointment. It could neither confirm nor refute any of the details of her profile, and it certainly didn't give any clues as to whether or not William Baine was the terrorist. Agent Marin seemed to be having better luck.

"I found something that you're gonna wanna see," he said, brandishing a worn, leather-bound book in his right hand. His other hand held a plastic evidence bag, and there was a laptop tucked under his arm. "It looks like some kind of journal. He had it tucked under the mattress, which has to be the single most common place to try to hide something. Our terrorist may be a brilliant scientist, but he's a lousy criminal."

"Unless he meant for us to find it," Seph said.

"Maybe, but I doubt it. It seems pretty important." Agent Marin flipped through the ivory pages crammed to the margins with chemical formulas, meticulously detailed drawings, and scrawled notations. "It's all Greek to me, but it sure looks like it has the scientific tidbits that your crew back in Atlanta could use to crack this thing wide open."

"Let's hope so. What's in the baggy?"

"Fleas. The bed is crawling with them." He laughed out loud at her horrified look. "Relax, Doc. We've all got non-O blood types here. That's why we were chosen for this assignment." He shot her a crooked, yet reassuring grin.

She smiled back, feeling a little sheepish at her overreaction. She should've realized the government would've taken that into consideration when assigning people to work on the investigation. Like every other department and institution, Homeland Security had been hit hard by a reduction in staff due to the epidemic. They couldn't afford to cavalierly assign a type O agent, only to have him or her fall ill mid-investigation.

"I think we're done here." Agent Marin gave one final glance around the room. "Let's head out. We'll keep the surveillance going. He's got to come back sometime. After we nab him, I suggest we evacuate and then flea bomb the entire building." He nodded at Seph. "Ladies first." He swept his arm toward the door.

They all headed out of the apartment and down the steps. As they rounded the landing to the exit, Seph bumped into someone coming up from the basement. She looked up to murmur an apology and found herself staring into the eyes of one Dr. William Baine.

She recognized him from his passport picture. Apparently, the Homeland Security agents did too, because for a split second, everyone froze. No one seemed to know what to do next, and they all required a moment to recover their wits, Dr. Baine included.

Seph thought she saw an element of surprise flash across his face, but it resolved almost immediately and was replaced by a mask devoid of any and all expression. The officers put their hands on their holstered weapons. Agent Marin opened his mouth to speak, but Baine beat him to it. His voice was perfectly flat in tone, measured in pace and inhuman in quality. "I believe you are looking for me," he said.

Chapter Nine

The Profile

Seph sat and studied Dr. William Baine through the thick, one-way glass of the interrogation room. He was tall and vaguely Nordic in appearance. Her prior research had revealed that his mother was Finnish, which was reflected in his sandy-blonde hair and piercing blue eyes. His eyes jumped out against his otherwise featureless face, one bland enough to allow him to blend in anywhere. He looked like her least favorite uncle.

The review of Baine's laptop yielded nothing, while the early part of his journal read like a prepubescent's diary. Most of the first one hundred pages or so had been torn out, presumably purged by Baine himself. About fifty pages of diary remained, dating from his late teens to early twenties, which mostly discussed his college education and early scientific endeavors. The most recently recorded scientific data in his journal related to a well-funded, university-affiliated research study he was currently conducting at his laboratory.

The rest of the journal was in code, and a cursory inspection suggested it was not going to be easily deciphered. Agent Marin had already contacted an expert in cryptography, who was to meet Seph back at command central upon her return to Atlanta. Seph watched as Agent Marin alternated between jabbing at his cell phone and exchanging terse words with the precinct captain, who finally threw up his hands and walked away.

"What was that all about?" she asked.

"They're sayin' we don't have enough hard evidence of Baine having committed a crime to hold him for more than twenty-four hours."

"But what about his travel history and how perfectly it matches up with the release of the virus?"

"From a legal standpoint, they consider it circumstantial evidence at best. They feel we're violating his rights, et cetera, et cetera. I, however, have no such qualms."

"So what's the plan?"

"The plan is to assume custody of Baine and transport both of you back to the CDC headquarters, so you and your research team can interrogate him at your leisure. The problem is they don't want to relinquish custody . . ." Agent Marin's voice trailed off as the precinct captain, with a gaggle of subordinates in tow, reappeared from around the corner.

They were all standing outside the interrogation room debating jurisdiction when Baine, who since the initial interaction in the stairwell had maintained a disinterested silence, began to speak. He stared straight ahead, knowing they could hear him through the bulletproof glass barrier, and in the same measured, flat voice he had used earlier, Dr. William Baine recited his confession.

The confession squashed any arguments over jurisdiction and resulted in a flurry of activity from both the police and the Homeland Security agents. While the others were distracted with their preparations, Seph took the opportunity to speak to Baine alone. She wanted to have the first crack at him, before he had the chance to develop the rote, rehearsed responses that suspects tend to develop after being asked the same questions over and over again.

Establishing an empathic connection with criminal minds was Seph's specialty, and the face-to-face interview, particularly if done one on one, was a key factor in the ultimate strength of that connection. Her uncanny ability to tap into their feelings, even subconscious ones, along with her attention to minute detail enabled her to understand and predict the actions of people like Baine—often before they knew their own intentions. This was the foundation upon which she had built her career, but it came with a stiff price. Being able to so acutely feel and process the emotions of such warped minds was not very comfortable.

She slipped into the interrogation room alone, and for a few moments, they just sized each other up, like a pair of poker players sitting down to play for the first time. They were separated only by a cold, stainless-steel table and a pair of handcuffs. *He must feel very at home here*, Seph thought, looking around at the grey walls and the otherwise empty room. *Time to shake that up a bit*. She formulated her opening words carefully, turning over various interview techniques and tactics in her mind before deciding that the direct approach was best.

"Dr. Baine, I'm Dr. Smith, and I'd like to ask you some questions."

He closed his eyes, and for a second, Seph thought she was going to get nothing but the silent treatment.

"*Doctor* Smith? Not Agent or Officer Smith?" he asked. There was another long pause. "You don't look like a physician or a scientist," he said finally.

"I'm a psychologist," Seph replied. She wasn't positive, but she was fairly sure she saw him roll his eyes, and she bristled internally. "You don't look much like a bioterrorist, either. I'd like to know why you created this pandemic."

"I already explained all that in my letter," he said, with a dismissive wave of one shackled hand. "You read it, I'm sure."

"I did. I understood your environmental concerns in regard to overpopulation. What I didn't understand was your discussion of natural selection, and how you are 'helping the Darwinian process of evolution.' How does that tie in with killing all the people with the O blood type? They are in no way evolutionarily inferior, at least to my knowledge."

Nothing. His eyes remained closed. His face was set in a mask of studied boredom.

Seph tried a different tactic. "Why do you like Nabokov so much?"

His eyes flew open.

Got 'im, Seph thought with satisfaction. It was the first natural, non-rehearsed response she'd seen from him.

He smiled at her in a most unpleasant way, forcing her to actively squelch her discomfort so it wouldn't show on her face.

"Why don't you read his books and figure that out for yourself?" he said. "You are, after all, the profiler. I see no reason to relieve you of your ignorance. I helped you enough with my letter." His voice dripped with disdain, and Seph struggled to remain cool and professional. She knew he was trying to distract her, to make her angry by rattling her in any way he could so she would fail in her mission.

"I intend to," she replied, smoothing her face into a placid smile, "right after I get done reacquainting myself with the music of Franz Liszt."

His eyes narrowed and then relaxed as the bored mask returned. "You do that, and let me know if it's to your *taste*, will you?"

His response confused her. He put a subtle emphasis on the word "taste," just enough to imply that he was hinting at something beyond her grasp. Seph decided she indeed needed to read Nabokov, listen to Liszt and maybe even figure out that damn code before interviewing him again. He was too tightly self-contained to slip up and divulge anything he didn't want to. She'd have to gather more information, more ammunition in order to effectively proceed. She stood to exit the room and was halfway out the door when he spoke to her back.

"You smell like flowers."

Seph paused but did not turn around, waiting to see if he would continue.

"Like *purple* flowers," he added, taking a deep inhalation through his nose and exhaling through his mouth with a satisfied sigh.

She finished walking out the door and slammed it harder than she'd intended, causing Agent Marin to give her a quizzical look. "It is my professional opinion that that man is just fucking weird," Seph said in response. "I'm heading back to Atlanta."

Chapter Ten

The Code

September 7th, 2016, 1100 hours
Atlanta, Georgia

Seph intended to read Nabokov's *Lolita* on the plane, but she underestimated how mentally exhausted she was from the tension of the last two days; instead, she slept most of the way back to Atlanta. By the time she arrived she felt calm, centered, and back to her usual self.

The strange interaction with Baine in the shadowy interrogation room seemed distant and unreal in the light of day, as if she had merely observed it happening to someone else. He was unnerving, yes, but she'd dealt with plenty of equally unnerving characters in her career. She couldn't place what was different about him, why he bothered her so much. Over the years, Seph had become an expert at creating mental barriers to protect her innermost self, and she attempted to banish her subjects' voices from her head at the end of the day and at the close of each case. Sometimes she was more successful than others. Baine's peculiar voice would stick with her for quite some time.

Seph would have ample time to refine her approach before interviewing him again. Homeland Security had prevailed in the custody battle, and they'd arranged for Baine to be on the same flight as her. At least he was seated clear in the back of the near-empty plane, discreetly surrounded by a gaggle of Homeland Security agents and an armed air marshal. Seph had been both amused and relieved when Agent Marin told her, tongue in cheek, that he'd ordered Baine to have a flea bath before boarding the plane. Better safe than sorry.

She met up with the team in time for the eleven o'clock briefing. The director was dour, Eric was scholarly and Dan was adorable. All was right with her world, at least for now. For the first time in a month, the atmosphere in the room felt positive, and everyone was buzzing with activity.

Seph noted a new face seated next to Eric at the center of the conference room table. The woman appeared to be about Seph's own age, with dark hair and eyes and a vivacious personality that commanded the undivided attention of all the men in the room. No one, not even Dan, seemed to notice when Seph entered to rejoin the team, which peeved her enough for her to trumpet her own arrival.

"Honey, I'm home," she said. *That got their attention*. Seph smiled with satisfaction when the director turned to scowl in her general direction.

"Seph, great, you're back," Eric said, still somewhat distracted by the beacon beaming next to him. "Believe it or not, a lot has happened just from the time you caught your return flight from New York. We've got a lot to cover. First off, this is Dr. Cecilia Peluso. She's a cryptographist from the National Security Agency headquarters in Maryland. I asked her here to help us with the code. I assume you brought the journal with you."

"Hi!" Cecilia jumped out of her chair to extend a hand towards Seph. "I hear you and I are going to be banging this thing out together."

Eric didn't wait for Seph to respond and hurried on with the briefing. "We've got cases on five continents now, and the numbers have exploded. China and India alone have about a million each, with Mexico not far behind. The US is just starting to see cases on the Northeastern seaboard, but the West Coast is reporting an exponential increase almost daily. Estimated total dead worldwide is now around six million. Some countries have declared martial law, and most are restricting imports and travel. The World Health Organization has instituted flea eradication programs; which, in my opinion, is akin to plugging a leaking dam with your little finger. The good news is that while we were making progress on our own toward the development of a treatment, we just received a big boost from Dr. Baine himself."

Surprised murmurs swept the room. Seph, who was still standing next to Cecilia, sank into a chair and eyed Eric skeptically. She raised a single questioning eyebrow at him, as if to suggest that perhaps they should discuss this new development before he divulged it to the other members of the team.

Eric ignored her implied request for discretion and barreled on with his explanation. "Homeland Security did a second sweep of Baine's apartment after you left, Seph, and this time they found a flash drive containing detailed information on the virus, including—get this—a complete description of the chemical composition for a vaccine! Apparently, our bioterrorist thought ahead in case he had second thoughts."

The murmur turned into a burst of chatter and nervous laughter as the tension of the last month dissipated in one fell swoop. Even Dr. Lee, whose home country had been so terribly afflicted, managed a smile. Only Dan was frowning. He rose from his seat, both palms planted flat on the table, and shook his head in emphatic disagreement.

"No. I'm not buyin' it. A man capable of killing six million people is not the type of man to have second thoughts," he said. "And do you honestly think someone so meticulous would leave a flash drive with his life's work on it just sitting around for us to find? He's setting us up for something. I mean, seriously people, why would he do that? He may as well have gone ahead and gift wrapped it for us!"

Eric did not appreciate the buzz kill. "Who cares why? And the flash drive wasn't 'just sitting around.' Homeland Security said that, unlike the journal-under-the-mattress scenario, the flash drive was well-hidden, so I don't know that Baine was making it particularly easy on anyone. He probably didn't expect us to find him as quickly as we did. I'm sure if he had known his apartment was going to be raided, he would've grabbed both the flash drive and his journal and run, right, Seph?"

Just as Eric didn't like Dan squelching his good news, Seph didn't appreciate being put on the spot. Truth be told, she didn't like the scenario either. Dan was right. Men like Baine did not have second thoughts. Insanity aside, they were far too self-assured for that.

The whole thing didn't feel right, and she wanted the chance to analyze the coded passages in his journal before rendering a professional opinion. Something told her this was where the truly sensitive information could be found. The exact nature of the contents was as crucial as it was unpredictable. For now, she deflected Eric's question in order to avoid taking sides.

"Baine probably didn't bother hiding the journal because he figured that, even if we found it, we weren't going to be able to decipher the code," she said. "In fact, I suspect he's taunting us with it."

"Great!" said Cecilia. "I love a challenge." She jumped to her feet, eager to get her hands on Baine's coded journal, and turned to address Eric directly. "You don't need me to tell you that you have an enormous amount of work ahead. Assuming the information you've received is legitimate, which, as Dan said, is a big assumption to make, it'll take weeks to mass-produce a vaccine, even if every lab in the world starts churning it out at the same time."

"That's not the only issue," Eric said. "We'll have to convince the FDA to bypass the normal safety regulations, which require extensive human and animal trials, in order to deploy the new vaccine rapidly enough to save lives."

"Exactly. That sounds like a job for you, Director Blanchard." Cecilia jabbed her finger in the director's general direction. "So I suggest that each of you keeps working on your little piece of the puzzle, and Seph and I will start working on ours as well. It's too early to celebrate." She smiled at Dan and gave his upper arm a reassuring squeeze. "With all of us putting our noses to the grindstone, we should be able to get you some of those answers, Dan."

Seph struggled to keep from laughing out loud. Cecilia, in true Italian fashion, talked as much with her hands as she did with her mouth. In those three sentences plus a few pointed hand gestures, she managed to tell the director his job *and* order everyone else off their asses and back to work. Cecilia's get-it-done attitude was admirable and refreshing, and Seph was lovin' it. She even forgave the touchy-feely bit with her boy, Dan.

Seph reached over and linked elbows with Cecilia. "We'll be in touch," she said, punctuating her words with a slow, solemn nod. She dared not look at the director's face for fear of dissolving into paroxysms of laughter. She and Cecilia turned together, and Seph all but dragged her out of the room, leaving the bemused team behind.

The door clicked behind them, and they made it about halfway down the basement corridor before Seph erupted. "That was magnificent! Well done," she said, gasping to recover her breath.

Cecilia shrugged and fluttered her free hand overhead dismissively. "We don't exactly have time for a cock fight right now, now do we? Besides, I'm dying to get my hands on that journal." She gave Seph's arm an impatient tug. "Lead on, girlfriend!"

Seph and Cecilia set up shop in Seph's airless basement office. Despite Cecilia's enthusiasm, Seph was at a total loss as to where to begin. The code was written in multicolored pen and pencil, which seemed odd considering the absolute absence of color in the drab apartment. The writing consisted of a mixture of upper and lowercase letters with some symbols thrown in for good measure. Seph recognized a few of the symbols as being musical in nature, while others looked as though they'd been lifted from a high school physics textbook, but for the most part, she hadn't a clue. She grimaced at the pages in front of her and ran her hand through her hair in exasperation.

"In case you haven't figured it out by now, I'm no Robert Langdon," Seph said referring to Dan Brown's Harvard symbologist.

"No worries—I'm not either, and that's my job!" Cecilia responded with a laugh. "In all seriousness, though, you use the same skill set as a profiler that I do as a cryptographist. We both look for patterns, themes, nuances—anything to help us crack the code. And don't forget a good computer. That helps." She was busily feeding data into her laptop, which was preloaded with some kind of top secret, code-cracking software capable of identifying patterns not visible to the human eye. "Tell me what objects you found in his apartment. I need personal artifacts of any kind—books, music, artwork or anything that just seemed out of place. All those things can help give me clues as to how Baine devised his code."

"Honestly, Cecilia, the apartment was a blank slate." Seph pulled out her files and flipped through them, trying to jog her memory. "He had no art and almost nothing in the way of personal articles. He did have a few books and CDs, but that was it. Nabokov and Liszt were particularly well-represented, for some reason."

They were interrupted by a rap on the door. Dan stuck his head around the corner and smiled. "Sorry to interrupt, Ladies, but I'm heading to Starbucks. I've deduced that whatever it is they're brewing in the conference room and passing off as coffee is deadlier than our virus! Can I get either of you anything?" His smile broadened, revealing a dimple in his right cheek.

"We're good for right now, but thanks anyway, Dan." Cecilia answered for both of them.

"All right, then. Don't say I didn't warn you. See you at the next briefing." He disappeared with a friendly wave.

Cecilia sighed. "Really, can that boy get any cuter?" She laughed at Seph's expression. "Don't worry. He's all yours. I prefer my conquests to have two X chromosomes. Now, where were we? Ah, yes—Liszt!" She punched a few buttons on her laptop, and the complex sound of Liszt's *Études d' exécution transcendante* filled the tiny room. "Life is only a long and bitter suicide, and faith alone can transform this suicide into a sacrifice." Cecilia clasped both hands over her heart in reverence as she recited the words. "Franz Liszt is infinitely quotable, but that one happens to be my favorite. Appropriate, don't you think?"

"So, you're an expert on Liszt as well as a cryptographist?" Seph asked.

"Not specifically on Liszt, but I do know more than my fair share about classical music. With a name like 'Cecilia,' I was expected to."

Seph was perplexed and must have looked it, because Cecilia expounded further.

"Cecilia was a martyr and the patron saint of music in the Catholic Church. My mother loved classical music and was as Italian Catholic as they come. Hence my name."

Seph vaguely recalled the story of St. Cecilia. She had been Catholic once as well, long before the atrocities witnessed on her job convinced her that God did not exist, or at the very least, didn't give a crap about mankind. As an atheist, she kept her mouth shut, though. Americans did not like atheists. She'd found that out on more than one occasion.

Cecilia continued with her explanation. "Of course, I had to learn an instrument, so I chose piano. Liszt pieces are technically difficult to play and always drove me crazy, but I forgave him because he was such an extraordinary character. He was a synesthete . . ." Her voice trailed off for a moment. "So was Nabokov." They stared at each other, thunderstruck, knowing they were on to something but not sure how to proceed with their new insight.

"I don't remember what that means," Seph said. "I've heard the word before, probably in a psychology class a long time ago, but I forget the details."

"Synesthesia is a rare genetic disorder where the five main sensory pathways in the brain are all intertwined. I first read about it in Liszt's autobiography, and I found the concept so fascinating that I researched it further online. Imagine being able to taste words and colors, see and smell music. I think it's beyond what the normal person can even attempt to understand. I know *I* can't imagine it, although I've been told trippin' on LSD is the closest one can get!"

"Just 'told'?" Seph smiled. "No personal research involved?"

"None whatsoever." Cecilia raised her right hand as if taking an oath. "That's my story, and I'm stickin' to it! The experts say a typical synesthete is highly artistic and intelligent, but socially backward. The condition is underreported because those afflicted don't understand how they are different from the general population; they just know that they are. They think they're weird or even crazy, so they learn to keep their mouths shut." Cecilia leaned forward, eyes ablaze with her passion for the subject, and she continued on, talking with both her hands and her mouth.

"Can you imagine the sensory overload from this? I mean, just daily life—the stimulation from rain drops on the window, a car horn honking or a dog barking—it blows my mind that anyone with this condition can function at all, much less thrive and create masterpieces like the one we just heard from Liszt! I'd bet anything our dear Dr. Baine is a synesthete, and this code somehow represents the things he sees and hears that we can't. You said he was confident we wouldn't be able to solve it. Now we know why."

Seph nodded in agreement. "So how *do* we crack it, then? Go find ourselves another synesthete?" Seph stumbled over the unfamiliar word. The whole thing seemed bizarre, but she had to admit it fit with her profile. Even the barren apartment now made sense.

"Nice idea, but they're not exactly standing around on the street corners," Cecilia said. "Especially right now." She flipped through a couple more pages of the journal, occasionally pointing to a symbol that caught her eye but saying nothing until she had finished devising her plan of attack.

"We should first attempt to break the code down into its individual pieces. Knowing Baine has synesthesia makes me suspect he has used five different types of symbols to represent the five senses, and that these are then all fused into one master code. Since we can't see the whole picture the way Baine can, our best bet would be to start with, say, sight and sound."

Cecilia pointed to one page of the journal. "A lot of the symbols in this section, for example, appear to relate to music. And these ones over here look like they relate to energy, light, wavelength and all that other squiggly-wiggly stuff. Since these two types of symbols make up the bulk of the text, I suggest we get additional input from people with expertise in the fields these symbols represent. I'm thinking a physicist and an expert in music theory would be the most helpful. Maybe you could see if someone from the research team has a physics background. I know just the right person to ask for help with the music theory part. Can we meet back here in, say, three hours?"

"Sure," Seph said, feeling a bit deflated. She didn't really want to crawl back to the conference room and admit that they needed help already. Wasn't Cecilia supposed to be the premier expert in her field? *At least she figured out the synesthesia part.* Seph dragged her feet down the long hallway and back to the conference room.

The room was dead silent when she walked in, despite the fifteen or so people in the room. All eyes were glued to the television monitor hanging on the back wall. The local news was playing. Paramedics were transporting a sheet-covered stretcher out of an apartment building in one of the poorer neighborhoods of Atlanta. Police officers had responded to a foul odor, the reporter was saying, and found the corpse of a woman who appeared to have died from the hemorrhagic virus approximately two days prior. The building was now under quarantine.

The cameraman panned to a close-up of one of the victim's arms, which had broken free from the stretcher's belt and was hanging rigidly out from under the sheet. It was grotesquely swollen and blackened, with gangrenous fingers.

That image was followed by shots of people crying, people panicking and people praying. Some carried signs that read "The End is Near." The message was clear. The virus had come to Atlanta.

With the stark images hanging in the air, no one in the room was in the mood to chatter, much less gloat over Seph's presence. Eric made some calls to a few of his colleagues, and soon Seph had secured the services of a physicist with ample time to spare. Armed with the new information about his condition, she decided to spend her extra time reintroducing herself to Dr. William Baine.

Chapter Eleven

The Genesis

Baine knew Dr. Persephone Smith would be back to talk to him again. He was a profiler's dream. He was looking forward to her visit. He hated chit chat, and he hated profilers even more, but he was also savvy enough to know that hers would be the definitive description of him recorded in all the scientific journals and layman newspapers. She was his personal biographer, and he wanted to make sure she got it right for the history books. Besides, he hadn't had this much attention from a girl since high school. He had hated high school, and not just in the normal acne-cursed, hormonally challenged way. His was more like Stephen King's *Carrie*. He was never popular, of course, and he spent most of his time trying to fly below the radar of the school's bullies. He'd failed miserably, particularly after that incident during the annual talent show.

He'd had a crush on a girl named Chastity, whose slutty behavior made a mockery of her name. She was pretty and popular with the jocks, and they passed her around like a dirty soccer ball. But she sang like the angel she wasn't, and he loved her voice. It was vanilla-scented, pure, with colors that glittered like sparklers on the 4th of July. He could still taste it today.

She sang at the talent show their senior year—a cheesy love song that to him sounded as magnificent as an operatic aria. He rocked back and forth to the music as if his auditorium seat were a rocking chair, unaware of his bizarre behavior. He had his eyes closed and his head up, ecstatically sniffing the notes as they bounced off the stage and into the audience. He opened his eyes when he heard a group of Chastity's friends snickering. The taunting started that day and never stopped until graduation. Their usual epithet was "Rain Man," but their verbal arsenal was replete with a plethora of other creative terms. He remembered each and every one.

Chastity took great delight in his torture, seeking him out to offer a song if only he would rock for her. He would scurry away, and she and her girlfriends would have a good giggle before moving on to the next target in their line of fire.

He ignored and endured to the best of his ability—except for one day. The one day in study hall when she tipped him over the edge with words long since forgotten. Baine walked out of the study hall, out of the school completely, and headed over to Chastity's home. He knew her mother would be there alone. He didn't have a distinct plan; his mind was swirling with a combination of the rage and embarrassment that had been building over the last few months. Looking back, he suspected he might have been going to tell Chastity's mother that her daughter was nothing but a feculent whore.

Instead he raped her, bludgeoned her to death and set the house on fire. It burnt to the ground. The small town cops never figured out who had done it. He was never even a suspect.

It was the one and only time he had committed a violent act against an individual being, not counting his lab animals. He went over and over it in his mind for weeks afterward before deciding he didn't enjoy it. The catharsis was nice, but the sensory stimulation was too intense. He also didn't appreciate the anonymity. He wanted Chastity to know he'd killed her mother, to describe the murder to her in gruesome detail, to see her reaction when she realized her mother's suffering had been all her fault.

But neither Chastity nor her mother were worth going to jail over, so he'd kept his mouth shut throughout the final weeks of school, and after graduation he'd left home for college, and he never went back. That singular event marked the embryonic creation of his current plan. The next time, however, the whole world would know it was him.

Chapter Twelve
The Interview

Seph rounded another dimly lit corner in the basement and breathed a sigh of relief when she realized she'd finally found the proper corridor. The basement was a maze of long hallways, identical in appearance, and she'd been wandering around lost for the last fifteen minutes, minutes she'd hoped to use to interview Baine. He was locked in room 8 B, a room that had once held the research dogs. It was the single most secure place in the building and the only room with a cage large enough to hold a human.

Homeland Security had posted a guard, and as Seph approached she saw a uniformed young man squirming on a hard wooden stool. Bored with babysitting a locked door, he barely looked up from whatever game he was playing on his smartphone when she requested admission. He handed her the keys without breaking eye contact with his electronic mistress. Seph unlocked the door and started shaking before she'd finished turning the knob to enter the lab. She opened the door and then paused to steady herself. Baine was only part of the problem.

The room smelled of wet dog and blood. The back wall was lined with small cages. Bits of dog fur lie scattered here and there on the floor. A dusty metal tray in the corner held a pair of menacing vice grips and other unrecognizable instruments of torture. Her stomach clenched as a wave of monstrous images flooded her brain. *How could "good," intelligent people do this?* She closed her eyes and pictured the words encircling her sister's ankle, tattooed just above Duncan's paw print. *The idea that some lives matter less is the root of all that is wrong with this world.* Grace lived by that quote. She could never enter a room like this, proving that one needn't be an empath to find vivisection abhorrent. Seph took a deep breath, gritted her teeth and walked in.

Baine was much as she'd left him in New York, sitting on a utilitarian steel chair with his eyes closed. The handcuffs had been removed, deemed unnecessary given the thickness of the steel cage that surrounded him. The faint odor of formaldehyde triggered a resurgence of the graphic images in Seph's brain which she worked to immediately and forcibly suppress. *Focus, Persephone. He can probably smell your fear.*

He opened his eyes, and the corners of his mouth twitched in recognition. For a moment, Seph feared he'd read her mind. He broke the silence first by sniffing at the air. "Violets. I've decided you smell like violets. Did you know that some *viola* species temporarily turn off the smell receptors in the nose, blocking any further sense of smell for a short period of time? They're also . . . edible," he added, with just enough of a pause before the last word to make it sound distinctly ominous.

"Fascinating," Seph said, "But what I really want to talk about is your synesthesia. What's it like? I want you to help me understand how it feels."

The ghost of a smile vanished and was replaced by the mask with which Seph was becoming quite familiar. Baine closed his eyes as he talked. "Spoken like a true psychologist." He paused again and began moving his head back and forth in a strange, wave-like motion, as if responding to some kind of internal stimulus. "My trying to explain to you what it's like to be synesthetic is like you trying to describe the color of a rose to a blind man. You can tell him it's red, but the image he 'sees' in his mind's eye is made up of only what he can smell and touch. He doesn't know what 'red' is. You can't understand what I perceive; I can't comprehend what you *don't* perceive. It's quite the paradox, isn't it?"

"Is that why you're killing off millions of innocent people—because they don't see the world the same way you do?"

"Of course not. I'm killing off half of humanity because the world has far more people than it can sustain, most of whom aren't worth sustaining anyway. If anyone should survive, why shouldn't it be the ones who are more highly developed? Isn't that what natural selection is all about?"

Seph pictured the images out of China and India. Young or old, healthy or infirm—all were equally affected by Baine's virus. The slaughter was indiscriminate, at least to her eye. "Natural selection is supposed to happen naturally. Your virus is man-made. There is nothing natural about your pandemic. It's murder, not evolution." She was being intentionally inflammatory, goading him toward a slip of the tongue.

"I beg to differ. I am simply the latest in a long line of scientists to affect the process. Mankind has been tinkering with evolution since we discovered penicillin in the 1940s. The difference is that my predecessors 'broke' natural selection. It doesn't work anymore. Why? We cure disease, and we help the weak survive when they should, in fact, perish." He paused to take a breath. Seph detected no emotion on his face, but his eyes were not entirely blank. They held expression, and the sentiment on display was not a nice one.

"We give handouts to disadvantaged adults. We promote the survival of all infants via heroic and expensive interventions regardless of the premature age or birth defects with which they are born. Many animals kill their own weak or genetically deformed young. We choose to create foundations and raise funds for them. I'm putting natural selection back on track. I think you'll find if you poll many of your scientist friends, they actually agree with me. But they're too afraid of the political consequences to say so. Society has made them weak as well."

Her tactic was working. The more he spoke, the more agitated and animated he became, and he was gradually letting his guard down. Time to twist the screws even tighter.

"You're implying that all the synesthetes, being more highly developed, will survive the outbreak to reproduce; which, in turn, implies that none of them have type O blood. Obviously, you must not be type O, but how do you know this is true of all the others as well? You couldn't have found them all, tested their blood types and warned them. Aren't you murdering your own kind?"

He jumped out of his chair and rushed toward her, grabbing the cell bars and rattling them violently. Seph jerked backwards in surprise and terror. The blank mask was gone now, replaced by a visage of muscles twitching in twisted rage. "You're a stupid, babbling bitch. You don't understand one iota of what's happening, do you? I've helped you, even guided you with my letter and journal, and yet you still don't have a fucking clue."

The outburst abated as quickly as it had surged. "I thought you were different. You managed to find me. In record time, I might add. You surprised me back in New York, and I'm not often surprised." He sat down in his chair and closed his eyes. "It doesn't matter. It won't happen again. You'll be dead in a few weeks. You and everyone you love will bleed like slaughtered little lambs."

The door to the room swung open. "Everything okay in here?" the guard asked. Seph was surprised he'd torn himself away from his Angry Birds or Candy Crush or whatever it was he was playing, but she was enormously glad he had. His presence gave her a few much-needed seconds to collect her rattled senses.

"Yes, thank you," she replied, striving to keep her pace natural and unhurried as she strode toward the open door. She turned back to face Baine before leaving the room. "Thank you, Dr. Baine. I think I have everything I need for today."

Seph was running late for her meeting with Cecilia, but the encounter with Baine had shaken her enough that she needed a moment to calm her nerves. She stepped outside and pulled a crumpled pack of cigarettes from the bottom of her purse. She'd smoked regularly for three or four years in the early days of her career when her ability to cope with her enhanced empathy and the long, stressful hours of her job was underdeveloped. Most of the cops she had worked with smoked too, and she'd been desperate to fit in with the boys.

She quit after her mother died of smoking-related lung cancer. Her mother had coerced her to do so, and Seph had kept her promise. She continued to keep a pack on hand, though, for emergencies like this one—emotionally traumatic situations that took their toll, no matter how well-honed a set of coping skills one possessed. All rationalization aside, sometimes she just wanted a damned cigarette. She took a long drag and concentrated on trying to slow her pulse back to a normal rate.

As she smoked, she went over Baine's words in her head, attempting to rationally dissect them as if they were no more than dead worms on a petri dish. By the time she finished her cigarette she realized there was a problem with their team's course of action—a big problem. Baine had a back-up plan, a fail-safe that was ready to go should they deploy a vaccine.

The devil was in the details though, and she lacked a single detail to work with. His confidence bothered her, as did his choice of words. He couldn't know her blood type and should surely know that only about half of all people have type O. Yet he specifically stated she and *everyone* she loved would die. There was an implication there, and Seph didn't like it one bit. She and Cecilia needed to break that code, and soon. If they couldn't, Homeland Security needed to break Baine, by any means necessary. Her gut told her that everything, including potentially her own life, depended on it.

Chapter Thirteen

The Martyr

Cecilia and the others were already hard at work when Seph rejoined them in the office. The room was far too small to hold four people, especially when one of them had just finished a cigarette. Luckily, no one seemed to notice.

"We've made a lot of progress, Seph," Cecilia greeted her. "Turns out the code is essentially a variation of a basic alphanumeric code: A=1, B=2 etc., but with a few special twists for those who happen to be able to see colors. I'd explain it to you, but I'm not so sure I understand it well enough myself yet. Dr. Vogel, would you do the honors? And keep it as down and dirty as possible for us unenlightened souls, will you?"

Dr. Vogel had a white beard and jolly red cheeks that made him look much more like Santa Claus than like any physicist Seph had ever met. He gave a deep, histrionic sigh and smiled indulgently at Cecilia, who had clearly charmed herself another admirer. "If I have to," he said. "The author of the code is using different wavelengths as his numbers. Each wavelength in turn corresponds to a letter of the Standard English alphabet. What makes this particular code confusing is that he's using the wavelengths of both sound and visible light and sometimes the combination of the two. The visible light spectrum has seven colors. You might remember the acronym ROY G BIV from high school physics?"

Seph nodded weakly, mostly to give the false appearance she was keeping up. Satisfied, Dr. Vogel continued on. "In addition, most modern pianos have seven octaves and seven different lettered notes per octave. This is where our music theorist helps us out." He nodded at an owlish woman sitting to the right of Cecilia. She was the polar opposite of her vibrant, outgoing neighbor, with mousy hair and round, thick glasses that made her eyes look huge. She hadn't made a peep, and she seemed to prefer it that way.

"Well, Saige?" Cecilia said, putting a hand on Saige's knee. They appeared to be old friends.

"I agree," Saige said. "When a synesthete plays a note on the piano—let's pick middle C as an example—he not only hears it, he sees a color, too. There are standard, readily available charts which list the wavelengths of musical notes. He adds that number to the wavelength of the color he sees, and voila—that's his A. I think this explains why some of the symbols in his journal are colored and some aren't. He needed a mixture of straight color wavelengths, straight musical wavelengths and a combination of the two to get the twenty-six letters of the alphabet."

"I also think some of the special characters he's embedded in his code correspond to punctuation marks and such, just to kick it up a notch," Cecilia said. "I suspect he's been refining this for years."

Seph was starting to feel like the clueless hick in a room full of urbanites. "Okay. So, if you've got it all figured out, how long until we know what the journal actually says?"

"The wavelength numbers are extremely close together, sometimes to the ten thousandth degree after the decimal point. I'm going to have to feed all the color and sound wavelength data into a special computer program to get us a graph of the alphanumeric code. Once we have that, then the actual decoding starts. I'd say it'll take us roughly twenty-four hours—thirty-six tops," Cecilia replied. Her confidence was marred by a paroxysmal fit of coughing that ended as suddenly as it started.

"Sorry about that." Cecilia wiped her hands and face with a tissue. Three faces stared at her, frozen in shock. She glanced down at the now-discarded tissue lying in the waste basket. It was soaked with blood, and there were tiny droplets scattered on the computer screen as well. A little trickle ran from the corner of Cecilia's right nostril, and she tentatively raised one hand to dab it away.

Saige's eyes welled with tears. She excused herself and hurried from the room. Dr. Vogel remained frozen, the color gone from his rosy cheeks. Finally, he, too, managed to mutter a few unintelligible words before exiting. Seph, now alone with Cecilia, found her voice first, though it was nothing more than a raw whisper.

"When did you know?"

Cecilia's responded in a light voice, but with a sad smile. "I started running a fever late yesterday afternoon, about an hour or so after I was asked to join the team. I guess I was hoping it was just a cold. You know what this means, don't you? Maryland and Washington D.C. are about to see an explosion in the number of cases."

They sat in silence for a few minutes, attempting to fully absorb the enormity of the situation to come.

"You know what else this means? I have fleas!" Cecilia's attempt to break up the somber mood with a dose of humor backfired when her forced laughter triggered another coughing fit and bloody nose. She blotted the red foam from around her mouth and nose as she regained her breath.

"I already told you St. Cecilia was a martyr, but did I tell you how she died?" Cecilia asked.

Seph shook her head. She was still having trouble fully finding her voice.

"The story has a couple of different versions, but basically she was to be beheaded, which is a quick and easy way for a martyr to die considering some of the other nasty and creative methods by which many were killed. But in her case, the sword simply would not cut through her neck despite several hacks at it. She slowly bled to death over three days. The townspeople considered her to be so holy they sopped up her blood with rags and sponges."

Cecilia looked down at the blood-tinged tissues in the paper can and smiled wryly. "Somehow I don't think that's going to happen with me—the part about collecting the blood, I mean."

Seph squirmed, unsure of the appropriate response. The religious aspect of death was not her forte. She was much more familiar with its criminal side. She blurted out the first unrelated thing that came to mind. "Why are you here?"

"Where should I be? Home waiting to drown in a pool of my own blood?" Cecilia fluttered her hands impatiently. "This thing is far from over, despite Eric's happily ever after vaccine crap. You and I both know this code contains something much more important than Baine's favorite lasagna recipe. It's mission critical we figure out what it says. I'm the best person for this job, just like you're the best person to get inside Baine's twisted skull. I knew I was dead the minute they determined the virus attacked type O blood. There's no point in whining about it."

"I'm sorry." A professional psychologist should be able to come up with something more profound, or at least more comforting, to say than those two simple words. But at that moment all Seph could do was repeat herself. "I am so sorry," she said again.

"You know what? I've got a lot of work to do." Cecilia glanced at her laptop. "And I don't need you sitting there staring at me with your sad puppy-dog eyes as if I'm already dead. Why don't you make yourself useful and go get us some coffee, would ya? It's going to be a long night, and I'm beginning to regret turning down Dan's kind offer." She flashed her brilliant smile in an attempt to take some of the sting out of her words. "Oh, and I think it's about time for the last briefing of the day to start. Do you mind filling them in on our progress so I can keep entering this information into the computer?"

"Sure." Seph needed a few minutes anyway to collect her thoughts. It was around five o'clock, and it had been a long and psychologically taxing day. The stress made her feel physically exhausted as well. Her legs were as heavy as concrete blocks, and she had to will them to take one step after the other down the long hallway to the conference room.

She reviewed the day's events in her mind as she walked. First, Eric had raised the hope of a cure; then came Baine's veiled threats, and then finally the revelation of Cecilia's terminal illness. The emotional roller coaster should have made her numb, incapable of being hit by any further emotional punches. Instead, one thought kept asserting itself, demanding to be acknowledged as it blazed its way through the fog of fatigue clouding her brain.

She hated Dr. William Baine. She hated him for creating his virus. She hated him for making her worry about Grace. She hated him for killing Cecilia and for disrupting her whole world. Mostly, though, on her most visceral level, she just hated his guts.

Seph had profiled dozens of cases over the years, but this primitive emotional response, this pure hatred for another human being, was new. It smoldered in the pit of her belly, giving her some much needed strength and fueling her resolve. Baine would not go unpunished, she vowed, if she had to drag him straight to Hell herself.

Chapter Fourteen

The Cross

September 7th, 2016, 1730 hours
Atlanta, Georgia

The room was strangely quiet when Seph walked in. The first thing she noticed was the empty space. There was a lot of it. Only seven people sat at the conference room table—Director Blanchard, Eric, Dan, Dr. Lee and three immunopathologists whom Seph had spoken to only briefly. Dan's eyes met hers as she entered. His worried look confirmed what she already knew.

"They're not all sick," Dan said. His words tumbled out in a rush. "Some of them just have sick family members."

Just. Her sister's face flashed into Seph's mind but was displaced by Cecilia's. The TV monitor in the corner was screaming apocalyptic scenarios brought on by the virus. Starving orphaned children and overwhelmed hospitals without adequate staffing blanketed the screen. Seph's legs quivered, and she slid awkwardly into the nearest chair, hoping the others hadn't noticed her near-collapse. Wasn't it just this afternoon that the local news reported the first known case in Atlanta?

Eric stood, signaling the official start of the meeting. "The vaccine and antidote production are in full swing, and the FDA has permitted us to waive the usual research trial protocols given the circumstances. Fortunately the chemical composition of the vaccine, as provided by Baine, turned out to be fairly simple to manufacture, so we should have a small supply to give to test subjects as soon as tomorrow. If that goes well, we should have enough made to be able to distribute to the military and other key personnel within a week. After that, it'll be doled out to the general public."

"What do you mean by 'antidote'?" Seph asked. "Do you mean you can cure this thing?"

Eric gave a curt shake of his head. "I'm afraid not. The antidote won't help someone who's already showing signs of the disease. It's an immunoglobulin, which prevents the illness from taking hold if given early after exposure to the virus. It's a treatment, not a cure. It does not provide long term protection. Vaccines, on the other hand, take a few weeks to kick in but will confer protection, making the recipient immune to the disease. We're recommending anyone with type O blood who is not yet ill get both the immunoglobulin and the vaccine, in case they've been bitten by a flea and don't know it. It's analogous to the treatment we give people bitten by a rabid animal. They get both the immunoglobulin and the vaccine at the same time."

"How soon after exposure does it need to be given to help? What's the time frame?" Seph asked.

"Seph, we don't know for sure. We don't know anything for sure, but if it acts like most immunoglobulins, typically

24 to 48 hours." He spoke to her like a weary parent placating his demanding child at the end of a long road trip.

"Cecilia's dying."

"I know, Seph. A lot of people are dying."

Something about the casual way Eric said it, combined with the fact that he didn't bother to look up from his precious papers, ignited Seph's smoldering fuse. She exploded. "You don't even care, do you, Eric? All you care about are the numbers, the big picture, but you know what? Some of them have names, Eric, and one of them is sitting right down the hall from here, busting her ass even though it's her last two days on this earth."

As soon as Seph erupted, she wished she could take it back. She bit down on her tongue hard enough that she could taste her own blood. It was her fatigue talking. She knew that. She hoped Eric did, too. When he finally looked up, the exhaustion and pain etched on his face made her flinch. He was at least as tired as she, and here she was screaming at him like a mad woman.

"I'm sorry," She rushed to apologize before Eric could respond to her outburst. "I'm just . . ."

"Tired. I know. I think what you were getting at is whether or not Cecilia would benefit from being one of the test subjects. The answer is 'no'—not if she's already sick. As I said before, it's too late by then. And we wouldn't . . ." He censored himself abruptly, but Seph had a pretty good idea what he was going to say. One of the dubious benefits of being an empath.

"We wouldn't want to waste one of the doses on someone who is already dead," she said, finishing his thought for him.

Eric turned his face away from hers and nodded his head. He took a deep breath. "Why don't you give us your update on the code and then go get some sleep? We don't have much else to do until we receive word that the vaccine is ready for its limited deployment tomorrow."

Seph hurried through her update, fetched Cecilia her coffee and walked out of the gloomy basement into the embrace of the Georgia sunshine. The warmth felt good on her arms. She hadn't seen the sun since she'd gotten off the plane from New York. She turned her face up toward the rays in order to savor them more fully, and she took her time strolling to the rental car.

Another wave of fatigue crashed over her as she fastened her seat belt. She clutched the hot steering wheel as if it were a life preserver, forcing herself to take several deep breaths in order to regain some focus before driving to the hotel. Eric was right. She needed some sleep. Things were looking good for tomorrow. The code would be cracked, and the first wave of vaccinations given. Hopefully, the announcement of the vaccine would restore people's faith that the world was not, in fact, coming to an end. Time to call it a day.

Seph *and* the rental car made it back to Holiday Inn in one piece. Once securely ensconced in her room, Seph kicked off her heels, took a long shower and raided the mini-bar. No tequila. Disappointing. She often found that when she was working a case, sobriety and insomnia held hands. Alcohol wasn't the healthiest way to get a good night's sleep, but for her it was the only way.

She crawled under the crisp sheets and waited for sleep to come. From the safety of her fluffy down cocoon, the events of the last few days seemed unreal, like something out of a bad science fiction movie. *At least there are no zombies,* Seph thought as she drifted off to sleep. *Not yet.*

The darkness gave way to a sun-kissed field of white narcissus and purple violets. A grand piano sat in the middle of the field, its blackness a stark contrast to the paperwhites. Baine was playing a cheerful Strauss waltz, his fingers bouncing skillfully back and forth across the keyboard. He wore a tuxedo, his hair slicked back and his head bent in concentration as he played. Bloated, rotting corpses lay scattered throughout the field, partially hidden by the blooms, so she danced gingerly, stopping to pluck any blossom that happened to grab her fancy.

Cecilia was there, lying among the dead; but unlike the others, her face was untouched and glowed with an angelic radiance. Grace was there as well, lying to the right of Cecilia. Their hands were tightly clasped together and Grace's face was turned toward Cecilia's, as if to share in her radiance. Seph knelt down and kissed her sister's icy forehead before placing the bouquet of freshly picked flowers into Grace's free hand, carefully folding her stiff, alabaster fingers around the stems so they wouldn't drop to the ground.

Baine looked up from his piano, his usually expressionless face replaced by that of a demon's, with eyes that glowed red and a contorted grimace for a smile. The music stopped, and the ground began to shake as if from an earthquake, opening a giant, gaping chasm into which everything—field, flowers, corpses and even the piano—was falling.

Seph clung to Gracie and Cecilia, digging her toes and fingernails into the earth for traction, but the three of them kept sliding toward the bottomless pit. The Demon Baine stood on the opposite side of the chasm, relishing their fear and desperation and laughing in great delight.

Then she woke up.

Normally the psychologist in her would require her to perform at least a cursory self-analysis of her nightmare, preferably over a leisurely cup of strong morning coffee, but Seph was far too anxious to get back to work to care. Despite the bad dream she felt optimistic and refreshed, which made for a nice change. She looked forward to seeing what progress Cecilia had made with the code. That, combined with Eric's promise of a vaccine, might make for a very good day.

The elevator to the basement offices had not seen this much use in decades, and it groaned its disapproval during Seph's descent to the bottom floor. The door lurched open to reveal a hallway hyperkinetic with the energy of a whole lot of people who shouldn't have been there. Her high spirits crashed and burned in response to the unexpected hubbub. Whatever was happening was not good.

Seph picked out Homeland Security Special Agent Marin's ramrod posture among the fray. For some reason, she'd assumed he'd gone back to New York. She should've known he'd stick around until he was sure her team had extracted all the necessary information from Baine.

She nudged her way through the crowd toward his location. He was talking to Director Blanchard, and both their expressions were particularly grave. She took another step in his direction and cursed as she nearly face-planted on the slick, wet floor. A drop of something landed on her forehead, and she looked up sharply. Water. From the sprinklers.

When she looked down again, Agent Marin was staring at her. He tossed his head sideways in a beckoning motion. She took a deep breath and closed the little bit of distance left between them. Just as with Eric yesterday, Seph knew what he was going to say before he opened his mouth to speak.

Agent Marin wasted no time on pleasant reintroductions or idle chitchat. "He's gone," he said. "He killed my guard, set off the fire alarm, and disappeared out a side door during the chaos. By the time we realized the fire was a false alarm and came to check on him, it was too late to do a lock down. He was already long gone by then. He left you a message, by the way." Agent Marin was wearing an outdated tan suit and had a notepad in one hand and a pen in the other. He looked more like a dime novel gumshoe than a modern Homeland Security agent.

"For me specifically? By name?" Seph asked.

"No, not by name, but I'm sure it was for you."

"How do you know that?"

"Well, the rest of us non-doctor types sure as hell don't know what it means, and you were the last person to talk to him. So, I figured he must have had you in mind when he wrote it. Wanna take a look?"

He led her into the room with the dog cages. 8B was flooded by the prolonged activation of the sprinkler system, and Seph had to step around several large puddles of water on the floor to get to the even larger pool of blood at the entrance to the cage where Baine had been held. She examined the scene. She noted plenty of spatter, but no body.

Agent Marin saw her looking around. "Justin—my junior agent who was guarding the door—he's already been bagged." His voice was matter-of-fact, but his face was grim.

The cell door was wide open, and the steel chair was still sitting upright in the center of the cage. The cage's emptiness screamed accusations about a situation gone wrong. "We don't know exactly how he tricked my guy into coming close enough to the cage for Baine to get a hold of him, but I'm guessing it happened when Justin was giving him his breakfast tray," Agent Marin said.

"We do know that Baine used the guard's keys to punch a hole in both carotid arteries. It was quick and surgical. Once Justin bled out, Baine unlocked the door with the key and just walked away. He used a lighter to set off the fire alarm and sprinklers as a distraction. He left this perched on Justin's forehead so we'd be sure to see it. He wasn't taking any chances." Agent Marin held up an evidence bag containing the dead agent's cell phone. One word appeared on the screen, typed in bold print: *KELL*.

"I'm assuming it's a typo. Surely he meant '*kill*'?" asked the director.

What is it with this guy and his typos? Seph thought in annoyance, flashing back to the day when she'd first introduced herself to the director—the day he'd assumed she couldn't spell her own name.

"With all due respect, sir, the man engineered a virus that's capable of killing off billions of people. I'm fairly sure he can spell," said Agent Marin.

Seph stifled a gratified smirk. She was tickled to hear Marin say exactly what she was thinking. They would make a great investigative team.

The director curled his lower lip like a petulant child. "None of this makes any sense. He practically begged us to capture him with a letter, and then he willingly gave us his confession. He seemed to be feeding off the attention.

Why run now? Your guard must have done something to him to trigger him to act like this. He was completely under control!"

Agent Marin's right hand curled into a fist, but his face did not change. He didn't suffer fools gladly, and Director Blanchard qualified as one such fool. Seph intervened for him, not wanting to risk having Agent Marin respond inappropriately and possibly being removed from the investigation. If they were going to find Baine again, she needed someone who knew what he was doing.

"We never had Baine under our control. You don't control men like him. He saw an opportunity to escape, and he took it. Baine accomplished his goals. We know who he is, what he's done and why he's done it. He doesn't necessarily want to pay for his crimes. I'm sure he had a contingency plan all along."

The thought of what that plan might entail sent shivers of anxiety down Seph's spine. The future, which had appeared bright just an hour before, now looked bleak. Baine had been one step ahead of them from the start. He'd most certainly been planning this for years, if not decades. His escape was his way of letting them know that, no matter how close they thought they were to deciphering his master plan, he was still in control, still pulling all the strings.

"So what, or who, is *KELL*?" asked Agent Marin.

"I'm not sure," Seph said. The word sounded vaguely familiar, but she couldn't quite put her finger on it. "I'll look through my notes, talk to the others and get back to you on that one. Do you think you have any chance of finding him?" she asked.

"He doesn't have a passport or driver's license on him, and even if he had a fake one stashed somewhere, my department has had the borders locked down since the pandemic began gaining momentum. His apartment is still under surveillance, so he can't reload there. The bottom line is he'll have limited resources at his disposal. He won't be able to get very far, very fast. Like you said though, Doc, he probably already has a plan in place, so we'll see."

Marin shrugged, the motion a tacit resignation to watchful waiting. Without any leads, it was his only option. He sounded weary and not at all as confident as Seph would've liked, especially when compared to the first time they'd met outside Baine's apartment. *Baine's getting into his head, too—the bastard*, Seph thought with a pique of anger.

"If you can give us any hints from that coded journal of his, we'd appreciate the help," Marin added.

The director looked like he was about to have a stroke. A "we'll see" from Homeland Security was obviously not going to be good enough for the bigwigs in Washington, and it didn't cut it with him, either. But, as with Agent Marin, "we'll see" was the director's only option. The situation was out of his control, and there wasn't a damn thing he could do about it. Baine was gone. Tough to put a positive spin on that. He scurried away to regroup in his office sanctum.

Seph looked at Marin, and Marin looked at Seph. Inadvertently, she burst out laughing. Once again, she could tell they were sharing the same unflattering thoughts about Director Blanchard. Marin raised one eyebrow. "Something funny?" he asked with a smile.

"Never mind. I'm going back to my office. Cecilia thought she might have the code broken by this morning. As soon as I find out anything you'll be the first to know, and if you come up with anything regarding Baine's location you call me first, okay?"

Marin nodded. "Deal." He pulled his cell phone out of his pocket and grimaced. "But first I need to call Justin's parents."

Cecilia was sitting staring at her computer screen when Seph returned to their cramped office. The printer was spewing out reams of paper that Seph hoped was the translation of the code. "We need some good news, Cecilia," she said. "What did you find out so far?"

Cecilia looked up from the screen. Seph was aghast at her appearance. She forced herself to shut her gaping mouth, hoping Cecilia hadn't witnessed her horrified expression. Her colleague's deterioration over the last twenty-four hours was painfully obvious. Her skin was albino white, her eyes bloodshot red. She had dark purple blotches on both fore-arms from where they contacted the desk, and she looked bone tired.

"I heard about Baine's escape." Cecilia's voice was flat, frail. She gestured with one hand toward the papers on the printer. "His code is broken, and the computer is translating it into text as we speak. I haven't read it yet. Figured we could share that particular pleasure. If it's really scientific, I won't under-stand it anyway. Remember, I'm just a symbologist." She flashed a ghost of her former smile.

"I'm thinking we should take it to the briefing and let Dan read it with us," Seph said. "I'm not sure that my psychology degree will help much either," she added, wrinkling her nose. "I tried reading up on immunohematology when this whole thing started, but I didn't understand much of what I read. At this point, what I do remember of it wouldn't fill a teacup. That reminds me—since you're sitting at the computer, can you do a search on the word '*KELL*'?"

"Sure." Cecilia strummed her fingers across the keyboard. "Looks like you have your pick of (a) an extinct volcano in Russia, (b) a dragon from *Star Wars,* or (c) a blood group system. I suspect option 'c' is our winner. Says it's the third-most potent antigen group at triggering an immune response, right after the ABO and Rh blood groups, which have become so near and dear to our hearts. So, I think that means it's another blood type. Why do you ask?"

"Because it's obviously important in Baine's plan. He left me that clue when he broke out of his cell. I'd like to have the mystery solved by our next meeting. Maybe we should try to skim through the journal and look for anything that relates to the Kell blood type. We might be able to figure out at least that much on our own. They've delayed the briefing by an hour anyway until all the Homeland Security agents finish up and clear out."

Cecilia cast a doubtful eye on the imposing stack of paper. "Be my guest. You read. I'll rest. I've been up most of the night deciphering the code, and my mind is fried at this point. Feel free to run things by me, though. I'll be right here." She pushed two of the office chairs side by side and curled her tiny frame into a fetal position to lie on her improvised bed. "Let me know if you figure it out," she said with a yawn.

Seph grabbed an inch off the top of the stack and propped her feet onto the desk. "Okay, Dr. Baine, let's see what's so important that it was worth all this trouble to hide." She took a deep breath and plunged head first into the darkness of Dr. William Baine's most private thoughts.

Chapter Fifteen

The Double Cross

Cecilia was sound asleep when Seph finished. Her breathing was barely perceptible, and she was so pale and still that Seph couldn't help but flash back to last night's bizarre dream. Seph wanted so badly to awaken her. What she had read in Baine's journal had shaken her to the point of near panic. She longed to hear Cecilia, with her breezy optimism, offer words of reassurance and emotional support.

Instead, Seph forced herself to take several slow, meditative breaths in an attempt to refocus her mind and quiet her racing thoughts. Seeking solace from a dying woman would be deplorable. It would be even more unfair for her to burden Cecilia with the sickening truth. Even to someone like herself, who didn't understand the specific scientific details about antigen receptor proteins and similar technical mumbo jumbo, the take-home message in Baine's journal was abundantly clear: They were all going to die.

Baine had told her as much from his cage yesterday. He'd had his end game in place long before he positioned his first flea-infested coat in the Shanghai airport, and he'd played the chess match with expert precision. She understood his

words perfectly now. *You and everyone you love will bleed.*
Now it would be up to her to tell the others.

Seph decided to let Cecilia sleep. With any luck she
would die peacefully with her ignorance firmly in place,
believing the world was going to survive because of her
efforts. She deserved that much. Seph kissed her gently on
one purple cheek and brushed a dark strand of hair off her
forehead. "Sweet dreams, Cecilia," she whispered. Then she
turned off the lights, shut the door behind her, and headed
once more down the long hallway that led to command central's dreary conference room.

The remaining team members were in command central,
standing with their arms crossed and watching the room's
television monitors. News channels across the globe were
broadcasting the initiation of the vaccination efforts, showing people lined up in desperation and anticipation even
though the vaccine had not yet been slated for release to the
public.

Eric's face beamed with satisfaction, and Seph felt another
irrational spurt of irritation with him; although this time, the
feeling was quickly replaced by pity. He, the architect of the
world's salvation, the yin to Baine's yang, was going to be especially crushed by her news.

The others were too wrapped up in their imagined success
to acknowledge Seph's presence. She grabbed the remote off
the conference table and clicked off all the monitors. Surprised, they turned around. Dan started to smile but saw the
look on her face and froze in anticipation of what she had
to say.

"Go ahead, Seph." It wasn't a command. He said it gently, encouragingly. Seph's eyes filled with tears. Dan was giving her permission to devastate them with her bad news. Dan, like Seph, had known all along that something wasn't right. He, for one, was prepared.

She launched into a halting recitation of the journal's translation, keeping her voice flat and her eyes fixed on an imaginary spot on the wall to circumvent any chance of seeing their expressions change once they realized the full impact of her words. Only after the expected period of shocked silence did she make eye contact in order to assess the damage her words had caused.

There were no surprises. Eric's face was paler than Cecilia's, his smug smile a thing of the past. Dr. Lee looked as if he might cry, faint, or both. Dan appeared pissed, but now was not the time for an "I told you so" speech. Instead, he said out loud the words everyone else in the room was thinking. "Now what do we do?" No one answered.

"Are you sure?" Eric asked Seph. His voice was calm, devoid of any signs of the inner turmoil he must be feeling. "What does Cecilia think?"

"She doesn't know. She didn't read the final translation. It wasn't done printing when she . . . she's . . . sleeping right now." Seph stuttered, unwilling to say the words out loud. She didn't need to. They knew what she meant. "And, yes, I'm sure, but I think we should all go over it together so we have the same level of understanding."

As a team, they read and then re-read the scientific data contained in the decoded journal to make sure Seph's interpretation was indeed correct. They sat in silence at the conference table, reading and scribbling notes, their faces etched in concentration and frustration. They spoke only when clarification was needed from a member with specific expertise in a particular area. Finally, Eric put down his pen, stood and walked over to the dry erase board.

Seph was struck by a strange feeling of déjà vu. This was exactly how she'd first met Eric on day one of her involvement; rumpled khakis, marker in hand, preparing to clarify details to his peers and brainstorm a solution at the same time. It had only been what—four, maybe five weeks ago? The whole world had changed during that time, and it was about to change again.

Eric reviewed what they'd learned, simplifying the biochemical details as much as he could for her benefit. "Baine created the virus with a membranous coating in place that makes it resemble type AB blood cells in order to fool our immune system. For people who have types A, B or AB blood, the virus circulates harmlessly and eventually degrades. However, people with type O blood already have anti-A and B antibodies circulating naturally in their bodies, so their immune system sees the membrane-coated virus as an invader. This immune system attack, not the actual virus itself, is what triggers the red blood cells to rupture, just like what happens in a transfusion reaction. It's the reason patients have to be typed and cross-matched to blood similar to their own prior to receiving a transfusion. If they get mismatched to a different blood type, BOOM! Their cells explode." So far, this was old news. Dan and the others had already figured that much out on their own. The subterfuge lay ahead.

"The vaccine Baine so conveniently supplied us with *appears* to block the immune system attack but in reality is designed to dissolve the virus's membrane, removing the cloak that makes it resemble the type AB blood cells and exposing the actual virus to the immune system. The virus is man-made, of course, and thus foreign to everyone, meaning no one has any natural immunity to it. It burrows into *all* types of red blood cells and acts much like malaria does, triggering the cells to explode. The disease presentation will be a little different than what we've been seeing in the infected type O's, but the end result is the same. Almost everyone who catches it will die."

"*Almost* everyone?" Seph asked.

"Everyone except those people with the rare Kell blood type system. He placed a receptor blocker on the surface of both the membrane and the virus itself that bonds to the proteins in Kell blood, deactivating the virus. So only the Kells survive. According to his journal translation, most people with synesthesia have the Kell blood type group, for unknown reasons. There'll be a few other random survivors, too—a few non-Kells. There always are."

"He assured his own survival and that of the others like him," Seph said, thinking back to her second conversation with Baine, where she had heckled him for dooming his fellow synesthetes. He'd called her stupid then, and no wonder. As usual, Baine had been several moves ahead. He'd been mocking her for not comprehending his master plan. Natural selection. Evolution. It all made sense now.

She jumped when Eric's next words echoed her thoughts. "It does make sense," Eric offered, "that Baine would have the Kell blood type, I mean. A variant of it causes 'McLeod Syndrome,' a condition associated with psychosis, among other problems. Some believe Henry VIII had it. The blood incompatibility would have caused his wives' miscarriages, and the psychosis contributed to his proclivity toward beheading them. It would also explain Baine's psychopathic tendencies."

Dan spoke for the first time since Seph had given the journal translation. "Once again, Eric, thank you for the history lesson. Great stuff. Very informative. On a more useful note, however, can you tell us what percentage of the world's population has the Kell blood type?"

"About two percent." Eric ignored Dan's sarcasm. "That leaves more than enough genetic diversity to continue the human species. He knew precisely what he was doing. Even the information he provided us on the antidote was useless. I'm sure his tactic was to slow down our research and remove any incentive to continue the hunt for our own cure. He knew we would devote our resources to quickly mass-producing the one he provided instead. Now we've got nothing and . . ." He paused before stating the obvious. ". . . and we're running short on time."

"But if we stop giving the vaccine, no one else with any of the other non-O blood types will die, right?" asked Seph. "Just the ones who got the vaccine? I mean, we only gave them out to the test subjects and the military. That's what you said we were going to do." Was that yesterday? The day before? She couldn't remember. Either way, it couldn't be that many people. A thousand, maybe. Her head was starting to spin. She was babbling, and she knew it.

Eric looked down at his feet. It was his turn to dole out the bad news, and he crafted his response carefully. "I wish that were the case, Seph. Yes, we only gave out the vaccine on a limited basis. But once again, Baine planned ahead. He played us."

"Explain yourself." She intended her words to sound business-like, but they came out shrill and hysterical instead.

"The vaccinated ones will spread the disease via the flea vector to the other non-O blood types." Her blank stare told him she wasn't following.

"The vaccinated ones become carriers of this new version of the disease, at least until they become sick and die. A flea bites the carrier, feeds on the blood carrying the new, uncoated virus and then hops away to bite another person, infecting them. Remember, the new, exposed virus doesn't care what blood type you have—everyone gets sick. Eventually the fleas carrying the new virus will also spread around the world, causing a second wave of the pandemic. Same virus, new disease. It'll happen a bit more slowly than the first wave because we won't have Dr. Baine trotting around the globe hand-carrying the fleas, but it *will* happen. I'm guessing we're looking at about a month before the next wave of illness hits."

"We could quarantine them. All the ones who got the vaccine." Seph was desperately grasping for straws.

"We can't quarantine fleas, Seph. Some of the vaccinated have probably been bitten already. Quarantine *may* slow down the spread a little, but it's not going to make a long-term difference."

"So, that's it then, Eric? Is that what you're saying? Checkmate. Now roll over and die."

Dr. Lee shook his head vigorously and stepped forward to speak. "No. We cannot and will not roll over and die. We can make a new vaccine. It will be easier now that the virus is exposed and now that we know it enters the blood cells like malaria. We were starting to work on our own before we got the information from Baine's laptop, and we were making progress. I know we can do it." Dr. Lee spoke with a quiet authority befitting his advanced age and professional stature.

"But can we do it in time?" Seph whispered the words, her voice choked with panic. "Is it even worth trying?" She imagined herself crawling home to die with Grace, unable to do anything but watch as her nieces' tiny faces grew purple and their eyes red. She imagined the reproach in Grace's eyes as her sister, too, faded away. *You were supposed to make this right.* Seph, gasping for air as her panic overwhelmed her, leaned over the table and braced herself with her right hand.

"Of course we can." Dr. Lee put one hand on Seph's and fixed her in his steadfast gaze. "We cannot afford to think otherwise."

His stoicism was contagious. It weaved its way throughout the room, restoring Seph's breath and permeating the group with a sense of calm determination. For a few moments, the room was silent.

"So what do we do?" Dan spoke first.

"We keep giving the vaccine," Eric replied. He seemed surprised at the shocked faces of those around him. "It'll placate the type O's and give us about a month to work on formulating our own vaccine. You saw what happened to society when the initial outbreak hit, and it only affected people with the O blood type. Can you imagine the repercussions, the mayhem that will ensue if the world finds out what we know right now? If we stop giving the vaccine, we're going to have to explain why, and the truth will likely kill us before the virus does. Civilization as we know it will not survive, and I'm not saying that to be dramatic."

Eric put both hands on the conference table and leaned forward for emphasis. "What we know has to stay in this room, between us and only us, for as long as possible."

"Let me get this straight. You're saying we should knowingly dispense a bogus vaccine to one group of people when that same vaccine has the capacity to kill off an entire group of other people just to buy us time and keep the peace?" Dan made no attempt to hide his disgust at Eric's recommendations. "Jesus, Eric!" Dan threw his pen onto the table where it landed with a clatter.

"I'm saying it's a solid, logical strategy. If we were to retract the vaccine now, then Baine, wherever he is, is going to know why. He'll know we've decoded his journal, and I guarantee you, Dan, he's got a contingency plan for that. If we've learned only one thing about him, it's that he leaves no loose ends. It also makes sense from a numbers standpoint. There will be no statistical difference in the long run whether we give the vaccine or not. As I said before, the virus is going to spread either way, and a few of the strongest people in both the O and the AB blood types will survive no matter what we do. Giving it buys us time."

"Now you sound like Baine with his Darwin bullshit." Dan was shouting now, his hands trembling with agitation. "What you're talking about is murder! You can't play God like that, Eric! None of us can." Mentioning God in a room full of scientists was like passing around a meat platter at a vegetarian banquet. No one wanted to take a bite.

"We already have. We gave the first set of vaccines this morning, Dan, in case you don't remember." Seph detected an uncharacteristic edge to Eric's voice, along with a barely perceptible note of condescension. Their little team was beginning to fray. No, it was beyond that. It was tearing apart at the seams.

"No one in this room will be making that decision." Director Blanchard's voice echoed from the back of the room. He had entered unnoticed while Eric and Dan were sparring. All eyes turned to his, which were unusually expressive. He appeared noticeably older and drawn, as if the burden of the last few weeks had caught up with him as well, forcing him to jettison his politically correct façade. The pretense required too much energy to maintain, and he no longer had any energy to spare.

He knows already, Seph thought. He hadn't been present at the beginning of the briefing, but she suspected he not only knew the details of their latest findings but had a plan already in place. This morning, Cecilia had mentioned in passing that she had sent the director an email with a file containing the decoded journal before she'd begun printing it out for herself. He would have had plenty of time to read it on his own. For the second time since they'd first met, Seph felt a rush of sympathy for him and his position. *With great power comes great responsibility*, the saying went, and for once in her life Seph was happy to be powerless.

"This task group is being disbanded. The Centers for Disease Control no longer has jurisdiction over this matter. The World Health Organization is taking over any and all future efforts with regard to the pandemic. Dr. Laird, you and

Dr. Dietz will join the World Health Organization's multinational research team in Geneva, Switzerland. You leave tomorrow. Dr. Lee, you are dismissed. Thank you for your service." Dr. Lee bowed at the group, nodded at Seph and shuffled from the room.

Next, the director turned to look Seph squarely in the eye. "We need to find William Baine, and we need to find him now. He created this situation. I suspect he knows how to fix it as well. With the proper coercion, he might divulge some additional valuable information capable of giving our research a jolt of much-needed momentum. I seem to recall that finding Dr. Baine was *your* job when you were assigned to this team. Agent Marin is waiting in my office to talk to you. You have been reassigned from the FBI to Homeland Security for the duration of this endeavor. Here are your papers." His voice was cool and detached, yet invited no argument. He could have been reciting his grocery list, if his grocery list included the capture and torture of one master criminal in an effort to extract secret formulas. He handed Seph a manila envelope bearing the official blue and yellow seal of the Federal Bureau of Investigation.

In other circumstances, Seph would have felt obligated to remind him that she was an independent contractor, not a civil servant, giving him zero authority to reassign her without her express written consent. However, for once, she and the director were on the same page. She did want to catch Baine, and working with Marin was the ideal way to go about it. She wouldn't be much help to the research team now anyway, not since she'd finished analyzing Baine's journal. She snatched the envelope out of the director's hand and stuffed it in the pocket of her pants.

"It's because we fucked up, isn't it?" Dan blurted out from nowhere. "Because of the vaccine."

Director Blanchard's face never flickered. "This is now a global crisis best managed by a global organization such as the World Health Organization. In addition, we no longer have enough staff to support the Special Pathogens Unit here in Atlanta. And, yes, this is because we *all* fucked up. I got my vaccine this morning." He turned on his heel and walked out of the room.

Chapter Sixteen

The Hunt

The shock waves from the director's bomb echoed and bounced off the walls of the conference room until finally dissipating into an uncomfortable silence. Seph stood for a moment with the rest of her now-defunct team before mutely turning to follow the director back to his office tomb. She was no good at long goodbyes anyway, although she was half afraid to leave Eric and Dan alone after their last hostile interchange. On the other hand, the two of them were going to be spending at least ten hours together in close quarters on their international flight to Geneva tomorrow, so they'd better get over it and get over it quick. *Besides, what are they going to do—kill each other?*

She cringed inwardly at her own morbid joke. They would all be dead soon enough thanks to Baine, and she feared it was going to take something akin to a miracle to change that outcome. Seph didn't believe in miracles, and she didn't believe much in luck either, so she was going to have to fall back on that which she held so dear—her training in the scientific method, with its foundation in careful observation and deductive reasoning. The drama of the last few days spent decoding Baine's journal while watching Cecilia bleed to death had distracted her from doing what she did best. Seph was going hunting.

Special Agent Paul Marin was awaiting her arrival at the director's office, fingering his wedding band with one hand and clicking a pen with the other. He uncoiled from his chair when she and the director walked in, happy for a reason to stand and eager to begin the hunt. He wore his usual buttoned down shirt, but he had the sleeves rolled up to his biceps as if he planned to get his hands very dirty in the process. Peeking out from under one pinstriped cuff was a faded tattoo of Chesty, the iconic bulldog mascot of the United States Marines Corps. The other arm bore a Christian cross with climbing red roses and the name "Peggy" artfully intertwined within the vines.

He greeted them both with a curt nod. "Looks like you're on my team now, Doc. Follow me." He led Seph through a doorway that adjoined the director's office to a spacious conference room, complete with plush leather chairs and floor-to-ceiling tinted windows overlooking the entire Centers for Disease Control campus.

A 3D interactive projected computer screen displayed a virtual map of the world, which seemed to hover in mid-air above the center of the mahogany conference table. The conference table itself had high-tech built-in touch monitors at each seat, and the table seemed to hum with an electronic life of its own. Seph wouldn't have been at all surprised to hear it say "hello." In three languages. She rested one hand on its highly polished surface. At least it wasn't breathing.

The director muttered something about having to make some phone calls and slammed the door behind her, leaving her alone with Agent Marin.

Marin caught Seph's look and grinned in response. "I know—pretty swanky, huh? Definitely a step up from where you've been working the last couple of weeks. Since Baine's escape, the director's been letting us use it as a staging area for our manhunt. You'll find everything you need here in both written and electronic form—copies of the data from Baine's laptop, the decoded journal, pictures of his apartment—basically, everything we know about Dr. William Baine is sitting in this room."

"So what have you got so far?" Seph asked. "Any leads?" Marin's face darkened.

"Not many. No credible ones, at least. We've had a few possible sightings, but by the time we've gotten someone there to check it out, the trail has gone cold. We're down a lot of manpower, either due to staff being sick or people going AWOL because they want to spend their final days churning out their bucket list instead of catching a mad scientist."

"So why are you still here?" Seph asked. Honestly, she surprised herself by asking the question. She wasn't profiling him. Old habits maybe, or maybe she was just curious.

"Because it's my job. My mission, if you like the sound of that better. Sounds more patriotic, I guess. You?"

"Same." Seph suddenly realized she'd asked Cecilia the very same question on the day she'd learned Cecilia was dying. Cecilia had responded something along the lines of "Where should I be—sitting around waiting to die?" At the time, Seph couldn't fathom why Cecilia would want to spend her final hours working a case, away from her family and everything she loved. That all changed when Seph learned that she, too, would be dead within a month. That powerful knowledge, along with Dr. Lee's resolute words, stripped away all the extraneous bullshit and gave her a renewed sense of urgency, purpose, and clarity.

The next month would define her, and its outcome would be her legacy. Now she couldn't imagine anything more morbid than returning home to Grace. She refused to sit around and worry about which body orifice would next begin spewing its bloody contents. No way. Instead, she was going to catch one more killer, one for the ages, even if Baine couldn't or wouldn't stop the plague he'd created. It was *their* mission—hers and Cecilia's and Dr. Lee's—not just Marin's, and she would see it through no matter what the personal cost.

Seph smiled at Marin, basking in the warm glow of their newly found kinship. Maybe she'd even get herself a tattoo when their job was complete! Her subconscious pounced on that thought, conjuring up an image of the paw prints tattooed on her sister's right ankle. She felt a twinge of guilt for not keeping up with her phone calls to Grace. She hadn't spoken to her sister in days, but they had exchanged a few texts, which was enough for Seph to know that everyone was alive and healthy, at least for now.

Seph picked up the folders containing the information from Baine's laptop and the early, unencrypted part of journal. She would read them again, dissecting them as if with a fine-tipped scalpel and paying special attention to any hints as to where he might have escaped. She abruptly felt lightheaded, and she realized she hadn't eaten all day. Now it was almost five in the evening. The day had started out with her presenting the journal translation, and any desire to eat had been lost in the resulting chaos. Agent Marin had been watching her closely, following the emotions that played across her face, and he grabbed her arm when she started to sway. "Are you okay?" he asked.

"I'm fine, really." Her stomach gurgled loudly in protest, and they both laughed. The moment of levity felt good. They'd been few and far between lately.

"You need to get something into that belly of yours, Doc! Why don't you take the files back to your hotel, get something to eat and call it a night? You have my cell. Give me a holler if you discover anything earth-shattering. Otherwise, we'll meet back here tomorrow at 0800 hours."

"Sounds like good advice." Seph gathered her belongings and headed out the double doors of the conference room. She had to walk past the entrance to the director's office on her way to the elevator, and she could hear the low rumble of his voice as he talked on the phone. Her step faltered when she heard him refer to Dr. Russo.

Seph strained to make out what he was saying but couldn't gather enough words to get the gist of his conversation. Cecilia. Seph looked at her watch. It had been six hours since she'd left her sleeping in their office. Seph knew she wouldn't be able to concentrate without at least checking on her, although she also knew it was unlikely she would find her still in the office.

Seph punched the button to the basement level. In stark contrast to this morning when she'd walked out of the elevator and into the chaos of Baine's escape, the basement hallway was empty. She strolled by command central, which was as dark and lifeless as a stagnant well. As she approached the office she and Cecilia shared, she was hit by the strong smell of chlorine bleach, the fumes stinging her eyes until they watered.

The office door was propped open by a chair, and she gasped as she rounded the corner and collided with a custodian in drab grey overalls. He was wearing a mask to protect himself from the bleach and had a mop in one gloved hand. She peered over his shoulder into the empty room, which was clean and tidy. He must have just finished up. His eyes met hers, and he answered the question she had not yet asked by slowly shaking his head back and forth. *No. Don't ask me. You already know. Don't make me say it out loud.* She turned and walked, then ran the rest of the way back to the elevator. She already knew.

Seph stood staring at her reflection in the mirror of the hotel bathroom, shoulders slumped, brain too numb to wonder why the glass wasn't fogging from the shower running behind her. No hot water and no one to call to fix it. She'd tried to order room service, but the front desk told her the kitchen was shut down due to "staffing issues." Instead, she'd raided the mini-bar and gorged herself on nuts and chocolate. And vodka. And wine. *But no tequila. Still no tequila. Damn.* She needed to erase Cecilia from her mind. Move forward. She had work to do.

She turned the shower off and sat on the edge of the bed, one hand resting on Baine's file. She'd peruse a few pages before bed. *Until the booze kicks in.* She'd barely cracked it open where her phone rang.

"Seph? It's Dan. I'm sorry to bother you, but I was hoping we could get together to talk about a few things." He sounded troubled and tense, just as he had when she'd last seen him during the final briefing. He obviously had not yet recovered from his spat with Eric.

"Um, sure. Of course. But I just ordered dinner in my room, and the place reeks of broccoli and garlic. Do you want to meet in the lobby?" Seph looked at the torn wrappers and empty bottles strewn around the room and lied like a politician. The room smelled like a bar.

"I can handle a little garlic. I have an early morning flight to Geneva, so I won't stay long. I promise."

"Um, okay." She threw her phone on the bed and raced to do a clean sweep of the room, tossing the evidence in the bathroom garbage can. A little perfume, a violent brushing of her teeth . . . she was almost presentable. What the hell could he want? Advice on how to work with Eric? A shoulder to cry on? Dan was cute but today had been a very bad day, and she was a wee bit too drunk to be providing professional counseling services right now.

He knocked on the door and Seph took a steadying breath, willing her erratic pulse to slow down. He stood in the hallway, shifting his weight back and forth and fidgeting with his watch. She gestured to one of the two chairs in her tiny room, and she sat cross-legged on the bed, her silence an open invitation for him to share his thoughts. Her training had always taught her to let the patient speak first, but Dan didn't seem to know quite how to start. She offered some gentle prompting. "Are you here because you're worried about traveling to Geneva? With Eric?"

"What? No." He seemed genuinely shocked by the thought. "Eric and I have our differences, but we'll be fine," he said, dismissing her hypothesis with a shrug of his shoulders. "What I'm worried about is you!"

"Me?" It was Seph's turn to be surprised. "Why would you be worried about me?"

"Oh, I don't know—maybe because you'll be hunting the most dangerous man in the world? Did I mention you'll be armed only with your intellect and accompanied by a cop who's old enough to be your father?"

"Now you're being disrespectful." Seph jumped to Marin's defense. "First of all, Agent Marin is not a cop . . ."

"You'd better hope Agent Marin doesn't develop angina from all the stress." His sarcasm morphed into sincerity, and he leaned forward to trap her in an intense stare. He looked very unlike his usual boyish self. "Promise me when you find Baine, and I have faith that you *will* find him, you won't do anything stupid like try to face him alone. He likes playing with you, Seph, and who knows what he would do if he managed to kidnap you."

Kidnap? Where the hell did that come from? She hadn't even considered that possibility, and she was certain Baine hadn't either. He expected her to die from his virus, along with the rest of non-Kell humanity. He'd told her that himself. What was confusing her at the moment was Dan. Apparently, she had no trouble second-guessing psychopaths but was completely incompetent when it came to deciphering the motives of normal young men.

Dan's concern appeared genuine, but they barely knew each other. She was aware that in intense situations, individuals tend to psychologically bond more rapidly than average, but still—this seemed excessive. She wasn't sure if she should feel touched, flattered or worried. And as far as how to best respond . . . She opted for a dollop of tough chick bravado. "You do know I hunt psychopathic maniacs for a living, right? This isn't my first rodeo, Dan."

"I know." He rose from the chair, raked a hand through his hair and started pacing in the narrow space between the bed and the dresser. Instinctively, she got up and put a comforting hand on his arm.

"Dan, it's *okay*. I can take care of myself. We're both going to be fine." The latter part was a lie, and they both knew it. He put his hands lightly on her upper arms so she was forced to look him straight in the eye.

"I wanted to make sure I said goodbye." His voice trembled on the last word. Seph knew he wasn't referring to tomorrow's flight to Switzerland. His underlying meaning was clear. Her eyes filled with tears. She looked away and swallowed hard, stifling a sob. These were the first tears she'd shed throughout this whole ordeal. She'd even managed not to cry over Cecilia, but now that the tears had begun, they would not be denied. Dan cupped her face with both hands and began kissing the tears away, tracing them with his lips as they ran down her cheeks. He held her for a long time, until the tears stopped flowing, occasionally murmuring words that Seph found unintelligible, but reassuring nonetheless.

They made love like two condemned prisoners consuming their last meal on death row: slowly, with desperation and sorrow. When Seph awoke at five a.m., Dan was already gone. He had left a note scribbled on the hotel's letterhead and taped to the front of Baine's file, where he knew she couldn't miss finding it. It simply read, *"I'll call you from Geneva. Dan."* For reasons she didn't understand, she started to cry all over again. She crawled back into the safety of the bed, pulling the fluffy white comforter over her head to block out the encroaching sunshine.

✚

When Seph awoke again at seven, she felt surprisingly calm and focused. Her long overdue sob fest had been cathartic; as for Dan, well, there was nothing like a good romp in the sack to clear the mind and release built-up tension. She hoped Dan *wouldn't* call from Geneva. They'd had their moment, and they both had some intense work to do. Distractions like him could be dangerous.

Seph had just enough time to take a cold shower, eat and grab some coffee before heading to the CDC's main office to meet Marin at eight a.m. as scheduled. She was hoping to beat him there so she could catch up on the work she had intended to accomplish last evening before she was derailed by Dan.

The lights were off when she arrived outside the conference room. She struggled with the heavy wooden door, awkwardly juggling her giant coffee cup, the light switch and her papers. She cursed as some of the hot liquid splashed onto her hand, and she tossed Baine's folder onto the conference room table. It whizzed across the highly polished surface and slid off the other side, scattering its contents across the floor.

Seph glanced around the room looking for security cameras and, seeing none, proceeded to swear in earnest, muttering every colorful word she could muster from her rather extensive and impressive collection. She attempted to collect the papers and reassemble them in chronological order before Marin arrived. As she did, one page caught her eye.

It was a seemingly innocuous vignette from the early part of his journal, the section that hadn't been coded. That section had been deemed irrelevant, containing typical diary musings from Baine's teenage years and early adulthood. It was non-linear and difficult to read, probably because Baine had heavily edited it, blacking out phrases and ripping out whole pages he thought too revealing of personal details.

Seph had only skimmed this early part of the journal, just enough to gain some background perspective on Baine's upbringing while she was developing his basic psychological profile. Even then, she had been convinced the more pertinent and interesting information was to be found in the coded section, and so after that initial cursory inspection, she'd put it aside to focus on breaking the code. This particular page mentioned his father's retirement:

"Father bought his fishing boat today, and it's beyond magnificent! He said I could christen it anything I like, as long as the name isn't too bright or too jarring to the senses. Friday is his last day at work, and I've a feeling we'll be spending more than just the summers in the Outer Banks now, on the water where it's quiet. Mother didn't have anything nice to say about it, of course. Said it was too expensive. The bitch is driving him to an early grave . . ."

Only a few months later, in dark ink that gouged and scarred the paper upon which it was written, Baine documented the sudden death of his father from a massive heart attack.

"She did it! The bitch finally killed him! She nagged him straight to death before he even got the boat to the water. She never understood him—or me, for that matter—and now she's killed the only person who did. She deserves everything that's coming for her, all the suffering

this world has to offer. The mother of the plague . . ." The rest of the page was blacked out.

The actual words, hastily scrawled in bold print, were barely legible, but the pain and rage contained within was clear. A traumatized Baine never wrote in the diary part of his journal again, and all subsequent recordings were purely scientific in nature, culminating in the coded master plan for his viral outbreak.

Seph set the paper on the table and, following a hunch, activated the touch screen to the 3D virtual map. It popped up to hover over the table like a genie released from its bottle, its green glow reflecting off Seph's face. She twisted one hand in mid-air, rotating the globe to the desired location and then used her other hand to zoom in over the Eastern Seaboard. She was still staring at it when Agent Marin walked in, interrupting her thought process. He saw the look on her face and smiled in anticipation.

"Thatta girl! Whaddya got for me?"

"He's on a boat along the Outer Banks, or at least he was. Cape Hatteras is only, what—about six hundred miles from Bermuda?" She pointed to the corresponding area on the map, and the projection accommodated her motion by zooming in even further. "I'm thinking he stashed a fake passport, some cash and anything else he thought he might need on the boat months ago, and then all he had to do when the shit hit the fan was sail away. Even if the boat was large enough to require it to be registered with the Coast Guard, he could have easily slipped into Bermuda and then flown off the island to anywhere in the world using his fake passport. With everyone so understaffed right now, I can't imagine the coastlines are being adequately patrolled."

"The boat would be registered under his, his father's or even his mother's name. She might have inherited it when Baine's father died. I'm sure Homeland Security did a records search but Baine is a common surname; and with him living in New York City, a boat registered in North Carolina under a different given name wouldn't have struck a suspicious chord with anyone."

Agent Marin was on the phone to the Coast Guard before Seph had finished her last sentence. A few minutes on his cell and a few computer strokes was all it took to confirm her suspicions.

"Strong work, Doc! We've got a hit with the North Carolina Wildlife Resource Commission for a cabin cruiser registered to one Gregor Baine, of New York City, New York. As of this morning, it was still docked at Santo's Marketplace and Marina in Rodanthe, North Carolina." He stuffed his cell phone back in his pocket, cocked his head and raised one eyebrow at her. "You ready for a road trip?"

"We're going to drive? It'll take at least ten hours to get there!"

"Not the way I drive," he replied with a crooked grin. "Besides, it would take a good six hours to fly once you figure in the wasted wait time, the connection and the drive to Rodanthe from the closest airport, and that's assuming the flights have on-time departures. If we stay on the ground, I can keep in touch with my partners, and we're not at the mercy of unexpected delays. I've alerted the local law enforcement agencies to stake out the boat until we get there." He was already heading out the door to the elevator, forcing Seph to run along behind to keep up. "So you just need to hop in, buckle up and pray like you mean it!"

Seph was an atheist, but she recognized a good piece of advice when she heard it. It didn't take her long, cruising at a hundred miles an hour and weaving in and out of I-95 traffic, to start praying like a Baptist. They were about half-way to the Outer Banks when Marin got a call on his cell. His stormy expression and furrowed forehead told her the news wasn't good.

"The local authorities went to the marina, but the boat wasn't there. The harbor master confirmed the boat *had* been there, but he wasn't sure the last time he actually saw it at the dock or when it might have left the area. Sounds like his activity logs are lax at best, and the marina security is even worse. He thinks it was at the dock early this morning when he did his last rounds, which means, if your theory is correct, Baine probably pushed off and headed to Bermuda with the sunrise. If that's the case, he should be close to arriving, if he hasn't gotten there already."

Marin proceeded to make several phone calls to the United States Coast Guard and Bermuda's Department of Marine and Boat Services. Meanwhile, Seph kept her head bowed, both hands clenched in her lap and her vision fixed firmly at her feet in order to avoid seeing the blur of traffic as they sped by car after car at breakneck speed. She continued her fervent prayers, mostly for the miracle of Bluetooth technology, which allowed Marin to keep both hands on the wheel while talking on his cell phone. Perhaps partnering with Marin hadn't been a good idea after all. She was beginning to think she'd be safer with Baine.

By the time she stepped out of the car in Rodanthe, her legs were wobbling, and she was in serious need of a barf bag. Agent Marin noticed her distress and responded with an unsympathetic grin. "Looks like someone needs to get her land legs back." His grin dissolved when she started dry heaving. "Um, why don't you go find a seat and get something to drink while I check things out with the local law enforcement?" he said, in a much more solicitous tone.

They'd pulled into the parking lot of the marina. The surrounding area had a few touristy shops and restaurants, and Seph spied a nearby café with a little outdoor patio. She took Marin's advice and made a beeline for the closest table, settling under one of the cheerful umbrellas and ordering herself a ginger ale to calm her roiling stomach. Once she felt better, she looked around, taking in her surroundings.

In other circumstances, the setting would have been ideal. It was early September but still warm. The ocean was blue and clear with a nice breeze coming off the water. Bright white sailboats and yachts bobbed and rocked lazily in the waves as they lapped the dock. The town appeared sleepy with little traffic and no one on the beach. The only noise was the occasional cry from the gulls circling overhead. Seph took a deep breath, inhaling the salty air and letting the serene setting wash over her like the ocean mist.

She had never been to the Outer Banks before, and she wondered if the calm was typical for this time of year or if the outbreak had thinned the crowds. She could see why Baine's father, himself a synesthete, would bring his family here on vacation and why William, even as an adult, would choose to continue the tradition. The quiet would be therapeutic for a brain like his, one so easily overwhelmed by the frenetic noise and pace of the city.

A gull landed on the patio beside her, its beady eyes imploring her for a handout. Receiving none, it flew away with a raucous caw of discontent, gliding effortlessly in search of a more gracious host. Seph closed her eyes, wondering how Baine would perceive all this with his interconnection of the senses. What would it look, taste and sound like to him? Her senses revealed nothing more dramatic than the sound of Marin's approaching footsteps, so she opened her eyes, took another sip of her ginger ale, and awaited his report.

"We may be in luck," he said. "The marina has security cameras posted at each end. They may have gotten a close enough image for us to at least confirm Baine was here and got on the boat. They might even tell us what time the boat left so we can estimate how far he got. That'll help the Coast Guard narrow the search area. Also, the police went store-to-store around the dock area showing Baine's picture to the locals. One of the owners recognized him. Said he was in early this morning and bought some supplies. Nothing suspicious—just 'touristy stuff,' she said. Paid cash. Unfortunately, her shop doesn't have a security camera, so we don't have any way to confirm it was actually him, but she seemed like a reliable witness. The police took the marina footage to the station, which is only a block or two from here. Would you prefer to walk or drive?"

Seph shot him a withering look in response to his too-innocent question, and he chuckled. "Walk it is, then."

The municipal building was next door to the historic Chicamacomico Life-Saving Station, the first facility of the United States Life-Saving Service, which later became the modern day Coast Guard. The station was a museum now, with a large bronze plaque outside the front door detailing the heroic lives of the men who'd formed the earliest corps in 1874. They responded, often during stormy and dangerous conditions, to the frequent ship wrecks and fires along the treacherous Outer Banks coastline in order to save the lives of those stranded at sea.

Baine would have spent his teenage summers here, immersing himself in maritime culture and learning to tie knots from the descendants of those brave sailors.

At first, Seph had a hard time visualizing someone like Baine, a lab rat from New York City, possessing the nautical skills necessary to flee the United States by boat, particularly leaving from an area so hazardous even the locals knew it as the "Graveyard of the Atlantic." But now that she was here, she could easily picture Baine sailing the coastline, reveling in the quiet solitude as he practiced navigating the area's unpredictable currents and learned the location of every rock formation by heart.

Seph and Marin walked by the museum and entered the lobby of the tiny municipal building. A little bell on the screen door tinkled their arrival, and a police officer waved at them from behind a glass door, gesturing for them to join him in his office. He already had the security foot-age up and running. The images were grainy but adequate, and they definitively showed Baine walking onto the cabin cruiser and pushing out to sea around five that morning. At one point he even turned, squinting into the rising morning sun, to look at the camera. His hand caressed the hull above the boat's lettering as he climbed on board. Both actions seemed intentionally contrived, as if he was playing to the camera. The words "*Chastity's Song*" were clearly visible in black boldface against the white hull of the cruiser.

"Vanna White," Agent Marin said, rolling his eyes.

"What?" Seph asked, confused.

"He looked like freakin' Vanna White right there. Does that name mean anything to you?"

"Yeah, she's from *Wheel of Fortune*, right?"

"Not Vanna White, Doc! *Chastity*." He nodded back to the lettering on the boat.

"Oh." Seph blushed, feeling thoroughly foolish. At least he didn't call her an idiot. She wouldn't have blamed him if he had. "She was a girl from his high school," she replied, calling to mind the details of a particularly memorable vignette in Baine's diary. The calmness of her voice belied the chill traveling down her spine at breakneck speed. "She's not pertinent to this investigation."

"Humph." Marin already had his phone up to his ear. "Time to deploy the United States Coast Guard."

Chapter Seventeen

The Flight

September 9th, 2016, 1600 hours
Off the coast of Bermuda

He wasn't far from the coast of St. George's Island. He could see it with his binoculars. The sun was beginning to set, and the fishermen were making their way back to harbor with their day's haul. He'd enjoyed the trip. He had passed no one else on the water during his voyage, and he saw none of the ubiquitous, megalithic cruise ships hulking in the harbor, nor any tourists on the beach.

He took this as validation of his vision, proof his plan was succeeding. Thanks to him, the world was already becoming a saner, more serene place in which to live. He'd spent most of the trip watching the *Chastity*'s turbulent wake expand into seemingly infinite ripples behind the boat as it traveled forward. To him, those ripples appeared to radiate vibrant colors that pulsed upward from the water's surface, and when combined with the smell and taste of the sea they became a veritable feast for his senses. He hadn't felt this relaxed in a long time.

He lowered the binoculars and sighed. As much as he would like to linger in this perfect moment, they would be looking for him by now, and he needed to keep moving forward. He gathered his essential supplies, stuffed them into a leather duffle, and set off the ship's emergency beacon. It took less than ten minutes for one of the small local fishing boats to reach his location and just shy of thirty seconds for Baine to shoot the first responder between the eyes. He turned off the beacon, doused the deck with gasoline, scuttled the ship and set it on fire. He watched for a moment, as the *Chastity* burned and sank beneath the water's surface, its reflection shimmering like a mirage against the setting sun. Then he turned the fishing boat toward shore and revved the engine to full throttle. He had a flight to catch.

Chapter Eighteen

The Flowers

September 9th, 2016, 1630 hours
Moosehead Lake Region of Maine

Grace Atwood had mail. She walked down the narrow, paved lane from her farmhouse to the mailbox sitting at the end of the road, periodically throwing a slobber-covered stick into the forest abutting her property so Duncan, her Irish setter, could retrieve it. He would amble into the woods, pick it up, and return to trot next to her for a bit, dropping it at her feet when he was ready for her to give it another toss. Then the whole process would start over again. It was part of their daily routine, and they loved it.

She'd just pulled the mail out of the box when a pickup slowed to a stop and rolled down its passenger window.

"Hey, Grace," Ben said. Ben was a park ranger, and his wife, Polly, owned the flower and gift shop on Main Street. Polly's great-grandfather had been a lumber baron back in the day, and that old money had been passed down through the generations. Polly didn't need to work, but she acted as if her little flower shop supported the entire local economy. Grace saw them at church once a week, and that was it. She couldn't imagine what Ben would want.

"Polly wanted me to tell you she's got a plant at the shop for you. Someone ordered you flowers. She was hoping maybe you could come pick them up. She doesn't have a delivery person anymore."

"Are you sure they're for me?" Grace had never, not once in her life, received flowers, not even when she and Tom were dating.

"Yep." Ben chuckled. "That's funny—she said the same thing when she got the order. Gotta head back to work." He waved and drove off.

Grace walked back to the house, Duncan wagging merrily at her side. Great. She had to go into town. She'd been avoiding town ever since the outbreak hit the States. Seph had told her to stay away from people as much as possible, and Grace always listened to her sister. Besides, she, Tom and the kids were pretty self-sufficient on their little farm. Even in happier, healthier times, they only needed to go into town about once a month for supplies. She used to take the girls to church weekly, but she'd even stopped doing that since Seph's last call.

Grace mentally shrugged and gave Duncan's stick a hurl. Oh, well. She could pick up a few things while she was there. No sense wasting the gas on a bouquet of flowers.

Polly's flower shop smelled like funeral flowers, which was pretty much the only business she was getting these days. The folks in her neck of the woods were too practical to spend their money on something that was going to die in a few days anyway. Polly was super-excited to see her when she walked through the door, but then again, Polly was super-excited about everything. She was just one of those excitable people, a rare specimen among her fellow stoic New Englanders. Grace was the transplant, having moved to Maine when she'd married Tom; but it was Polly, with her vintage Pucci print dresses and teased-up blond hair, who looked as though she'd just rolled out of a 1960s New York City transvestite coterie.

"Grace, can you believe it? I got an FTD order, a *same day delivery order* for you! Do you know how expensive that is? Somebody obviously thinks you're pretty special!" She pushed a potted African violet across the counter at her and batted her faux fur eyelashes with such velocity that Grace expected them to fly off and land among the foliage.

Grace eyed the purple blooms with a doubtful eye. No way was that thing going to survive at her house with the kids and the dogs. "Who's it from?"

"Oh, I hadn't gotten to that part yet. Let me see what they wanted on the card." She rifled through her papers for the order. "Here it is. It says, 'Get well soon, B. Baine.' Oh my God, Grace, you're not sick, are you?" She clasped her bejeweled hands in front of her heart, and her expression was one of such mock horror that Grace almost applauded the performance.

"No, I'm not sick. Are you sure this isn't some kind of mistake?" B. Baine sounded remotely familiar to her, but she couldn't place it.

"Absolutely." Polly frowned at Grace's lack of enthusiasm. "Just take them. If you don't want them, I know Mrs. Taylor has a thing for African violets, and she just got out of the hospital. You could give them to her; pretend they're from the church auxiliary or something. I won't tell. Cross my heart."

"That's exactly what I'll do. Thanks, Polly." Grace picked up the vase and carried it out to her car. If Polly hadn't been watching her out her shop window, she would have tossed the plant right in the trash. Instead, she braced it in the trunk while she ran her errands and then paid a visit to Mrs. Taylor, who was thrilled to take it off her hands. On the way home, she tuned the radio to the national news, and it was only then she remembered where she'd heard that name before. She needed to call Seph right away.

Chapter Nineteen

The Island

September 9th, 2015, 2030 hours
Rodanthe, North Carolina

Several hours had passed since Agent Marin first contacted the Coast Guard, and the inactivity, combined with what had turned out to be a very long day, was making Seph cranky. She'd never been good at cooling her heels, and Marin wasn't exactly a sparkling conversationalist. She finally excused herself from the municipal building and planted herself back at the outdoor café, which by night had assumed an entirely different vibe.

The umbrellas were strung with cheerful multicolored lights, and candles flickered on the wrought iron tables. This, combined with the salsa music blaring from a set of outdoor speakers, gave the cafe the feel of a cozy Mexican cantina, its warm glow protective against the evening chill coming off the water. From here, the ocean looked dark and forbidding. The sea birds, undaunted by a breeze that was picking up both speed and intensity, were still circling about, searching for their evening meal. She was sitting alone, nursing her third cup of black coffee when Marin finally appeared and presented her with an update.

"So I've got good news and bad news," he said, flagging down the lone waitress with a flick of his wrist. "The good news is that the Coast Guard confirmed receipt of an emergency distress call from Baine's boat emanating from near the Bermudan coast. The bad news is that the boat now appears to be on the bottom of the ocean floor. I've been in touch with the authorities there. A few fishing boats saw the ship in flames, but by the time they got there, it had already sunk."

"Baine wasn't on it when it went down," Seph said with certainty.

"No. At least, I don't think so. The authorities also reported receiving a missing person report a short time ago. One of the local fishermen never returned home after work this evening. They found his boat docked in the harbor near the airport. It had some blood splattered on the deck, and the ship's log indicated he had responded to a distress signal from a cabin cruiser around five p.m. That can't be a coincidence. It'll take time to run the DNA on the blood, but I think we can safely assume it is not Baine's."

The waitress tore herself away from the television behind the bar to stalk over to their table. She didn't want to be there, and it showed. *We're in the middle of a plague, and you two go out for Mexican.* Seph smiled as she read the waitress's attitude. Marin, ignorant of the silent conversation going on around him, ordered himself a Guinness and pointed to Seph's near empty cup. "You good, Doc? The next round is on me."

Seph nodded. "So, if you're assuming Baine made it to shore on a hijacked fishing boat, where do you think he would have gone from there?"

"That's the other bad news. I think he's already managed to hop a plane off the island. He had his arrival timed perfectly. Two flights took off before we could convince the Bermudan authorities to lock down the airport. One was a red eye going to London, and the other was headed to Toronto. They're reviewing the passport data as we speak, along with the limited security camera footage they have, to see if they can confirm Baine boarded one of the flights using a fake ID. We're going to have both planes detained upon arrival until we can sort this whole thing out. Luckily, no more planes are scheduled to depart tonight."

He smiled at the waitress as she delivered his beer and received a scowl in return. A sudden gust of wind blew his paper coaster off the table, and he watched it flutter away into the darkness. "A storm's coming, the remnants of the hurricane that hit the Gulf yesterday. It's tracking up the coast. Luckily, it's movin' pretty quick. We should be able to make it to Bermuda, or Toronto or London—wherever the hell Baine is heading—tomorrow, no problem. But we're not goin' anywhere tonight." He raised his glass. "Cheers!"

As tired as she was, Seph wasn't able or willing to turn off her brain and call it a night. She frowned as she considered the scenario Marin had presented. "I don't think he's on either of those planes," she said. "It's too obvious. He has to know we would follow the trail he left us exactly as you just described. Why would he set himself up to be captured right off the plane? There's no point in that. He *wants* us to think he's on one of those planes, just like he wanted us to think he'd given us the cure to his virus. It's a distraction. He's buying himself some time to get to wherever he's really going."

"Well, if he's not on one of those planes, where is he? He wouldn't risk staying on an island as small as Bermuda. A tall, white American traveling alone outside of the normal tourist season? He'd stick out like a sore thumb, and I'm sure he's smart enough to know that."

"Bermuda has a lot of tiny surrounding islands where he could avoid detection for a while, maybe ride things out until the virus takes its toll," Seph said, thinking out loud. "But I agree. Bermuda is not an ideal place to hide, and even if it were, hiding is not Baine's style. Our sociopath has a sense of the dramatic. I think he's leading us somewhere, but I have no clue as to exactly where or why. He's testing us to see if we can keep up with him and his game."

"No offense, Doc, but this doesn't feel like much of a game to me." Marin scowled as he clanked his empty beer glass back down onto the iron tabletop. "My guess is he'll leave the island eventually, if he hasn't already, and he can do it only one of two ways—by boat or by plane."

"A boat would be too slow and noticeable," Seph replied. "And as far as a plane goes, you said all of the commercial outbound flights at the Bermudan airport are locked down now. That leaves a private charter as the only other possibility. I sincerely doubt Baine has a pilot's license, so he'd have to hire someone to fly him out of the country. I suggest that's the angle we pursue."

Marin grunted in agreement. "I suspect we're gonna have to beat the bushes for a street level informant willing to snitch on the creepy American who paid 'im big bucks for a little help sneaking off the island. That usually requires some hands-on persuasion, so it looks like we'll be heading to Bermuda after all. We can get the information on the privately registered aircraft on our way there tomorrow morning. But for tonight . . ." Marin looked over his shoulder for the waitress who had disappeared behind the bar. "I guess I'm getting myself another beer." He stood and gingerly picked up Sephs' porcelain coffee cup, holding it by two fingers as though it were a dangerous foreign object. "You sure you don't want anything?"

Seph acquiesced with a shrug. "How about a margarita?"

"How do you like yours? Let me guess . . ." Marin's eyes twinkled devilishly. "Frozen and fruity?"

Seph leaned forward in her chair. "Do I look like a frozen and fruity kind of girl to you?"

Marin chuckled. "Not at all, Doc. Not at all." He headed off in search of the missing waitress.

As Seph settled back in her chair, her cell phone started vibrating, and she glanced down at the caller ID. Her eyes widened in surprise. It was Grace. Her sister never called when she knew Seph was busy working a case. Never. Something was very wrong.

"Hey, Marin!" He stopped mid-stride on his way to the bar. "Better make it a tequila. Patrón. Straight up."

It was Marin's turn to look surprised. "Yes, ma'am," he said, with a mock salute.

Seph picked up her phone just before it went to voice mail. "Okay, Gracie. Spill. What's going on?"

"I got flowers."

"Okay. That's nice. *That's* why you called?"

"From Baine."

Seph's chest deflated as if she'd been kicked by a horse.

"Seph, are you still there?"

"Hold on a second, Grace. I'm putting you on speaker." Seph cupped her hand over the mouthpiece and called to Marin. "You need to hear this." She set the phone on the table. "Okay, Grace. Go ahead."

"There isn't anything else to say. I got a call from the florist in town. Someone sent me an African violet. The card was signed B. Baine."

"You didn't take the flowers home, did you?"

"No. Oh, God! I gave them to Mrs. Taylor! Is something going to happen to her?"

"No, no . . ." Seph was distracted by Marin, who was signaling that he wanted to speak to Grace. "Grace, I'm gonna turn it over to Special Agent Paul Marin from Homeland Security. He needs to ask you some questions, okay?"

Within minutes, Marin had obtained enough information to trace the FTD order to Justin's credit card, which Baine had stolen during his escape. The order had been placed early this morning, either before Baine had pulled up anchor or when he wasn't far off shore and still had web access.

Seph spent the remainder of the phone call trying to calm her sister down. "Grace, you and the kids are not in any danger, I swear. Neither is Mrs. Taylor. The violet was directed at me; you were just the conduit. He's making a point." *You smell like purple flowers.* Seph heard Baine's atonal voice and shuddered. "You studied *The Art of War,* didn't you?"

"No."

"I thought it was mandatory reading at the Naval Academy."

Silence.

"Well, 'know thy enemy,' right? You remember that much, I'm sure. Baine's telling me he's done his homework, and now we're equal. I know him, and he knows me."

"So now what?"

"Now Agent Marin and I head to Bermuda and haul Baine's ass back to the States."

"Right." Grace was unconvinced.

"I find your lack of faith disturbing." Seph did her best Vader impression, but it landed flat.

"I find a bizarro psychopath sending me flowers disturbing!"

"Grace, I'm telling you, it's fine." Seph seethed internally, furious at Baine for dragging her sister into this. She glanced over at Marin and lowered her voice, hoping he wasn't paying attention to what she was about to say. "Look, remember that scientist I told you about?"

"Dan?" Grace perked up.

"I have a story to tell you . . ."

Marin responded to Seph's teasing tone by looking up and raising an eyebrow.

"Don't change the subject!" Pause. "Are you still on speaker phone? Is it juicy?"

"No, I'm not. And yes—you might say that." Seph pictured her last night in Atlanta—the agony over Cecilia, the booze and the tears. She'd have to edit the details a bit.

"When are you coming to visit?" Grace liked such stories to be told face-to-face over a cup of tea.

"As soon as we wrap this thing up."

"Make it quick."

"I'll do my best." Seph hung up and met Marin's inquisitive gaze.

"Do I want to know?" he asked.

"I'm sure you do." Seph tossed her cell onto the table.

"But you're not gonna tell me, are you?"

Seph raised her empty glass and clinked it against his. "There's not enough tequila in the world."

September 10th, 2016, 0700
Hamilton, Bermuda

Working with Homeland Security certainly has its perks, Seph thought as they touched down in Hamilton early the next day. Agent Marin had secured an eight-seater government aircraft for just themselves and the crew, so she was able to stretch out and enjoy the flight. She had never been on a private plane and also had never been to Bermuda before, so their little excursion allowed her to check two items off her bucket list.

While Marin had chosen to work non-stop throughout the short flight, she was glad she'd managed to settle down into the comfy reclining leather seat and catch a catnap. Her coffee and tequila binge had not been conducive to a good night's sleep, and the phone call from Grace hadn't helped matters.

Their flight arrived just as the sun was rising over the horizon, and the view of the blue sky, clear water, and the white boats in the harbor was breathtaking. Seph pressed her nose against the glass like a child, craning her neck to see as much as she could during their descent. A little voice in her head reminded her to enjoy these moments while she could. Mortality loomed like a dark cloud overhead.

Her phone alerted her to a voice mail from Dan, who'd called while she was in flight. He'd left a message indicating the team of scientists at the World Health Organization headquarters in Geneva was making rapid progress toward the development of a new vaccine and an antidote. He sounded certain they'd be successful, but whether they'd be done in time was another matter.

So far, they'd had no reported cases of a second wave of illness, but Eric conservatively estimated they had less than two weeks left before it would hit. The research team guessed they would need about the same amount of time before the vaccine would be finished, in full production and distributed. It was going to be desperately close. Dan kept his voice neutral throughout the message, and he ended the call with a "happy hunting," which for Seph was a relief. "I love you" would have been infinitely more complicated.

Throughout the trip, Agent Marin remained in constant contact with the US Coast Guard and Air Force, as well as the Bermudan authorities, and together they turned up some interesting information. They found out that L. F. Wade International Airport had a separate terminal on the north side specifically for corporate jets, and one such jet had taken off during the time frame in question. In addition, the Bermuda Aircraft Registry listed eight helicopters, all registered to private yachts docked in the various harbors around Hamilton. The corporate jet had filed a flight plan and was headed to London where it would be detained upon arrival. Tracking the helicopters presented more of a challenge.

Upon landing, Seph and Agent Marin were met on the tarmac by the governor's official chauffeur, a very British appearing elderly gentleman wearing a formal jacket and tie with his pleated Bermuda shorts. He assisted them into the back of a black sedan before whisking them away to meet with the governor at the parish's parliament building. He led them into the posh lobby and offered them some tea before discreetly exiting the room, leaving Seph and Marin to await their audience with the governor.

Marin paced back and forth over the polished marble floors, his shoes squeaking on the tile as he fumed over the delay.

"What exactly are we doing here?" Seph asked, carefully sipping her tea. The fine china cup she held in her hand was probably older than she was.

"We're supposed to be meeting with the governor and a contingent from the Bermuda Police Service to develop an action plan. Obviously I have no jurisdiction here, so I need to work in concert with the local authorities. The governor doesn't have to be involved per se, but he asked to be present for the initial meeting. I suspect he wants to make sure that we brash Americans don't sully his island." He resumed his pacing.

Seph glanced at her watch. "I guess we're on what they call 'island time.'"

"This isn't hang loose Hawaii, Seph." Marin fumbled with trying to make the requisite two fingered salute. "This is Bermuda. Their sphincters are much tighter here."

"I can see what you mean," Seph replied, looking around the lobby's stuffy colonial decor. "I'm half expecting to hear *God Save the Queen* blaring over the loudspeakers. And how about our driver? Do you think his name was really Jeeves?"

Seph tried her best to distract Marin into relaxing a bit. His tension was contagious, and the constant clicking of his heels on the floor was becoming highly irritating.

Marin wrinkled his nose but said nothing. A faint noise emanated from behind a set of heavily carved wooden doors in the back of the lobby, and he swiveled around in response. "Thank God," he said. "Looks like we're finally gonna get some movement."

The doors swung open to reveal a secretary in the tightest pencil skirt Seph had ever seen. She waved them in, smiling becomingly at Marin and ignoring Seph completely. "The governor will see you now."

Seph had imagined how the governor might appear; this was not it. Short and bookish, he looked more like an accountant at a New York investment firm than the governor of a British colony. Standing at attention next to him was the chief of police, and they were surrounded by a few other men and women in business attire, some with note pads and official-looking files in hand. Agent Marin waited impatiently for the formal exchange of pleasantries to end and then jumped in with both feet.

"I need all the information on who owns those helicopters including their whereabouts for the last twenty-four hours," he said. "I also need to know the names of the actual pilots employed by the owners. We have to look for any connection to Baine or for anyone susceptible to being bought out—like someone with gambling debts, for example."

The governor and the police chief exchanged glances. The governor peered over his owlish glasses and down his nose at Agent Marin, as if the detective had just crawled out from under a hay bale at the county fair. "I appreciate the gravity of the situation, Special Agent Marin," he said in his most formal Queen's English. "However, those yachts are owned by wealthy, powerful and private individuals who do important business with the banks and corporations of Bermuda. We can provide you with the information from the Registry with regard to whom the ships are registered, but as far as interrogating the owners as to their whereabouts, I'm afraid that won't be happening."

It was Marin's turn to exchange a look with Seph. She stifled a smile. This was going to be good.

"I see," said Marin. He paused reflectively and put one hand on his chin, stroking it with his fingers while appearing to ponder the governor's statement. His posture and voice shifted as he did his best John Wayne impersonation.

"Well, I reckon we could always release a press statement asking the good people of Bermuda to give us a holler if they see any tall, white men who could be Baine spreading his pox around the island. As far as we know he's still hangin' around these parts, and since we don't know his reasons for coming to Bermuda, it's possible he's chosen your island as ground zero for round two of his little rodeo. I'd bet that news would make your international investors wet their britches, huh? You fellas just give me a call if anyone starts to get sick, and I'll send the cavalry a'runnin' your way."

Marin stood up, tipped an invisible hat, and turned to walk out the door, gesturing for Seph to follow. They hadn't made it as far as the doorway before the governor called them back.

"Wait." He cleared his throat and removed his wire-rimmed glasses, which he proceeded to wipe vigorously with the fine silk handkerchief from his breast pocket. "I suppose under the dire circumstances, we can assist with your interview process. I assume I have your complete and utter assurance you'll be as discreet as possible with any information you obtain."

"You have my word, Governor." Agent Marin's face and voice were oh-so solemn, but his eyes were dancing with laughter, and Seph could tell it was all he could do to keep it together.

"Excellent. Chief Riddings will assist and accompany you while you are on the island. If you will excuse me, I have another meeting to attend." He placed his glasses back onto his nose and walked stiffly out of the room, followed by his herd of minions.

His exit was accompanied by an uncomfortable silence as Chief Riddings and Agent Marin surveyed each other. The chief was a tall, distinguished appearing black man with intelligent eyes and, from the look on his face, little enthusiasm for babysitting a cowboy and a shrink. Marin dropped the John Wayne persona, returning to his no-nonsense self.

"So, Chief, this is your island. How do you suggest we begin?" he asked.

Chief Riddings' deep voice had the kind of resonance that, when combined with his British accent and neatly-pressed uniform, could make the average American woman melt into a puddle of hormones. Seph found his accent to be particularly lovely, a delightful mix of proper English with a barely discernible lilt she assumed was indigenous to the island itself. She swooned, lost in the beauty of his voice, until he smiled at her doe-eyed expression. Embarrassed, she tore her eyes from his mouth and pretended to pull a speck of lint off her shirt. As long as he didn't speak much, she'd be fine.

"First, we go to the tobacco shop next to the airport." He smiled at their perplexed expressions. "Trust me. It doesn't matter if you don't smoke. Silvino, the owner, is what you would call 'well connected.' His shop is next to the airport for a reason. He knows everything that goes down on the island and is willing to share—for a price, of course. I suggest you buy something Cuban," he said to Marin. "It'll let him know you're 'open' to his kind of business."

Agent Marin raised both eyebrows. "His kind of business would be smuggling, I assume?"

Chief Riddings frowned. "Smuggling is such a pejorative term. I prefer to think of Silvino as an importer of fine and rare merchandise."

"And you don't reel him in because . . ."

The chief shrugged nonchalantly. "Silvino is harmless and often quite useful. Let's see what he might have for us today."

They navigated the narrow, cobblestoned streets to the tiny shop tucked between touristy T-shirt stores and open air cafes. The sign overhead read *Trece Ladrones*—"thirteen thieves." A smaller sign in the window trumpeted the fact that the shop was the only one in Bermuda officially licensed by the Cuban government to sell Cuban cigars.

A bell announced their presence as they pushed open the steel reinforced door and stepped inside. They appeared to be alone. The air was hazy with smoke and the light was dim, so it took several seconds for Seph's eyes to adjust. As the room came into focus, she saw floor-to-ceiling shelves lining three out of the four walls.

Every square inch of every shelf was covered by row after row of cigars, all neatly nestled in their colorful square or rectangular boxes. The fourth wall was covered by a heavy red velvet curtain which puddled like a pool of blood on the wide plank floor. In front of that was a counter lined with glass apothecary jars containing what appeared to be loose-leaf tobacco. A display case sold cutters, lighters and other paraphernalia. An old-fashioned radio crackled noisily from the corner.

If Seph closed her eyes she could easily imagine she'd been transported back to Havana, circa 1920. She inhaled deeply through her nose and felt her head start to spin. The smell could only be described as intoxicating. Seph had a sudden flashback to when she had opened the humidor in Baine's apartment. Then, just like now, she'd been overwhelmed by the heady scent of the tobacco, although there had only been two cigars in the box.

She opened her eyes and started rooting through the messenger bag she had slung over her shoulders. She'd been carrying Baine's file with her everywhere she went. She pulled out the folder containing the snapshots from when they'd searched Baine's apartment and flipped through. She found what she was hunting—a picture of the open humidor with the cigars clearly visible—but the image wasn't close enough for Seph to make out the names on their bands. She was about to hand the picture to Chief Riddings when the red velvet curtain swept open to reveal a doorway to the back office. Like the Wizard of Oz presenting himself to Dorothy and her motley crew, a small, dark figure emerged from the folds of fabric. He hobbled into the room.

Silvino was humpbacked and as shriveled as an old raisin that had baked too long in the island sun. Seph guessed him to be about eighty-four. He flashed a toothless smile at her and nodded in recognition at Chief Riddings. She could see why the chief considered him harmless. Tottery appearance notwithstanding, his eyes shone with a shrewd intelligence which was obviously well intact despite the ravages of his advanced age.

"How may I be of assistance today, Constable?" He addressed the chief, but his eyes followed Agent Marin, who was walking around the store and examining the items in the display cases. Chief Riddings nodded toward Marin, redirecting Silvino's attention to the Homeland Security special agent. "And what about you, my friend? Can I interest you in the highest quality steel cutter, or perhaps even a cigar?" His voice was as smoky as his store but with a terminal rasp that spoke of too many rum swizzles.

Agent Marin ignored the old man's sales pitch and instead responded with his preferred approach—direct and sharply to the point. "We need information on a fugitive named Dr. William Baine. He arrived from America by boat, and we think he's trying to buy his way out of Bermuda."

It was the shopkeeper's turn to be direct. "Mmm. Never hear of him. But you know how it goes. You shop, I talk."

Agent Marin looked back and forth between the shopkeeper and the chief, who was leaning against the display case, placidly watching the scene unfold. Marin waited a few moments, expecting the chief to intervene on his behalf. When it didn't happen, Agent Marin finally caved, sighing heavily and rolling his eyes in a Broadway-worthy performance signifying his defeat. He dug his wallet out of his pants pocket. "How much for the cutter?" He gestured to the one closest to him in the display case.

"An excellent choice. It is three hundred and fifty dollars. I accept both American and Bermudan dollars and credit cards, of course."

Marin tossed the money on the counter, and the shop-keeper retrieved the cutter from the case. While Silvino was packaging it, Seph leaned forward with the picture of Baine's humidor. "Can you tell me what these cigars are, please?" she asked. "I'd like to buy one."

Silvino picked up the photo and held it closer to the light. A slow, sly smile spread over the shopkeeper's face as he perused the picture intently.

"I'm afraid, Miss, that these cigars are no longer avail-able for purchase, even from a store as well-stocked as my own. Only one man has any left, and he gives them out only to his special clients. It's his calling card, so to speak. Your friend, this Dr. Baine, he had one of these?" He pointed to the larger of the two cigars.

"Yes, he did," she replied.

"Mmmm." Silvino paused, and he appeared to be mentally weighing the value of his information against the amount of money he just collected from Marin. His eyes shifted over to Chief Riddings and then back to Seph. "The cigar is an *Ani-versario Gran Corona*. It is from a limited line of Davidoff cigars made in 1986 to celebrate Zino's 80th birthday. Appro-priately, only eighty of them were made."

"Who is Zino?" Seph asked.

"Zino Davidoff, the head of one of Europe's oldest and best-known cigar manufacturing families. His cigars used to be made in Cuba, but in 1989 he had a falling out with

Cubatabaco, Cuba's state-run tobacco monopoly. He burned over 100,000 cigars and moved his cigar production to the Dominican Republic in 1990. He was first my boss and then a good friend. He taught me everything I know about all of this." He gestured grandly about his shop.

"After the bonfire, it became difficult to get a Davidoff cigar in Bermuda or anywhere else in the Caribbean, outside of the Dominican Republic, of course. Most are sold in America, or in Europe, where the corporate headquarters remains. He took me there once, to Geneva, as a thank you for all my years of loyal work. The scarcity of the new Davidoff cigars in this area has led to an active counterfeiting and smuggling trade. The man who supplied your Dr. Baine with his cigar is one such smuggler. He has connections in both Cuba and the Dominican and operates out of a yacht in the marina. If anyone knows where your friend is, he does."

Seph had stopped listening when she heard Silvino mention the word "Geneva." That single word scrambled her thoughts into chaotic bursts of anxiety, and she couldn't concentrate on anything else the shopkeeper was saying. Marin also appeared stunned; but Chief Riddings, oblivious to the significance of that particular fact, remained focused on the task at hand. Seph distantly heard him thanking Silvino for his assistance, and they all stepped back into the morning sun and clean air. The darkened tobacco shop had engulfed Seph in its smoky air of intrigue, but her senses cleared quickly in the light of day.

"That can't be a coincidence, can it? That he's going to Geneva," she said, still bewildered. "I mean, I guess there's a small chance he's staying in the Dominican, but I doubt it. Why in the world . . ." Her voice trailed off as her mind struggled to find a logical explanation.

"Do you suppose he means to undermine the vaccine production?" Marin asked.

"I can't see how he could," Seph replied, "but it seems obvious that he's going there because he knows the mission has been transferred there."

"Maybe, maybe not. He might have made his escape plan long ago and couldn't care less that the World Health Organization's center of operations happens to be in Geneva. Or he could be counting on the fact that we'll follow him there," Marin said. "Maybe he wants the original team back together for some reason. He seems to have a bit of an unhealthy fascination with you." A long pause ensued as they considered the options and what each one might mean.

Seph broke the silence first. "I don't know," she said, with an air of finality. "Everything I come up with just generates more questions than answers."

Marin nodded, running a hand wearily across his eyes. "At least our passports are getting a work out."

Chief Riddings had been silently listening to their interchange. "I think it would be wise to first confirm Silvino's intel before you take the path of least resistance and fly off to Geneva. It sounds like your perpetrator is good at leading you down the path he wants you to follow. Silvino is suggesting Baine left Bermuda in a privately-registered helicopter from a smuggler's yacht and flew to the Dominican. We can assume that from there, he took a commercial flight to Switzerland. A visit to the owner of the yacht should provide the needed concurrence."

"Good advice. But as I recall, the marina has eight helicopters registered to private yachts, and Silvino didn't give us a name. Researching and interviewing them one by one would take too long." Any delay would let Baine get any farther ahead of them than he already was.

Chief Riddings nodded. "Six of those yachts are registered to respectable businesses. The other two—not so much. I have a pretty solid idea who our smuggler is. Silvino didn't give us a name because he knew he didn't need to. I suggest we start there, and we'd better hurry. Silvino plays both sides if it suits him and the money is right. We don't want him tipping off our smuggler. I doubt the governor would approve of us intercepting a private yacht in international waters should our suspect choose to pull up anchor." Chief Riddings opened the door to the back seat of his vehicle and motioned for Seph to get in. "Whenever you're ready, then."

The city's cobblestoned streets, with their right angles and hairpin turns, were not meant to be traveled at a high rate of speed. By the time they arrived at the marina, Seph was white-knuckled from clinging to the door handle, and she swore to herself she would never complain about Marin's driving again. It didn't take them long to locate the smuggler's gleaming multimillion dollar yacht, tethered to the dock like a prized Derby winner in his stall. The owner, who identified himself only as "Manny," turned out to be surprisingly cooperative, hospitable even. He invited Seph on a tour of his "humble, little dinghy" and offered each of the men a dark 'n' stormy, Bermuda's traditional cocktail of black rum and ginger beer. He seemed genuinely disappointed when they declined both offers.

Manny was able to identify a picture of Baine but claimed not to know his name or that he was a fugitive. He'd given Baine an "aerial tour" and then dropped him off at the *Las Americas* airport in Santo Domingo as requested. Baine had paid with cash. "Business has been slow recently, what with *la pestilencia* and all," Manny explained, so he thought it best not to ask his customer too many questions. He sent them on their way with a cheery wave and a rain check good for a future tour, should they change their minds.

Once back at the parliament building, Chief Riddings telephoned the Dominican authorities. After two hours of intense diplomatic negotiations, they finally confirmed they'd let an international fugitive successfully board a flight to Geneva using a fake passport. Agent Marin, already convinced of Baine's final destination and not content to sit around and wait for the chief to complete his telephonic castigations, forged ahead, notifying the Swiss authorities and the World Health Organization's director of Baine's imminent arrival. The governor authorized his private diplomatic aircraft to take Seph and Agent Marin to Geneva, and soon they were once again alone onboard a swanky government plane; except on this go-round, they were jetting to Europe.

Through her tinted window, Seph looked back at the tiny island, growing smaller and smaller and then finally disappearing into the blue ocean as they continued their ascent into the clouds. They'd spent less than twelve hours in Bermuda, and Seph vowed to return for a vacation if she lived long enough. As an independent contractor, she could've taken all the time she'd wanted in between accepting new cases, but she never bothered to take even a single week off. And for what? It all seemed so silly now.

As usual, Agent Marin worked throughout most of the seventeen hour flight, leaving Seph to marvel at his endless stream of concentration.

"They're beefing up security and surveillance," he said. "Baine's picture is being disseminated as we speak, and they're placing plain-clothes policemen and security cameras in every nook and cranny of the World Health Organization campus. There's no way Baine will be able to set foot on the property without being noticed."

Seph nodded in polite agreement, but she was convinced that sabotage was not on Baine's agenda. She'd developed her own theory, and it was just as disturbing. Baine knew they were going to fail, and he wanted to bear witness to an outcome he predicted was imminent. He wasn't worried about their puny attempts to save the remaining fifty percent of the world's population.

In his mind, he was already the victor, and they were the vanquished. He had opened his Pandora's box, afflicting the world with its evils, and now he wanted to watch and gloat. His ego demanded it. Hiding on an island somewhere would simply not do. Seph could only hope that, as with Pandora and her *pithos*, the spirit of hope remained.

Chapter Twenty

The Reunion

September 11th, 2016, 1000 hours
Geneva, Switzerland

The flight over Switzerland, despite the marked difference in topography, was just as spectacular as that over Bermuda. They descended over Lake Leman, its cobalt blue waters starkly contrasted against the backdrop of the snow-covered Alps. Seph took it all in, mulling her imminent reunion with the American members of the research team; which, of course, included Dan. She'd spent the flight alternating between catnaps and fits of angst over their brief *pas de deux*. But now, while absorbing the majesty of the Swiss Alps, their encounter seemed trivial, and even more so when considering the horror yet to come should she and the team fail in their mission.

She now understood, at least a little bit, the mentality of the type O's after the plague first hit. In their final weeks many had chucked everything they owned, everything they'd worked their whole lives to achieve, just for a taste of some exotic, elusive pleasure, some experience they could've never otherwise afforded. A few even took it to the criminal extreme, indulging sadomasochistic and pedophilic urges long hidden under their proper suits and ties and held in check only by the civility of modern society.

Seph shuddered at the memory of those first two weeks of the outbreak. She'd been relatively sheltered from all the mayhem, holed up as she was in her stuffy basement office, too absorbed with her work to really, truly feel the impact of the pandemic. Only Cecilia's death had given her any reason to pause. This second wave would be different. This time, the devil was coming for her, too. She pushed Dan out of her mind and concentrated on the beauty around her. Their impending reunion, awkward or not, was of no consequence. Life was too short for regrets.

Like many European cities, Geneva looked better from the air, where the awkward juxtaposition of modern and historic was not so obvious. Even with the initial outbreak thinning the population by about 40 percent, the city was bustling with traffic and alive with the babble of French, German and English speaking crowds—a fact Seph attributed to so many international agencies, including the Red Cross, being based there.

She and Agent Marin split up as soon as the taxi dropped them at the World Health Organization's headquarters, a nondescript postmodern building that looked like a series of metallic rectangular compartments all stacked inside a shoe box. Marin went straight to security while Seph was directed to yet another upper level, high-tech conference room to meet with the research team.

After fretting for the entire transatlantic flight over the possibility of an uncomfortable reunion with Dan, the fact that he was not present was a bit anticlimactic. Eric, however, was there, and he greeted her with the same welcoming smile and, by appearances, the same rumpled khaki trousers as when she'd first joined the team back in Atlanta. As they exchanged updates on their interim individual activities, Eric mentioned that Dan was stationed in the research laboratory with the other virologists and was not needed at this particular briefing.

He looked away as he said it, and his tone seemed overly casual, causing Seph a brief flash of panic as she wondered if Eric knew. After all, the two men did sit next to each other for at least ten hours on their trip to Geneva. They had to have talked about something. Not that it really mattered. It was none of his business anyway. But still, she had a professional reputation to uphold for however long the civilized world continued to exist, and she'd worked too long and too hard to foster her tough-as-nails image to let one indiscretion ruin it.

She furtively monitored Eric's demeanor as he ran through the most up-to-date information with marker in hand, stopping only to scribble the occasional salient point on the flip chart at his side. He was midway through a discussion on the World Health Organization's global surveillance program for the appearance of a second wave of outbreaks when he was interrupted by the urgent sound of heavy boots pounding down the hallway. The door to the conference room flew open, and a ruddy faced security guard rushed inside, hunching over as he tried to catch his breath.

"Dr. Smith, we need you right away," he said in heavily accented English. "We got Baine."

"We got Baine" turned out to be something of an exaggeration. Instead, Baine had strolled through the front entrance on his own volition, approached the security guard at the information desk, and asked politely if he might speak with Dr. Persephone Smith. The guard picked up the phone to call command central and was in the process of dialing when her partner, mouth agape, recognized Baine's face from the bulletins circulating throughout the buildings.

Exactly what happened next was unknown, because the scene erupted into mass chaos, with the panic alarm blaring a dissonant soundtrack. The lobby overflowed with officers of every nationality and variety, including the organization's own security guards, the local Swiss police and the American Homeland Security agents. Rubberneckers peeked curiously out of their office doorways and over the upstairs banisters as law enforcement jockeyed to see who could gain control over the situation first.

Baine stood in the eye of the hurricane, as still and expressionless as a stone moai, watching the pandemonium swirl around him. When the alarm finally hushed and the movement ceased, he was in handcuffs. He was in the process of being escorted out of the building when Seph made it to the main lobby.

"Wait." She hurried after the Swiss police officers, trying to get their attention and failing. "Please, wait," she called out again, waving one arm in the air.

A familiar face detached from the crowd and grabbed her by the elbow. "It's all right, Doc," Agent Marin said. "Believe it or not, the situation is under control. They don't have anything here suitable to use as a holding cell, so they're taking him to the closest secure location—a building once used as a Medieval prison, stone dungeon and all. Baine should feel quite at home there." He gave her a wry grin as he guided her through the throng and toward the exit. "Just what the doctor's overactive senses ordered: dark, drab and quiet."

"The guard said Baine asked specifically for me."

"He did." Marin's affect stiffened, and his tone became brisk. "I don't like it. I hope you have a better idea of what's going on in that whacko brain of his than I do. Obviously, this has been part of his master plan all along. He didn't just happen to fly in from the Dominican, hear we were in town, and spontaneously decide to drop by for a visit. Anyway, we're supposed to meet the local police at the jail to assist with the interrogation and processing. I also have the pleasure of attempting to iron out some rather complicated international legal issues—who has jurisdiction, whether or not he can be extradited to the United States—that sort of thing. You ready to go through this again?" His eyes searched hers for signs of weakness or fatigue.

"Of course. Round three, right? First was New York, then Atlanta, now here. I get a clearer picture of how he thinks every time I interview him."

"Interrogate, Seph, not interview. Remember? And make sure that process doesn't work in reverse, okay? You get into his brain. He doesn't need to get into yours. Protect yourself and your family. The less he knows about you, the better."

Seph bristled at the implication. She would never knowingly place her sister at risk for harm. "You do realize I didn't just roll off the back of a turnip truck, right? That I actually have a degree which says I know what I'm doing? That whole thing with the violet wasn't because of me, because of something I said or revealed. Baine is perfectly capable of using the Internet."

Marin smiled at her indignation, which annoyed her even more. "I'm just saying that even an old leatherneck like me can recognize that this Baine character is not your average criminal. You said it yourself—we've been one step behind him the whole way. Neither of us knows what's coming next, but I do know he seems pretty interested in you, so it's plain common sense not to reveal too much about yourself. Don't give him any fuel for whatever bonfire he's planning on lighting next."

Marin struggled to hail a cab, but finally prevailed, and he and Seph rode together in silence for the trip to the *Vieille Ville,* the Old Town, where the prison was located. The upbeat Euro pop playing on the radio contrasted sharply with the darkness of Seph's mood, but she was too preoccupied with her own thoughts to care. They pulled up to the curb outside the massive stone building, which cast a jagged shadow over the entire cab as they disembarked. They paused outside to survey the ominous structure.

Perfect, Seph thought. *All we need now is Vincent Price, a howling werewolf and a black cat.* Marin pulled the heavy, arched door open by its iron lever and motioned for Seph to enter.

"Ladies first, of course."

"Thanks. You're all heart," Seph replied, still feeling a bit cross. She stepped gingerly over the threshold.

After the imposing exterior, the interior was a let-down. It was completely modernized save for the original stone flooring, and it hummed with fluorescent lighting and computer monitors. Agent Marin met with the Swiss chief of police, and then he and Seph were escorted through the narrow corridors and down some old stone stairs into the basement chambers.

Here the modernization ceased, and it was as Agent Marin had suggested it would be—dank, drab and dreary. The only upgrades were the overhead light bulbs, which flickered on and off at random intervals, doing little to alleviate the darkness. Drops of moisture collected on the thick stone walls and dripped onto the floors forming black puddles.

"If I'd have known we were going spelunking . . ." Agent Marin said, trying to punch a hole in the oppressive atmosphere. Seph smiled but did not respond. She didn't like being underground.

Their footsteps echoed loudly as they worked their way down the row of iron-barred cells to the end unit where Baine was being held. To Seph's surprise, Marin gestured for the door to be unlocked so they could enter. She glanced at him quizzically, trying to gauge his thought process, but his face was as impassive as Baine's.

The door clanged shut behind them, and Seph jumped, hoping the darkness hid her jitters. *He's just a man. A regular, flesh and bone man just like all the others. Agent Marin's here, the police officers are here* . . . Her pep talk did little to tamp down her nerves.

It had to be the flower incident with Gracie. Never in her entire career had a criminal targeted her family. His doing so had upset her professional equilibrium—the intended effect, for sure. *He's a piece of shit.* Seph conjured up all the hatred she had felt when Cecilia died, killed by Baine's virus, and added it to her anger over Gracie. The strength of her rage did what her intellect could not, squelching the gut-wrenching anxiety. She glared at the target of her enmity and reminded herself to play it cool. He didn't need to know how much he bothered her.

Baine was seated on a hard chair with his ankles shackled to the legs. His wrists were handcuffed together, and his hands rested in his lap. For a moment, the three of them contemplated each other in silence. Then Baine slowly tilted his chin upward into a sniffing position and closed his eyes, as if he could sense something she and Marin could not. She strained her own ears in the silence and her eyes in the darkness, trying to discern the external stimulus to which he was responding, but she could find nothing. Finally, he lowered his chin and his steady gaze met hers.

"So nice to see you again, Dr. Smith. I've been waiting for you. I trust your sister received my present?" He ignored Agent Marin completely.

"What do you want?" Seph snapped. So much for playing it cool. He knew exactly how to push her buttons.

He smirked at her obvious discomfort before turning his gaze to Marin. "Perhaps you could leave the doctor and me alone to talk? We have some business to address."

"Perhaps you can stick that thought right up your ass," Marin responded. "Save your flirting for some other time and place. You have precisely one minute to start telling us how we can put the brakes on this virus of yours."

"Flirting?" Baine seemed genuinely fascinated by the concept. "I didn't realize I was. As far as my creation goes, I have no reason to give you any information unless you have something to give me in return. What's in it for me?"

"You get to keep all your fingers and both your balls." Marin took a step toward Baine and pulled a sinister-appearing metallic object out of his pocket. Seph recognized it as the cigar cutter he'd bought from Silvino at *Trece Ladrones*. Baine also appeared to be aware of its purpose because his smug amusement disappeared. A faint hint of fear settled in his grey eyes. Marin glanced at the Swiss police officer standing guard on the other side of the bars who, without a word, abandoned his watch and walked down the dimly lit hallway, vanishing into the blackness at the other end.

"You and I both know you can't do anything like that," Baine said. His voice was calm, but the beads of sweat forming on his upper lip gave him away.

"Wrong. No one gives a rat's ass about your rights, Dr. Baine. Not a goddamned soul. That's the only good thing I have to say about you and your virus. You wiped out most of the lawyers and the mamby pamby's behind the ACLU, which makes my job a whole lot easier. Welcome to your new world order."

Baine's eyes narrowed in thought as he considered his options. The pause was too long for an impatient Marin, and he stepped forward to imprison Baine's right hand, slipping the man's little finger into the jaws of the metallic cutter.

"I underestimated you." Baine had his eyes fixed once again on Seph's face, holding her in his gaze. "I'll tell you everything you need to know on one condition—you come visit me monthly for as long as I'm incarcerated."

Marin answered for her. "You're not in any position to make any demands." He tightened the cutter just enough for several tiny droplets of blood to appear on the surface of Baine's skin.

"And you're not in any position to cure a plague, are you?" Baine replied. His face remained impassive, but the bulging veins in his neck disclosed his pain and anxiety.

"That's enough," Seph said, stepping forward to put an arresting hand on Marin's arm. She motioned for him to remove the cutter from Baine's finger. Marin hesitated but then reluctantly obeyed, slipping the cutter into his pocket. He studied her face, trying to ascertain her next move. She looked down at Baine, now sucking on his right pinky in an effort to quell the sting from the paper-thin lacerations he had sustained.

"Fine. Give us the information we want, and I'll visit you every month in your cell if you live long enough for that. I have a strong suspicion, though, that someone will take you out long before you make it to prison."

The smirk returned. "You and I both know I'm far too valuable not to protect. Your psychologist peers will be falling all over themselves for the chance to profile me. And as for you . . ." he nodded toward Marin. "Your friends at the CIA will try to recruit me to work in one of their secret labs developing biological weapons. I suspect I will not lack for company or attention. But if it makes you feel better to think of me rotting away in solitary confinement, then by all means, run with it."

Marin whacked Baine across the mouth and nose with the back of his hand hard enough to draw blood from both

Baine's right nostril and a cut in his lower lip. "Funny, that special synesthetic Kell blood of yours doesn't look any different than anyone else's. Does it, Seph?" He crouched down so that he and Baine were on eye level and thrust his face forward so he was only inches away. "Maybe it tastes different, huh?"

Baine spat as hard as he could, spritzing Agent Marin's face with a gush of blood. "Why don't you tell me?" The blood sprayed from his lips and dribbled down his chin as he spoke.

Marin grabbed Baine by both shoulders and pulled him to his feet. Seph started screaming for the policeman down the hall. She didn't speak any French, and he spoke no English, but the urgency in her voice was enough for him to come running with two other guards in tow.

"Marin, stop!" Agent Marin punched Baine a second time, opening a cut above Baine's right eye. "Paul, we need him!"

Seph's unfamiliar use of his first name surprised Marin enough to pause his attack. The police officers unlocked the cell door behind them, and Marin, cognizant of their presence, pushed Baine back into the chair with enough force to nearly tip him over. Marin backed away, straightening his tie while regaining his composure.

Baine was making funny gurgling noises as he tried not to choke on the blood running down the back of his throat and clotting off his pharynx. He hunched as far forward as he could in his chair without falling over and managed to expectorate a few of the larger clots. He slowly returned to an upright position, breathing hard, face covered in blood and sweat. He managed to focus his eyes onto Seph's face. "You see, Per-Seph-O-Nee." He enunciated each syllable like a sommelier sampling a fine wine. "We are all monsters." His eyes shifted to Marin's face, still spattered in droplets of Baine's blood.

Agent Marin gritted his teeth and curled both hands into tight fists but did not rise to Baine's bait. "May I have a word with you?" he said to Seph. "Outside." He spun on his heel and exited the cell.

He and Seph hustled down the hallway toward the stairs at the other end, her sensible heels clicking a staccato rhythm on the stone floor as she tried to keep up with his rapid gait. She heard the heavy metal door slam shut behind them and then the undertones of the guards worriedly discussing the situation in rapid-fire French.

On the other side of the doorway, Agent Marin let 'er rip. "Are you out of your mind?" He spat out the words in a fury. Seph took a step back. "You don't make deals with someone like him. Didn't you hear anything I said to you earlier? He called you by your first name, for Chrissake!"

"Am I out of my mind? You're the one who was playing bongos on Baine's nose back there! I mean, really—so I visit him in his cell once in a while. It's a small price to pay to cure a pandemic that's wiping us out as we speak. Besides, who says I have to keep my end of the bargain after we get what we need?"

"But you will. You and I both know that." Marin pulled a handkerchief out of his pocket and, grimacing in disgust, began wiping Baine's blood off his face.

"Maybe. A lot's going to happen between now and then, so who knows if the situation will even arise. Let's just get what we need and move on."

"May I remind you that the research team is closing in on a cure of their own *without* you having to make a deal with the devil?"

"So they say. We've been through that before. Didn't turn out so well, if you recall."

"What makes you think this will turn out any better?"

They stared each other down, neither willing to blink. Agent Marin broke the stalemate by turning to pound his way up the stone stairs, taking two at a time. "Have it your way," he said over his shoulder. "For the record, it's a mistake. Let's hope it doesn't come back to bite you in the ass." He disappeared into the light at the top of the stairs, leaving her standing alone in the faint glow of a dying bulb.

She made her way back to Baine's cell, taking her time in an attempt to develop *en route* an optimal way to approach the next stage of the interview. *Interrogation!* She could practically hear Marin hissing the word into her ear. Whatever. After how poorly the first part of the *interview* had gone, she'd be lucky if Baine could speak at all.

The officers were still standing guard outside. She motioned for them to leave. They resisted, shaking their heads and exchanging worried glances. She made another, more impatient motion for them to go. This time they acquiesced, receding into the background just far enough to give the appearance of privacy, but close enough to be of immediate assistance if needed.

She stood outside Baine's cell, watching him. His nose had stopped bleeding, but it was already turning ugly shades of purple and green, and his upper lip appeared painfully swollen. He had his head tilted backward into the sniffing position again, with his eyes closed as per his usual, and he labored to breathe through his blood-encrusted nostrils. Every now and again, he would run the tip of his tongue over the cut on his upper lip, tasting his own blood. The dim fluorescent lighting made his pale skin appear unnaturally sallow.

He looks like the victims of his own plague. She rattled the cell bars, making him aware of her presence. Without looking her way, he slid his eyes open as best he could and then smiled, the action grotesquely distorted by the swelling of his face and mouth. He spoke first.

"You already know I hate psychologists." His words were slurred. "Now I'm beginning to hate Homeland Security, too." He lowered his head to look at her, and it struck her that he was trying to be funny without knowing how, given his utter lack of social acumen. Sensing a vulnerability born of physical pain, Seph decided to go with a gentle hand and innocent approach.

"So why make an exception for me? You can't hate me too much if you want me to visit you every month," she asked, batting her eyelashes in what she hoped was a beguiling manner. She suspected she'd fallen woefully short of goal, because she was neither gentle nor innocent at heart. Luckily, Baine was so distracted by his own discomfort that he didn't seem to notice her insincerity.

"We've discussed this before. I need you to tell my story. You seem competent. You passed the test by tracking me to Geneva. You notice the details and connect them, like a synesthete interconnects the senses. And besides, you smell better than the other psychologists with whom I've dealt."

Another pathetic attempt at humor, which Seph ignored. She forged on, abandoning her false naiveté. Too much work.

"That's a load of crap. You expect me to believe you turned yourself in so I could do a cover story on you for *Psychology Today*?" So much for being sweet.

Baine shrugged. "I accomplished my goal. I just reassessed my end point. Originally, I did intend to fully cull the human herd of all but those with the Kell blood type, but now I realize such drastic measures aren't necessary. The new world will be a more interesting place with a few non-synesthetes like you in it."

Baine leaned forward and lowered his voice as if he were sharing a secret. "You're different, Dr. Smith. Just like me. We're the same in our difference. Your empathy compliments my synesthesia."

How did he know about her condition? Seph pictured Baine reviewing her own high school psychological evaluations, much as she had reviewed his. Stunned, she remained silent. Baine mumbled on.

"I have an obligation to educate, guide and lead the residual population to a new level of human development. It'll be easier now that the population is thinner. The struggle for natural resources is over, and my agenda can take precedence. I sacrificed myself to the world by turning myself in. I cannot lead from exile."

"You make it sound as though people will flock to you like you're the second coming of Christ after the Rapture. You're a criminal, not a god, and the populace despises you. You will never again see the light of day after Homeland Security finishes prosecuting you."

"I *am* a savior. I have, in fact, already saved mankind with my actions and that of my virus. The populace just hasn't realized it yet. You can help them to see. You can help me guide them by being my voice." Baine smiled and winced at the effort. "You're manipulative, too, you know. You read people, feel them out, and then use their emotions against them. I could use your interpersonal skills."

Are you insane? It took every gram of self-control in Seph's possession to keep her from screaming the words out loud. She would rather be tortured to death in thirty minute increments with old *Hee Haw* reruns than assist a delusional psychopath with a God complex. But she still didn't have what she'd come for, and she wasn't leaving the dungeon without it. She needed the cure for Baine's plague. She could scream later. She steadied her voice, attempting to rid it of any traces of the emotional turmoil roiling within.

"I see," she replied. "That's quite an offer. But first we need to start with the formula for the vaccine, or no one will be left to care about your new world order."

He stared at her, attempting to read her face and voice. She pulled her smartphone out of her pocket and held it up to him, indicating she was ready to record whenever and whatever he was willing to share. She must have passed his examination, because he closed his eyes to assume his familiar chin up position and, in his usual methodical and dispassionate way, began to dictate into the machine.

By the time Baine finished, it was early evening. His face was unrecognizable, courtesy of Agent Marin. He appeared fatigued, as if divulging all his secrets had deflated what little energy he had left. He was even too weary to make his usual distasteful parting comments to Seph, for which she was grateful. He did manage to open his left eye—the right having long since swollen shut—and watch her as she backed out of his cell. He nodded his head ever so slightly at her as she closed the door, and then he closed his eye again. The tiny but deliberate gesture could have been interpreted in several ways: a dismissal, a good luck, or even a thank you, but she would have to analyze its meaning later. The interview had taken longer than expected.

Seph hurried out of the dungeon and called Eric to request he reconvene the scientific team ASAP. It was imperative they review the potentially crucial information Baine had supplied, and she didn't want to wait until the next scheduled briefing to do so. The precise chemical formulas and detailed algorithms meant little to her, but she had no doubt Dan and the others could put the data to good use. A breakthrough, a *real* one this time, would be very, very nice.

Eric came through for her. At least thirty people representing the top scientific minds in the world were already assembled in the headquarters' mini-auditorium when she arrived, including Dan. Their eyes met briefly as she stepped to the podium to announce her findings. Eric took notes on an overhead projector, and she ran the microphone, starting and stopping the recording at the request of anyone needing to discuss or clarify some of the more obscure details.

Baine had taken three hours to dictate his secret formula. The team took six to review and dissect it. By the time they were done, Seph was emotionally and physically fried. She stepped away from the podium and turned the meeting over to Eric. His steady hand could guide the team the rest of the way. She'd completed her part of the mission. The scientists would be working all night, further breaking down each bit of information into tiny pieces, but she could be of no further assistance, and, in Dan's case, she might even be an unwanted distraction.

Seph slipped out of the auditorium to head to the hotel. She considered calling Agent Marin to update him on these latest developments and maybe attempt to patch things up a bit, but she thought the better of it. He'd come around on his own. Besides, it was the tail end of a brutal day, and there'd be another briefing first thing in the morning. He'd be there. They could talk then.

She stepped out the door of the World Health Organization headquarters and shivered. The September air had turned cold with the setting of the sun. She tucked her chin down, burying it in the collar of her jacket to protect her face from the chilly breeze coming off the lake. The hotel was only a few blocks from headquarters, so she hurried down the dark street, now barren of the government workers that made it bustle during the daylight hours.

She walked past an old stone building, and her thoughts involuntarily returned to the medieval prison and her earlier interaction with Baine. Despite her years of experience, her initial psychological evaluation had been way off. She blamed his synesthesia for her failure. It confused his profile and made him more complex than anyone she'd ever studied. He was an enigma upon whom her innate empathetic gift did not work, and this hobbled her ability to understand him. Even worse, Agent Marin was right—Baine *was* interested in her, maybe even liked her, if he were capable of such a thing. Seph squirmed at the disquieting thought. If there weren't so much at stake, she would've welcomed the challenge of evaluating someone so unique, but instead, given the current situation, he frustrated her to the nth degree.

She was so wrapped up in her self-flagellation that she missed her turn into the hotel and instead wound up in a dead-end alley leading to the hotel's service entrance. Now seriously irritated with herself, she spun around and looked up just in time to come face-to-face with a two-legged predator.

He was a rough-looking young man, with a crooked nose that implied he'd been on the losing end of more than one fistfight. He muttered some words in French which Seph did not comprehend, but his tone and his leer were universally understood. He deliberately moved one gloved hand to the front pocket of his baggy, black jeans and flashed the handle of a knife sheathed within. Seph swallowed to quell the panic and did a quick assessment of her potential assailant. He was clad in a long, fur-trimmed, grey leather parka, as old and as ratty as a dead raccoon. The hood was cinched tightly under his chin. His knee-high, fringed boots were of the same grey leather and in the same sad state of disrepair. By appearances, he seemed more likely to harpoon an Arctic whale than to steal her wallet.

She glanced over his shoulder and spotted the hotel entrance, its safe haven tantalizingly close. He must have followed her the entire way, and he looked quite pleased that she'd boxed herself into a corner without his having to make any effort at all. Impatient with her lack of response, he took a menacing step forward and opened his mouth to speak, but she beat him to it. Her assessment was complete. No serious criminal would be caught dead in a coat like that.

"Fuck off, asshole. Do I look like a damsel in distress to you?" She shouted at him with such force the pigeons pecking at the garbage in the corner flapped away in terror. He was caught off guard, and she took the opportunity to brush by one of his fur-trimmed shoulders and make a sprint for the hotel lobby.

She didn't look back until she was safely inside, skidding through the front doors with an undignified kerfuffle. The man at the front desk questioned her in French, stepping around the corner to offer his assistance. Seph smiled sweetly in return, straightening her jacket with a tug and brushing a bit of imaginary fuzz off her lapel while waiting for her pulse to return to normal. Alone in the elevator, she sagged against the wall and took a deep breath. She needed to be more vigilant. In her world, it seemed, there were monsters everywhere.

Chapter Twenty-One

The Savior

September 11th, 2016, 2100 hours
Geneva, Switzerland

Despite his ankle shackles and the constant throbbing of his broken nose, Baine managed to get some rest. He was able to half-hop, half-slide the chair over the cobblestoned floor from the middle of the cell to the darkness of the far back corner, and this allowed him to lean against the wall. There was a cot in the opposite corner of the cell, but the guards had neglected to undo his restraints, and he didn't bother to complain. He wouldn't be here long.

The thick stone walls of his underground chamber muted the noise from the city above, and the stone itself felt cool and soothing to his swollen face. Occasionally, a droplet of water would fall from the ceiling and ping off the floor, resulting in a welcome burst of color and light only he could see. He needed to sleep. They would be coming for him soon, and despite the bravado with which he had taunted the American agent, he knew if he didn't quickly convince the Russians of his brilliance, of his worth, he himself might not live to lead the new world he had so carefully crafted. The ultimate of ironies.

He closed the one eyelid he could move. As a rule, he did not dream. Dreaming for him involved an uncomfortable activation of all five of his interlinked senses. The end result was much the same as being awake, except in a dream, he couldn't control his level of sensory exposure. He'd trained himself at an early age to avoid it at all costs. At first, this required intense exercise until he dropped from exhaustion, but it got easier with practice, and now he could slip into a deep, dreamless sleep upon will and with little effort.

Tonight, though, his pain was too distracting, so he resorted to letting his tightly controlled mind wander freely. As he loosened his mental vice grips, he experienced an immediate rush of sensory information—the smell of flowers, a pulsating purple haze behind his eyes and a complex taste on the back of his tongue that could best be described as dark chocolate mixed with cayenne pepper. Dr. Persephone Smith. He sniffed the air and licked his lips, then smiled at his own gesture. He knew it would have made her squirm, which in turn would have made her angry.

He pictured her face and was rewarded with another rush of sensations, warmer and somewhat more erotic than before. They would meet again. He'd make sure of it. He was glad his virus hadn't killed her, and now the information he provided would save her from the second wave. He hoped she realized that. Someday, she would have to acknowledge that he was, indeed, her savior. It was a shame he would be unable to keep their monthly engagement. He'd made prior plans.

As if on cue, he heard a faint scuffling in the distance, followed by the jangle of metal keys hitting the stone floor. Someone had dispensed with the guards.

Chapter Twenty-Two

The Scientist

September 12th, 2016, 0400 hours
Geneva, Switzerland

She had another nightmare that night, thanks to the encounters with her would-be mugger and Dr. Baine. She'd struggled with nightmares for decades. During the day she had attitude and self-control to spare, but at night her fears and insecurities came out to play, often warping the day's events into a perverse facsimile of reality.

In this particular dream, Seph visited Baine in his cell, presumably during one of their upcoming monthly tête-à-têtes. However, once the door closed and locked behind her, she found herself not in a modern-day, steel and cement maximum security prison, but in a subterranean maze of narrow, unlit passages with randomly appearing doors and mirrors set at odd angles. This phantasmagoria reflected just enough light to be disorienting, but not enough to alleviate the smothering blanket of darkness.

She stumbled through the black labyrinth, trying to escape from what she did not know, because even though she imagined the hot breath of a Minotaur on the back of her bare neck, she saw nothing chasing her. Instead, the doppelgangers materialized directly in front of her as she rounded each dark corner, seemingly able to anticipate her every turn. They took various forms: the rotting, blood-soaked corpse of a plague victim, the leering face of the ratty-coated mugger; and Baine, his eye sockets hollow yet somehow still able to pierce her soul with his stare.

The apparitions drove her forward, deeper into the maze. She strained her eyes into the inky abyss, searching for a way out. Sometimes she could see a faint light shimmering at the end of the passage, a light she was sure indicated a safe exit. Invariably, though, no matter which way she turned, crashing through the darkness with arms and fingers splayed wide in front of her in a futile attempt to feel her way toward the beacon ahead, another demon, each more terrifying than the last, appeared to snuff out the light and block her way. She would never escape; this gradual realization drowned her in a flood of abject hopelessness that welled from within and washed over her like a tsunami.

Seph awoke in a sweat, tears streaming down her face. She took several minutes to settle down and reacquaint herself with her surroundings. Four a.m. in a hotel room in Geneva. Too late to try to go back to sleep at this point, and she wasn't sure she wanted to anyway. She got up, ate the complimentary Swiss chocolates on her nightstand, and made a cup of strong coffee.

She pulled back the black-out curtains and, cradling her drink with both hands, gazed out of her third story window at the city below. She had a view of the lake, and although it was still dark outside, she could see the street lights around the dock reflecting off the water. Her coffee warmed her from the inside out and braced her for the day ahead; a day she hoped would finally see the end of the prior month's madness by revealing a cure for Baine's virus.

She considered what might be next for her, after all this was over. She hadn't afforded herself the luxury of thinking that far ahead until this moment, but now she had a modicum of hope that she and the rest of humanity would live to see the new year.

The disconcerting images from last night's nightmare flashed back through her mind, and she grimaced at her coffee mug. Maybe she should make a career change. Cake decorating sounded nice. Tough to have a nightmare about fondant.

Seph left her room with the sunrise, eager to meet up with the scientific team and assess their progress. She stepped out of the hotel elevator to find several of the night shift employees silently gathered around the lobby's television, their faces somber. She joined them, although she had a sinking feeling she knew what she would see. Round two had begun.

The footage was from India and broadcast the growing hysteria in Mumbai, where the streets overflowed with mobs of desperate people. They gathered in front of hospitals and local government offices, blocking traffic and clamoring for assistance while a decimated military stood by and watched.

One sobbing woman, her sari torn and blood-stained, carried a prostrate child covered in horrific bruises. The camera panned to the child's mask-like face before focusing on the reporter's subtitled words typed in bold print on the bottom of the screen. *Too Little, Too Late.* Seph didn't stay to see if the statement represented a warning, an accusation or both. She'd already seen enough.

She hurried out the revolving door and ran the entire distance through the empty city streets to the World Health Organization headquarters. They were too late to prevent a second wave, too late for Mumbai, but they still had time for containment. At least, she hoped so.

At the prior briefings, Seph had been forced to interrupt the constant hum of activity in order to announce her own arrival. This time, she walked into a roomful of zombies. They sat stone-faced and mute around the long conference table. Even for a group not known for their dapper attire, they looked rough: unshaven, hollow-eyed and utterly exhausted. The elation she was hoping for was absent. Instead, they moved their heads in her direction like fuel-deprived automatons incapable of generating an emotional spark due to their low energy state. It had obviously been a tough night.

"Where's Agent Marin?" she asked, more to break the uncomfortable silence than anything else.

Dan answered. "He's not coming. Said he had other business to attend to."

"Oh." Like a jailbird shuffling to the guillotine, Seph felt all eyes following her to her seat. "Were you waiting for me?" Her radar told her they were. *Why?* She had nothing to offer their research. She had a not-so-funny feeling she was about to be put in a difficult position.

"We were." Even calm, cool, and collected Eric seemed spent. He moved to the front of the room to address the team. He kept his eyes fixed on Seph, and his diction was stiff and formal.

"We were able to use Dr. Baine's information to formulate updated versions of both an antidote and a vaccine which should be effective against the new strain of virus. If we begin production today, we'll be able to start vaccinating as soon as next week. The Eastern hemisphere will suffer casualties in the meantime, but we are hopeful we can limit the damage and prevent further spread. What we cannot do is conduct the appropriate testing."

Eric cleared his throat and treaded delicately with his choice of words. "There has been some discussion as to whether or not we should proceed, given the negative outcome that occurred the last time we utilized Baine's data."

Seph rushed to interrupt. She could see where this was going. "What's the alternative? How close are you to coming up with your own solution, and how closely does your research match his? If it looks like your outcome is going to be the same as, or at least similar to, his, then it makes no sense to drag your feet."

Eric's eyes shifted around the room, touching on the impassive faces of the other top scientists. "Because we had to halt work on our own vaccine in order to analyze the new data you provided from Baine, I can't really say how much longer we have yet to go. Days, maybe a week or two. . . . It's hard to tell. So far the research seems consistent, so in all likelihood, we will end up with the same solution, but . . ."

Dan jumped to his feet. "That's an overstatement, Eric, and you know it." The room erupted into a buzz of interpersonal conversations. "Do I need to remind everyone *again* that we created this second outbreak with our cavalier approach to standard research protocols the last go 'round? That we trusted a homicidal maniac who double crossed us into doing his dirty work for him? And now you're seriously asking us to trust him again?"

Eric did not respond, and Seph knew why. He was waiting for her to run interference. This conversation was just a continuation of the tense discussions they'd had last night, and the resulting rift had the team stalemated. Eric was promoting forging ahead; Dan was urging discretion. Eric had surmised that she had Dan's trust and, based on that supposition, was thrusting her into the role of the expert mediator, hoping she could sway Dan and the others into agreeing with Eric's plan to move forward using Baine's data. As the team's "superstar" criminal psychologist, she should be the one to know Baine's intentions best. Eric was counting on it. He was putting her talent to the ultimate test. She was to be the deciding factor, the tie breaker.

Like a pair of dice bouncing down a craps table, Seph let the options roll over and over in her head. If they didn't use Baine's data, tens if not hundreds of thousands of additional people would die before the team could develop and distribute their own vaccine. On the other hand, if they used his data to immediately deploy a vaccine, those lives could be saved. The televised image of the hollow-eyed infant from Mumbai rushed to her mind. But what if Dan's concerns were valid, and the cure came with a catch, another ploy that could cost them all their lives?

She shuddered to realize the fate of humanity was quite possibly in her hands, a prospect that made her both hate

Eric and want to vomit at the same time. Her gut told her Baine had given her the truth yesterday in his cell, that he had no intention of killing off the rest of the non-Kell humans, but what if Agent Marin was right again? What if Baine had gotten into her head and was using her? Eric was using her, and he wasn't even a psychopath.

Her head started to pound, and she glared at Eric. She detected a hint of an apology in his eyes, but she wasn't buying it. She took a deep breath and stood up, then rigidly walked to the head of the oblong table to stand in projected solidarity next to Eric. She turned to face the team of scientists and steeled herself so she could speak with an air of professional authority. *Fake it 'til you feel it.* It was the first rule a psychologist learns in Counseling 101, and today it would serve her well.

"I am completely, one hundred percent convinced the data Baine gave me is accurate and without underlying malicious intent. Time is running out. We have already lost almost half of the earth's population. The first wave nearly destroyed society as we know it. We cannot afford a second. We merely need to observe the television images from India to see what our future holds. Just releasing the information to the public, telling the world we have the means to gain control of this situation and to cure this disease could be all we need to stop the chaos. Hope is more powerful than any drug we have. We need to use it. I suggest we proceed."

Silence. Seph was certain a full minute passed before anyone made any effort to speak. She struggled to keep her head up, shoulders back, chin out and face set in a determined gaze. Her panic bubbled like molten lava, threatening to spill over her, over Eric and over the entire room. What in God's name had she just done?

A man she did not recognize broke the silence. "We will proceed, then," he said in a thick, Russian accent. His authoritative voice invited no further comments. "We have a lot of work yet to do," he added, addressing his scientific peers, more so than Seph. His opinion appeared to carry considerable weight, because his colleagues responded by rising and filing out of the room, presumably to return to their individual laboratories.

The Russian gazed at Seph and gave a slight nod before he, too, turned and exited the room. The innocuous gesture was eerily similar to the one Baine gave her yesterday before she'd left his cell, and it was enough to put Seph over the edge. Her legs refused to hold her upright any longer, and she slumped into a heap on the floor next to the conference table, tucking her head down and holding it between her hands. She had completely forgotten she wasn't alone in the room until Eric's soft voice interrupted her catatonia.

"Thank you."

Anger had always been Seph's salvation in moments like this. She summoned it from somewhere deep within and wrapped it around herself like a protective shield. When she felt the familiar flush reach her cheeks, she jumped to her feet and, bristling with adrenal-fueled rage, turned on him, pounding one fist against his upper chest. "How dare you! How could you put me in a position like that? You manipulated me, Eric! Do you know what I potentially just did?" She uncurled her fist and pushed him away.

"Yes. I know exactly what you just did. You did the right thing, Seph. You saved the world."

"Bullshit. Don't patronize me, Eric. How do you know that? How can any of us even know that? With everything that's happened the last few months, with nothing turning out the way it was supposed to . . ." She was babbling, and she knew it. Her surge of energy was ebbing fast, and she was in imminent danger of collapsing again.

"Seph, listen to me. I trust you and your gift. You said Baine was telling the truth this time, and I believe you. Now you have to believe in yourself. It's going to be all right."

Thank you, Dr. Phil. In normal circumstances, Seph would have crucified Eric for his amateur attempt at reassurance, labeling it psychobabble of the most pedestrian kind. What right did he, an epidemiologist of all things, have to be telling her, a seasoned psychologist, to believe in herself? But what was done could not easily be undone and Eric, based on the earnest look on his face, was being sincere. She decided to just let it go. Her shoulders sagged, and she ran a shaking hand over her forehead.

"Who was that, anyway?" she asked, intentionally changing the subject.

Eric, relieved to be let off the hook, followed her lead. "Dr. Dmitri Kosov. He's from a family that has produced multiple generations of renowned scientists, and he's one of the world's most respected viral geneticists in his own right. He and his family members are well-connected with the Russian elite. If he recommends we proceed, Eastern Europe will listen."

"I didn't even know viruses had genes," Seph said, unsuccessfully suppressing a hysterical giggle. Oh boy, she was losing it. Eric obviously thought so as well.

"Every living thing has genes." He frowned. "Look, why don't you head back to the hotel to ride the rest of this thing out? You've done everything you can do and more. We have another briefing tomorrow morning, and I'll call you before then if anything new develops. Okay?"

Seph nodded but made no motion to leave. Eric hesitated, not quite sure what else to do or say. He finally decided to just walk away, hoping she would follow along behind him. Instead, she stood alone at the far end of the quiet conference room, gathering her thoughts and her strength. She was calm now. Eric was right. There was nothing more she could do. Perhaps she'd check with Marin and see if he felt she could head back to the States. Most commercial air travel was stalled, but he seemed to have good government connections. Surely, even though they hadn't separated on the best of terms yesterday, he could talk someone into sparing a helicopter or something.

The thought that she might soon be home curled up in her own bed was enormously comforting to her, and she clung to that mental image as she shuffled out of the conference room and down the hall toward the elevator. She rounded the corner to find Dan waiting for her, leaning against the wall with his arms crossed over his chest. Eric would have also had to walk right by him, and she imagined the choice words they might have said to each other. It was a wonder she didn't hear them.

She stood before him with no emotion left to muster and waited for him speak, like a prisoner prepared to accept her sentence. He, too, appeared to be waiting for something, so she hurried it along, eager to get the whole damned scene over with. She'd been nervous about their reunion since the flight from Bermuda, but now she couldn't care less. She was prepared to say what she knew he wanted to hear. It was the right thing to say anyway. What she was worried about was his response.

"I'm sorry," she said.

"You should be. If we're both still alive by the end of next month, I'll forgive you." He left her standing alone in the hall.

Chapter Twenty-Three

The Abduction

September 12th, 2016, 1000 hours
Geneva, Switzerland

After her run-in with Dan, Seph wasn't ready to head back to her hotel room just yet. It was still early in the day, and she was too agitated to hang out in her hotel room doing nothing; instead she strolled around Geneva, exploring the city the way most European cities were meant to be seen—by foot. Maybe it was her imagination, or her current state of mind, or perhaps a combination of the two, but the crowds seemed even thinner than when she'd first arrived in Geneva. The news from Mumbai had spread in a flash, and in response, the usual vibrant international chatter of the city's streets had dulled to a subdued hum.

She had the city to herself, and she walked for several hours, burning off her nervous energy until she was finally tired enough to rest. She passed a park on the way back to the hotel, but it was devoid of life. No children played on the swings, no lovers cuddled on the grass, and no one sat on a bench reading the daily morning paper. She knew why, and it brought tears to her eyes. They were all at home, waiting to die. Cecilia would not have approved. Once again, Eric was right. The vaccine needed to be announced ASAP or what was left of modern society was going to disintegrate.

She reversed her path and walked back to the park, trudging up to the closest bench, her face set in a stubborn scowl. She plopped down and crossed her arms in an act of pure defiance. The park was surrounded by high-rise apartment buildings, and if she strained her eyes, she could see the occasional movement of a curtain or a flicker of light caused by someone walking by their window. She hoped they could see her sitting below. *Come outside.* She beckoned to them mentally. *I'm going to be all right, and so are you. This time, the vaccine will work like it was supposed to. I promise.* But no one came.

A cool wind rushed off the snow-capped mountains and brushed past her face, its chill reminding her of the fact that winter, and therefore Christmas, was coming. She always spent Christmas with Gracie and her family, and this year would be no different. Determined to break the melancholic spell of the empty park, Seph decided to give her sister a call. Maybe once she shared the good news about the latest version of the vaccine, they could have a normal conversation about something other than the outbreak. It would make for a nice change. She pulled her cell phone out of her jacket pocket, nearly dropping it again when it started to ring. Agent Marin. Perfect timing. He could help arrange her flight home.

He didn't waste time with hellos. "I need to talk to you in person and as soon as possible," Agent Marin said. His voice was purely professional, without a hint of warmth or even a trace of familiarity. *Surely he wasn't still upset over the incident in Baine's cell?*

"Of course," Seph replied in what she hoped was an equally crisp tone. "I'm available now. Do you want to give me a heads up as to what's going on? I expected to see you at the briefing."

"Meet me in the hotel lobby in fifteen," he said. Then he hung up on her.

"I'll take that as a 'no,'" Seph said out loud, staring at her cell phone. She was only a few minutes away by foot, but she jumped from the bench and hurried to the hotel to position herself in its posh lobby. She was alarmed. Something was amiss, and she wanted a few moments to collect herself before Marin arrived. She didn't want to appear as uptight as she felt. Although their relationship was only a professional one, now that she'd alienated Dan she considered Agent Marin to be the sole team member she could lean on. He was as steady as Eric but with the added and reassuring ability to kick someone's ass into tomorrow if he deemed it necessary to do so. As silly as it seemed, she didn't want him mad at her.

A fire roared in the oversized fireplace as she entered the gleaming lobby, vacant except for a solitary reception-ist behind the white marble check-in counter. The televi-sion was thankfully turned off, making the space blissfully serene save the occasional pop of a spark shooting off the burning logs.

Seph settled into a plush velvet sofa and let the fire warm the September chill away. She closed her eyes, took a few deep breaths and practiced her self-guided imagery, a psychological technique designed to help decrease anxiety. She drifted back to the beaches of Bermuda, recalling the warmth of the sun on her face. She hadn't felt truly warm since she'd touched down in Switzerland, and it wasn't even officially autumn yet.

The receptionist broke her reverie by offering her a cup of herbal tea; and instead of mentally returning to Bermuda, Seph allowed herself to pretend she was on a luxurious European vacation, awaiting the arrival of her paramour while being pampered in an exclusive boutique hotel. She smiled at the thought and felt the muscles in her shoulders relax as she sipped her chamomile.

She considered her long-overdue vacation and decided she would make that her utmost priority after the outbreak was resolved. After visiting Grace, of course. Maybe her sister could ditch the kids for a week, and the two of them could go on vacation together. They'd never done that, not even as children. It was a luxury their mother could never afford.

Seph had her back to the lobby's revolving door, but the sudden whoosh of cold air followed by the brisk cadence of approaching footsteps told her Agent Marin had arrived. She hid her face by taking another calming sip of her tea. He sat down on the sofa opposite hers, his face inscrutable, as he pulled a pen and notepad out of his front jacket pocket.

"What time did you leave Baine's cell last night?" he asked.

"Why?" She knew why. There could only be one reason he was asking her these questions.

"Just answer me, please. What time?"

"I don't know exactly. I was there about three hours after you left, and it was just getting dark outside, so I'd guess about seven o'clock or so."

"Did you talk to the policemen on your way out?"

"No. I don't speak any French, remember? I nodded at them, and they tipped their hats at me, if I recall. Why don't you ask them?" A sharp edge crept into her voice despite her best efforts to keep it neutral. Although she didn't appreciate being interrogated by her supposed partner, she was trying hard to keep her attitude in check. Sarcasm would not benefit her in the long run, especially if she wanted to stay in Agent Marin's good graces.

"I would, if their throats hadn't been slit from here to here." Marin gestured from the right side of his neck to the left with the tip of his pen.

Seph swallowed hard and lowered her gaze. She'd figured from Agent Marin's affect that Baine had escaped again, and she should've realized the guards would have been killed in the process. This couldn't be easy for him, having Baine escape from his custody twice.

"How did he do it?" she asked. The Swiss officers seemed a lot more competent than the guard at the Centers for Disease Control laboratory in Atlanta, the one whom Baine had tricked into opening the cell door and then killed with his own set of keys.

"I don't think he did, at least not directly. The police officers were in their original positions at the end of the hallway opposite Baine's cell. Neither of them had defensive wounds, and the blood spatter pattern indicated they both had their necks sliced from behind. This means there were two assailants—stealthy ones at that, and most likely professionals given they left no recoverable fingerprints behind."

Once the cops were dead, Marin explained, the rest was easy. The assassins unlocked the cell door and Baines' leg shackles using the officers' keys. "Whether he escaped with them or was taken by them is unclear," he said. "Knowing what we know about how Baine operates, I'm assuming the former, but I can't rule out the latter possibility just yet. I believe there was also a third party involved. They would've needed someone to feed them the inside information; necessary details like the location of Baine's cell within the building and the extent of the security around him."

Marin paused and inspected Seph's face for any kind of response to his information. Seeing none, he continued. "The building has a few security cameras located outside the main entrance and on the main floor, but the basement has none. You and I know from personal experience that the basement is nothing but a dark maze of stone corridors, yet it's estimated the perpetrators made it in and out with Baine in less than fifteen minutes. They had to have known exactly where they were going. My team, in cooperation with the Swiss team, is still analyzing the security footage, but given the skill of these guys I doubt we're going to be lucky enough to get anything useful. If they knew where to find Baine, they also knew the location of the cameras and how to avoid them, I'm sure."

Seph was confounded by this latest turn of events. "I find it hard to believe Baine was working with anyone. He's too much of a loner and a megalomaniac to be part of any team."

"That's what I thought at first," Agent Marin said, "but he's double-crossed us before. He seems perfectly capable of negotiating a deal when the terms suit him. How do we know the bastard hasn't already sold himself to the highest black market bidder in exchange for a get-out-of-jail-free card? I'm sure there's no shortage of scum willing to make that deal. I keep thinking back to when Baine was bragging about how he'd never spend a day in jail . . ."

"But then he made me agree to visit him monthly in exchange for the vaccine intel, remember? As if he were planning on staying imprisoned. I think he was just yanking your chain about the men in black whisking him away to a clandestine lab somewhere. I . . ."

"Of course, I remember." Agent Marin cut her off with a brusque wave, cramming his pen and notepad back into his shirt pocket. He fidgeted in place for a moment before finally meeting Seph's eyes. The intensity of his gaze was a testimony to the gravity of his words. "What happened after I left yesterday, Dr. Smith? What else did Baine say to you, and what did you say to him? Did you make any other kind of deals or promises that I should know about?"

His implication was clear, and Seph was, for the first time in recent history, shocked totally speechless.

"Seriously?" She sputtered in her attempt to string two words together. "You think I'm your 'third party'? You can't honestly believe I had anything to do with his escape. Do you? *Do you?*"

Marin's face remained still, and his voice stayed neutral. "You two seem to have some kind of understanding," he said. "If you know anything, said anything, told *anybody* something, even inadvertently, about his location—now is the time to let me know."

Seph knew it was critically important for her to stay calm, even though inside she was reeling. Admittedly, she *was* the only person to have spent any appreciable time alone with Baine, but that was part of her job as a psychoanalytical profiler. It should not be enough to make her a person of interest. There had to be a dozen other people on the security force who knew of Baine's location.

She was too hurt to be angry, too hurt to even argue with him. She thought she and Agent Marin shared a mutual trust and respect, but obviously she had been wrong. Never before in her career had she been accused of conspiring with a criminal whom she was profiling, and the allegation stung. She considered her response. She could sob hysterically or launch into an effusive proclamation of her own innocence, but neither was likely to affect him much. As usual, the cast iron bitch approach was her best option. For the second time that day, Seph pulled herself up to stand as tall and straight as she could. The ice in her eyes met the steel in his.

"I am a psychologist and an empath, Agent Marin. Understanding criminal minds is what I do. That doesn't make me a sympathizer or a criminal myself. I want to see Baine rotting away in solitary confinement as much as you do. I believe he was taken by someone with a vested interest in his intellect and prior research. Whether this was part of a specific pre-existing escape plan, I don't know. I do know he is, as you suggested, overly attached to me, and I wouldn't be at all surprised if he didn't try to drop me some kind of clue as to where he was being taken and by whom. He wants me to follow him. His plan is complete, and he's accomplished his goal. All of this is just a game now, icing on his cake. I suggest we review the security camera footage together. It's his game, but it's our move."

"Fair enough." Marin stood as well. "But I've never cared much for any game that doesn't involve a ball and a referee. You understand what I'm sayin'?"

Seph nodded.

"Good. Now let's go see who's been playing on Baine's team."

Chapter Twenty-Four

The Escape

They sat next to each other in uncomfortable silence during the cab ride back to the medieval stone building, Seph staring out the window at nothing and Marin fiddling with his phone. When they finally arrived, Seph leapt from the vehicle in an effort to escape the tension. They strode through the massive front door and were met by a bevy of activity.

While Agent Marin did a brief huddle with the chief of the Swiss security force, Seph descended the narrow stone staircase to the basement and surveyed the scene of the crime. The dead bodies had already been removed, leaving little to see at this end of the hallway. She tucked her gear close to her side and scuttled through the corridor of blood-spattered stone walls until she'd reached the empty cell, the keys still hanging in the door.

The metal chair was upside down and Baine's ankle shackles dangled from its legs, but nothing else seemed amiss. She knew enough about the workings of Baine's psyche to have faith in her conviction; he'd left her some sort of clue, assuming he had the time and ability to do so.

Seph paced up and down the long corridor and around the cell, squinting against the dim light while methodically sweeping her flashlight from side to side in an effort to uncover something, *anything* hiding in the moldy corners of the dark room. But the basement was bereft of bread crumbs. Perhaps the cameras had caught something upstairs. She turned and retraced her steps, the click-clacking of her heels echoing off the stone floors as she ascended the stairs to rejoin Marin.

He'd managed to secure the video footage, so Seph and Agent Marin packed themselves into the chief's tiny office to begin the tedious task of reviewing it frame by frame.

"Find anything downstairs?" he asked.

"Not a thing. What about you? Anything?"

"The Swiss force reviewed this once already." He gestured toward the monitor. "And they gave me a brief rundown. At around nine o'clock last night, two men wearing hats and long coats disabled the alarm system and entered through the front door. They pretty much roll up the carpets in this section of the city after five o'clock, so they were able to enter unnoticed."

The building had been empty except for the two guards and, of course, Baine in the basement. "The men never looked directly at the cameras, which lost them from view when they entered the basement stairwell; but obviously, we know that from there they proceeded to kill the guards and release Baine from his cell. The cameras picked them up again as they exited the basement door onto the first floor. The perpetrators followed the same path out as they'd taken in—right through the front door of the building—but this time they had Baine walking in between them. They exited the building at 9:16 p.m."

"Did we get a license plate number off the getaway car?" Seph asked.

Marin ran his hand over his forehead. "Unfortunately, this building has only one security camera outside the front door, and its angle doesn't reach all the way to the curb. So, in a word, no. We couldn't see the vehicle at all. The Swiss police checked the surrounding buildings for security cameras that might've been able to give us any additional information, but they got bupkis. Given how little we have to go on, and the fact that Baine now has more than a twelve hour lead on us, I'd say we're royally screwed. The *only* good thing is that there isn't much movement in and out of the country—any country—right now."

The latest wave of infection had put a screeching halt to most non-essential travel. "Unless you're government or military, you may as well forget about flying, and the few civilians that are traveling stand out like cabbages in a rose garden, so whoever's got Baine would have to employ some highly creative methods in order to smuggle him out of Switzerland. Their best bet would be to hole up and lie low for a while, which could work in our favor." With that, Agent Marin pressed the play button on the recorder. "Let's get this over with, shall we?"

Seph nodded and focused on the small screen as Baine's grainy, black-and-white image appeared. She watched his every step as he marched in slow motion down the main corridor of the first floor toward the exit. The entire processional took exactly four minutes.

At one point, he turned his mottled face toward the camera and ogled the black lens, giving the secretive half-smirk with which Seph had become so familiar. Then he stumbled and jerked forward, grabbing onto the forearm and wrist of the man walking to the left of him in an effort to avoid falling. He righted himself and continued walking, gaze forward from that point on, until he exited the front entrance of the building and was lost from the camera's view.

"Not a goddamn thing," Agent Marin said. He tossed his pen and notepad on the table and leaned back in his chair. "Just as I expected."

"I'm not so sure," Seph said. She was lost in the footage, her voice nothing more than a murmur and her eyes still glued to the images on the screen. She reset the recording to the beginning, and then paused it when Baine stumbled, configuring the video to loop over and over again at that specific moment in time. "There's got to be something here. He looked right into the camera just before he stumbled, like he was trying to emphasize something. I don't think it was a coincidence. In fact, I think he tripped on purpose. Something's here he wanted me—us—to see."

"And that would be what, exactly?"

Seph responded to Marin's sarcasm by pulling her eyes off the screen long enough to cast him a withering look. "First of all, in my experience, there is no such thing as a coincidence. A coincidence takes far too much effort and planning to occur spontaneously. Secondly, you're the detective here. I read minds for a living, not camera footage, so why don't *you* tell *me* what you see?"

Agent Marin expelled something between a snort and a sigh before turning his trained eye back to the screenshot in front of them, where Baine remained frozen mid-stumble. Marin surveyed the image in silence for a few seconds, and then pointed to Baine's left hand, which was encircling his escort's forearm for support. "There. Can we zoom in a bit more right there?"

Seph zoomed the screen to its maximum level of magnification, a view that included only Baine's hand and the perpetrator's lower arm. Marin leaned forward and squinted at the pixelated images.

"Baine pulled up the guy's sleeve when he grabbed his forearm, which showed us that the assassin's wearing a wrist watch. See how Baine's fingers are curled just above it? It's not just any wrist watch, either. It's a Russian-made Vostok and a highly collectible version at that. They were made in the mid-1960s and only for the military. That's why it's called a 'Commander's' watch. See those markings?" Agent Marin used the tip of his pen to point out the small lettering barely visible on the face of the watch. ЗАКАЗ МО СССР.

"It stands for 'Ordered by the Ministry of Defense of the USSR.' Those things are not cheap. By wearing one, our perpetrator is advertising that he is an experienced, highly compensated upper echelon kind of assassin—probably retired KGB, and now a gun-for-hire. Your average Joe Schmo criminal cannot afford a timepiece like that."

Agent Marin looked up just in time to catch Seph's amused expression. She glanced down at his right wrist, sullied by a battered, old Timex that looked as if it had been rescued from the clearance section of the local Walmart.

"Hey, I like wristwatches, okay? That doesn't mean I can afford a nice one. It's no different than you women with your shoes. I don't see too many of you actually running around in those Johnny Choos!"

"*Jimmy* Choos." Seph corrected him with a gentle grin. "I'm actually quite impressed. Baine wanted us to see that, but I would've never noticed it—too subtle. It helps, though, right?"

"Well, it helps some. It gives us a place to start by narrowing down the players in the field. Instead of the whole world, we can focus on the Russians."

"So what's next?" Seph's cell phone chose that exact moment to chime, and they both jumped. "Sorry. I thought I had it on vibrate." She cursed under her breath as she rummaged through her bag, trying to find her phone. She stepped out of the cramped room to answer the call. The ring tone told her the call was from Eric, and she hadn't been expecting to hear from him again so soon. Whatever he had to say must be important. "Hey, Eric. What's going on?"

"I know I told you to go get some rest, so I hope I didn't wake you, but I heard Baine escaped again. Guess that's why Agent Marin wasn't at the meeting this morning. I'm assuming you've been made aware," Eric said. He sounded troubled.

"I am aware, and I'm on it." *Thanks for the courtesy wake-up call, Eric; in fact, I not only know of Baine's disappearance, but I've been accused of being an accomplice.* Seph wasn't sure why Eric should care. He had everything he needed from Baine. She waited for the other shoe to drop.

"Do you remember Dr. Kosov from this morning? He was the Russian geneticist who supported our plan."

"Vaguely." The morning was a blur. Too much had happened since then.

"He's missing as well."

Boom! Seph perked up.

"He didn't return to the laboratory after lunch, and he isn't answering his phone, so I sent one of the research assistants to check on him at the hotel. She reported back to me that his door was propped open, and the room was empty. No luggage, clothing, or personal articles of any kind. Dr. Kosov has been an integral part of the vaccine deployment team and a key liaison for acceptance of the vaccine in the Eastern European countries, so his sudden absence seems odd, to say the least. Even if he had to urgently return to Moscow, I would've expected him to leave me some kind of message, but I didn't get so much as a brief text. I'm not sure if or how his disappearance relates to Baine's escape, but it seems somewhat coincidental."

"The coincidences appear to be piling up," Seph said. She leaned into the office where Agent Marin sat glowering at the security monitors and signaled for him to pay attention. He clicked off the monitor and stood up when she asked Eric, "Are you concerned something may have happened to him? I guess what I'm getting at is—do you suspect some kind of foul play?"

"I don't know what to think," Eric replied. "I'm not familiar with him on a personal level besides what I told you earlier today about his family. We have a working relationship only. I've been aware of his research for years, of course, but I'd never met him face-to-face before the World Health Organization cobbled this team together."

"Agent Marin and I are going to need every shred of information you have on the good doctor. We'll be there shortly." Seph disconnected and shoved her cell phone back into her bag.

"What was that all about?" Marin asked.

"We have another lead, and I think this one shows even more promise than the Vostok. In fact, they mesh together quite well. Let's go."

They left the building in search of a cab. En route, Seph briefed Agent Marin on the details of her conversation with

Eric, and Marin generated a flurry of phone calls and text messages to his contacts around the globe. "You think this is a coincidence?" Marin asked her between calls.

"No way. Don't believe in 'em. Or in fate, luck or destiny, for that matter. 'Where some people see coincidence, I see conspiracy. That's my job.' Anthony Horowitz. I think that quote about sums it up, don't you?"

Marin grunted and continued pounding on his keypad with pugilistic resolve. Finally, he clicked his phone back on his belt clip. "'Coincidence is God's way of remaining anonymous,'" he replied. "You can't argue with Einstein."

Maybe not, but Seph was sure going to try. The game, it seemed, was afoot.

They trotted through the lobby of the World Health Organization headquarters, spotting a security guard who directed them to the fourth floor laboratory that Eric had made his home away from home. It was a so-called "dry" laboratory— no beakers or body fluids—but was still filled with a flotilla of complex and expensive computers, analyzers and other noisy machines. All were churning, humming and spitting out data, creating a virtual sea of information.

A utilitarian stainless steel table sat like a stolid anchor in the middle of the turbulence. One wall was adorned with a démodé chalkboard, decorated by a simple line graph with the word "Merlin" scrawled underneath in pink chalk. The laboratory door, propped open with a garbage can, also bore a handwritten sign: *Please keep door shut.*

This, Seph imagined, was Eric in his natural environment, before all the upheaval had torn him out of the lab and into a rotating array of conference rooms. He was hunched over the table, which had scattered upon its surface various photographs and articles from a dossier he'd gathered on Doctor Kosov. Seph and Agent Marin entered the lab after a perfunctory knock on the open door.

"I'm not much use now in regards to fighting the outbreak since I'm not a clinician. At this point, my role as an epidemiologist is just to monitor new cases and adjust the statistics as the numbers role in. So I played detective and tried to track down some information on Dr. Kosov for you. I didn't come up with much, I'm afraid." He grimaced. "Mostly just public information pulled off the internet. I also picked the brains of the other team members, but despite the doctor's level of renown within academic circles, no one seems to know much about his private life."

Eric started rearranging the papers on the steel table, beginning with a picture of the Russian scientist, followed by images of Dr. Kosov's family and then finishing with a timeline of the major milestones in his career. Eric pointed to each corresponding image as he summarized his findings.

"From a wealthy, well-connected family based in Moscow. Divorced. No children. Went to university in St. Petersburg. Internationally famous for his research on sequencing RNA viral genomes and how they mutate. His father, now deceased, was a former minister of science. He has one sibling, a younger brother, who is a particle physicist. Rumor has it the family has long been friendly with both the Communist Party *and* the *Bratva*—the Russian mob—which is probably how his father got the ministry job. It's also how some people think his brother managed to get hired by the

European Council for Nuclear Research even though the Russian Federation is not a member of their organization. No known criminal record, but the *Bratva* has ways of burying those kinds of details deeper than anyone cares to dig."

Eric paused for questions. He shrugged at their silence. "That's all I have. Sorry it's nothing earth-shattering. So do you think this situation with Dr. Kosov has anything to do with Baine's escape, or not?"

Seph intended to punt Eric's question to Agent Marin, but he appeared to have drifted away. He continued to nod his head even though Eric had stopped speaking, and his eyes flickered back and forth over the contractor-grade drop ceiling tiles as if they were the most interesting ones he had ever seen. She'd witnessed this look at least once before, and she knew better than to interrupt. She and Eric exchanged glances and waited to see what kind of crack investigative insight Agent Marin was birthing from within. Oblivious to their expectations, he broke the silence with a question. "You say his brother works at CERN?"

"Yes," Eric replied. "Vladimir. Not nearly as famous as his older brother. Still trying to make his mark in the world of theoretical particle physics. According to one of my colleagues, he's assisting with the recalibration and upgrade of the Large Hadron Collider during its latest shutdown."

Agent Marin's head continued to bob up and down. "I seem to recall saying their best bet would be to hole up and lie low for a while," he said under his breath, "but I didn't expect them to go literally underground." His bobbing head ceased, and he lifted a picture of the Kosov brothers off the table and held it at arm's length. "You say it's not working right now?"

"What's not working?" Eric asked. "I'm sorry—I'm not following you."

"The collider." Marin jabbed his finger at Vladimir Kosov before tossing the picture back into the pile with the others. "You said the collider is offline for maintenance, which means that between the shutdown and the pandemic the CERN campus is operating on a skeleton crew. Smuggling somebody in and out would be relatively easy, especially if the smugglers had access to an insider with an ID badge, such as the junior Doctor Kosov's. And the collider's so deep underground we couldn't follow a cell signal, or any other kind of tracking device. Baine could hide out forever down there, wait until the dust settles, then emerge again to a whole new post-apocalyptic world. It'd be like living in a bomb shelter on steroids! It's a huge facility, right?"

"Massive," Eric replied, "and it's on a sixteen month shutdown, so in theory they could hunker down there the whole time and remain undetected and undisturbed. I've toured the CERN campus a few times, and I remember the guide saying that the Large Hadron Collider alone has over twenty-seven kilometers of tunnels and over a thousand magnets. The repair technicians have specialized bicycles to maneuver around the tracks, and they use x-rays to do their repair work because, as you said, the magnets disrupt a lot of other signal types. The campus is so large, with so many buildings and accelerators that it actually spans two countries—Switzerland and France."

Seph's face froze, mouth agape, as she processed the implications of what Eric had so innocently revealed. Agent Marin closed his eyes, put his elbows on the table, and covered his eyelids, nose and mouth with his palms. He mumbled as he rubbed his hands up and down over his face like a man awakening from an all-night bender.

"This is getting worse and worse," he said. "So, if I'm understanding you correctly, they could enter the CERN campus here in Geneva, traverse the property's buildings and tunnels and exit the facility in France, thereby smuggling Baine out of the country?"

"I'm not sure who you mean by 'they,' but I know they can," Eric said, "because even if you or I would decide to take a tour through the CERN campus, we'd have to have our passports with us. It's required."

Seph filled Eric in on what she and Marin had discovered to date. "'They' are the Russians who escaped with Baine. We're not sure if he was kidnapped or if Baine pre-planned the whole thing, but either way he's traveling with at least two Russians."

Eric nodded as he put two and two together. "Now I understand why you were so interested in Dmitri Kosov's disappearance. I'm glad I called you when I did."

Marin lifted his face out of his hands and swiped one palm across his forehead. "I'd bet my last dollar the CERN campus has at least as many entry and exit points as it has buildings, which means our chances of containment are slim. This is going to be a logistical nightmare."

"Well, I'm sure the property has some smaller entrances," Eric said, "but I know of only two main entrances here in Switzerland and one exit into France, which has a customs agent. Even with the shutdown and the outbreak putting the kibosh on staffing, the Russians would still have to fool or kill the guards at one of these entrances to gain access. That gives you a place to start. Also, the campus has a facility control center that monitors all the activity everywhere on the grounds—fire alarms, automatic doors, and so on. I saw it on the tour once years ago, and it was pretty amazing. Every machine, from the smallest computer to the biggest particle accelerator, is observed for any sign of malfunction. The person babysitting the monitors might be able to help narrow your search to a particular sector if he's noticed any kind of unusual aberrancies, even subtle ones, develop in the last twelve hours."

"We also have the element of surprise on our side," Seph added. "The men who took Baine are clearly not expecting us to follow them. In their minds, they made a clean snatch with no trail to follow. As a matter of fact, Dr. Kosov was stupid to leave so hurriedly. It waved a bright red flag. If he were smart, he would've . . ." She was interrupted mid-sentence by Eric's cell. *Dun dun dun dah da dun* . . . Darth Vader's theme song.

Eric shot them a sheepish grin before answering. The conversation lasted only a few seconds. "He would've called in." He finished Seph's previous thought for her when he hung up. "Guess who that was about? My research assistant says Dr. Dmitri Kosov just called from Moscow. He apologized for his rapid departure and said he had to go home for a family emergency. He will not be returning to Geneva."

"Everyone has a family emergency right now," Agent Marin said. "We're in the middle of a fucking plague! Dmitri Kosov's only 'family emergency' is that his brother sold himself to the Russian mob, along with access to the Hadron Collider." He shook his head back and forth, muttering several nasty words under his breath. He looked sidelong at Seph. "Pardon my French."

"No apology needed," Seph replied. She put her hands on her hips and assumed a pseudo-stern posture. "You, however," she said, addressing Eric, "are much more of a nerd than I gave you credit for. I mean, the *Imperial March*? Really?"

"I changed the ringtone when the pandemic started. It seemed appropriate at the time." Eric turned a rosy shade of pink. "I apologize. Very unbefitting someone of my scientific stature, I know." He covered his discomfort by looking over his glasses and matching her stern affect with a faux intellectual countenance of his own. "I assume you are aware, however, that *Star Wars* was nominated for an Academy Award and was considered groundbreaking for its time. It's straight up pop culture, not the stuff of geekdom."

Seph was unimpressed. She crossed her arms and grinned at Eric's defensive posturing.

Agent Marin reached for his own cell and shot off some rapid-fire texts. "Are you two done? You know we have a killer to catch, right?"

Seph's smile faded as she snapped to attention. "Right. So what's next?"

He answered her without looking up. "I have to make some phone calls. We need to establish a perimeter around the entire site so no one can get in or out without our knowing it. Next we seal off the entrances and exits to every building on the CERN campus and we talk to the control center, where we'll set up our command hub. Then we begin combing the corridors and tunnels, one by one if necessary. I'm hoping the control center people have some kind of thermal imaging setup that can distinguish human heat signatures. If so, it'll make our lives a lot easier. The key is to try to accomplish all this without tipping them off that we're coming for them."

He turned his attention to Eric. "You need to stay here and carry on business as usual. You talk to no one about this—got it? As far as you're concerned, Dr. Kosov's departure was legitimate, and you know nothing about Baine's escape or current whereabouts. That's for your own safety. You understand?"

"Got it. I may be a science nerd, but I'm not stupid. I have no desire to meet up with anyone associated with the *Bratva*. I don't want them to even know I exist." Eric focused on Seph. "And you shouldn't either, although I have a sneaking suspicion you're going to head to the CERN campus no matter what I say."

Seph nodded affirmatively. "I could be useful, depending on what happens with Baine," she replied. "Besides, I'm used to crime scenes. You belong here, in the lab. We'll let you know what happens."

"Yes, please do. I'd prefer not to hear about it on the evening news."

"Ditto," Seph said over her shoulder as she hustled after Agent Marin, who had already exited the laboratory and was halfway down the hall. "See you on the other side." She stopped, turned back around, and grinned at Eric. "May the force be with you!"

Seph was surprised to find a government vehicle waiting for them outside the main entrance. It was driven by a well-armed Swiss soldier, and the rear windows were heavily tinted, guaranteeing complete privacy for the passengers. She glanced at Agent Marin, one eyebrow raised. "What happened to the taxi?"

"Taxis are inching toward extinction in this city. Besides, no one outside of the mission needs to know where we're headed. We can't have a cabbie blabbing to all his friends about an incident going down at CERN, especially if our perpetrators are somehow monitoring the situation. Like you said, right now we have the element of surprise on our hands, and that's about all we have going for us. No sense screwing it up by being stupid."

He identified himself to the driver and, once they were cleared, motioned for Seph to enter the vehicle. "*L'Conseil Européen pour la Recherche Nucléaire.*" He instructed the driver on their destination while he and Seph buckled themselves in. His accent was flawless.

"Where did you learn to speak such perfect French?" Seph asked. She was equal parts impressed and envious.

"I'm fluent in three languages." He caught Seph's surprised look out of the corner of his eye. "I may look like a simple-minded jarhead," he said, "but even old Devil Dogs can learn new tricks."

"I didn't mean to imply anything," Seph said, embarrassed that she'd been caught pandering to the Marine stereotype.

"I know. Just yankin' your chain, Doc." He smiled at her for the first time in what seemed like ages. "I learned to speak French on assignment about twenty years ago, long before the Department of Homeland Security even existed. 'Nuff said."

Seph was happy to let it drop; happy just to be back on friendly terms with Marin after the last couple of tense days. She trusted his expertise. Now, more than ever, they needed to be a cohesive team at the top of their game if they were to have any chance of nabbing Baine for a third and, hopefully, final time. She relaxed back into the sedan's leather seat, luxurious by comparison to those she'd experienced in Geneva's taxis. She listened to Agent Marin as he made what seemed like dozens of phone calls to coordinate the surveillance, road blocks, and all the other arrangements needed to seal off the CERN campus.

By the time they arrived at main entrance A, several teams, representing police and military personnel from at least a half-dozen different organizations and jurisdictions, were already milling about. Agent Marin was right—this was going to be a logistical nightmare. They hadn't even reached a complete stop before he dove out of the car and into the fray, barking orders in every direction like a drill sergeant on the first day of boot camp.

While Marin organized his crew, Seph surveyed the surrounding area. She noted entrances A and B, both of which had already been cordoned off by the police. This section of the campus had two conspicuous features. The first was a huge building shaped like a giant golf ball. "The Globe" reminded Seph of a similar structure at Disney World's EPCOT theme park. Both buildings served the same purpose; namely, to represent Mother Earth and serve as a visible hub for educational facilities and exhibits.

The second was a six-and-a-half foot tall bronze sculpture of the Natarja, the dancing Shiva. The depiction of the ancient, multi-armed Hindu deity, with its greenish blue patina, seemed anachronistic in a place such as this; a place containing the Large Hadron Collider, which by some estimations represented the highest pinnacle of human scientific achievement. This strange juxtaposition drew Seph closer for a more detailed inspection of the plaque mounted next to the statue.

According to the description, Lord Shiva was the god of cosmic destruction and rebirth, and his dance represented the elements of eternal energy—creation, destruction, preservation, salvation, and illusion. It was this relationship to eternal cosmic energy that convinced the CERN architects to situate the statue on the campus more than a decade ago.

Seph doubted Baine believed in any god at all; but if he did, it would have to be Lord Shiva, whose dance of destruction, executed in order to create the birth of a new age, aligned perfectly with Baine's master plan. Some believed the collider itself would bring about the destruction of the universe, its smashing of atoms into subparticles somehow triggering a black hole that would consume them all. She remained lost in her uneasy thoughts, staring at the statue's bronzed snakes, until Agent Marin snapped his fingers in front of her nose, breaking the image's hypnotic spell.

"You still with me, Doc?" Agent Marin asked. Seph nodded, turning her back on Shiva and his destructive circle of fire.

"Of course. How are things going?"

"Well, despite all the people you see running around, we're understaffed for an operation like this. And by understaffed, I mean there aren't enough people with guns. This damn place has too many buildings with too many entrances and exits. We don't have enough personnel to cover them all. Interpol and the other big agencies are stretched mighty thin just trying to manage their own back yards. They'd have to be understaffed to allow an American like me to run what should be a European operation." Agent Marin paused to give her a lopsided grin. "It might just be you and me against the world, Doc! You up for that?" Seph raised both eyebrows but did not respond, so Marin continued on.

"Thus far, in an effort to keep things as quiet as possible, we decided against contacting the few employees currently working inside the buildings. The only CERN employees who know what's going on are the security personnel at the gated entrances." He nodded toward one such guard standing by with a dazed expression on his face and, more importantly, an access key card in his right hand. "First stop is the control center. If Eric is right, we should be able to find what we need there. I can't imagine these guys could evade all the different tracking systems without causing some kind of electronic blip, no matter how clever they are or how much inside help they had."

The guard led them to a nondescript building next to the Globe. He swiped his access card and held the heavy grey metal door open so Seph and Marin could step inside. Seph took a few tentative steps inward and then halted, gasping at the sight. The room was pitch-black with no windows. The only ambient light came from the monitors of the control panel, which covered two whole walls of the room in a half-moon pattern. She had never seen, outside of a science fiction movie, such a dizzying array of machines, screens and buttons, all burbling and flashing in response to stimuli known only to themselves. This room made the equipment in Eric's tiny laboratory look like Stone Age tools in a prehistoric cave.

Seph picked out a few familiar terms on the control panel, such as "magnetic field strength" and "core temperature," but most of the flashing controls were as mysterious as they were blinding. She felt as though she were standing on the deck of the starship *Enterprise,* complete with a swiveling captain's chair sitting in the middle of its semicircle.

Seph was so entranced with the technological wizardry she failed to notice that the captain himself was lying on the floor in a pool of his own blood, his head clinging to his neck by a few residual tendinous threads. The image registered on her brain when she heard the guard retching his way out the door.

"Well, at least we know we're on the right track," she said with a wry smile as she knelt down to take a closer look.

"Better check his pulse," Marin said. Seph glared in response, which only served to broaden his smile. "Seriously, though—same M.O. as the others. The Russians took the necessary precautions to keep from being detected. They figured none of us would know how to retrieve any meaningful information out of this." He frowned as he swept his arm around the roomful of monitors. "They figured right. I'd bet there aren't too many people out there who can, especially since the outbreak. And this guy ain't talking. We need to develop a Plan B. I'll be back." He stepped outside to speak to the guard, leaving Seph alone with the corpse and the machines.

She stood in the dark for a moment, absorbing the crime scene. The intermittent flashes of red light bounced freakishly around the room, reflecting off the pool of sticky, coagulated blood on the floor and illuminating the corpse's face, frozen into an eternal grimace. She closed her eyes, trying to channel Baine.

Seph could smell the blood, and she wondered why she hadn't noticed that when first she walked in. She felt dizzy from the overlap of the humming machines and the pulsating lights, which still managed to penetrate her eyelids although they were closed. The smell grew in intensity, making the hairs on the back of her neck stand on end and her stomach churn. This must be how Baine felt all the time, surrounded by flashes and smells and noises, all swirling into an overwhelming, symphonic crescendo of the senses. She opened her eyes, blinked hard and swallowed.

Somehow, her brief, synesthetic moment presented her with a flash of clarity; insight into the working of Baine's mind. He was far too smart to leave anything to chance. He particularly would not allow his own fate to be dictated by others whom he undoubtedly considered his intellectual inferiors.

He needed the Russians to smuggle him out of France. After that, they were of no use to him. Perhaps they had offered him a safe haven, maybe even a research lab of his own, but nothing said he had to follow through on his end of the bargain. He was one step ahead of them, too. Manipulating them. That's what she would do. The door clicked open behind her, and Marin reentered the room.

"The guard says, because of the outbreak, their staff has been reduced to a skeleton crew, and those who've remained healthy have been working the control room in twelve hour shifts. This unlucky stiff . . ." Agent Marin nudged the dead man's shoe with his own. ". . . reported to duty around 8 a.m.

local time, roughly eight hours ago. I suspect he's been dead about seven of those hours."

"They wanted to buy themselves as much time as possible before the second shift showed up," Seph said. "This implies they did *not* intend to hunker down and hide somewhere but wanted to keep moving toward a preplanned destination, which is most likely the portal into France. They're probably halfway there by now."

"Mmmm." Marin muttered his assent and started pacing, doing laps around the dead man's body. "We have the only other available control technician on his way in to help us retrieve any meaningful data we can from these machines, but it's going to be at least an hour until he gets here. I'm no good at waiting around. You've probably figured that out by now." He fidgeted with his cell phone, nearly dropping it onto the corpse's red shirt. "Especially when we're behind the eight ball already."

Seph perused an eighty inch map of the entire facility, projected on one of the largest screens in the room. "Maybe we won't have to just wait." She stooped down to pull a laser pointer out of the dead man's front shirt pocket and aimed the red beam at the screen.

"We know they want to travel through the underground tunnels as much as possible in order to avoid detection. This will slow them down substantially. We, on the other hand, don't have to do that. We can also assume if they're underground far enough that we can't detect them electronically, they can't detect us either. That means we can set up whatever trap we want above ground without them being aware of what's going on."

"This map indicates the most direct underground route to the French border is via the northern loop of the Large Hadron Collider—here." She traced the path with the pointer. "Assuming a rate of travel of two miles per hour, they could have gotten as far as this—give or take." She pointed the light to the corresponding area and drew a squiggly circle representing their approximate location. "There appears to be a service entrance to the collider just before that, right here. We could drive to that entrance in a fraction of the time it took them to walk it and, in theory, trap them between us and the French border agents waiting at the exit into Saint-Genis-Pouilly. They wouldn't have any place to go."

Marin stroked his chin while considering her analysis. "I don't know, Doc. That's a lot of assumptions," he said, eyeballing the map.

"I know, but I'm also not suggesting you send an entire battalion surging down the service entrance. A few men would do, just in case I'm right. Everyone else can maintain their positions until we get more detailed intel from HAL here." She patted a panel of lights, which flashed and burbled a cheerful response. They were interrupted by a rap on the metal door. Agent Marin opened it to reveal the still-nauseated appearing guard standing outside, working hard to keep his eyes averted from the corpse on the floor. Marin and he had a brief conversation in French, which ended with Marin's curt nod of dismissal. The guard beat a hasty retreat, and Marin slammed the metal door behind him. He raked his hand through his hair in frustration.

"The other controller is now showing signs of the virus and will not be coming in. He picked a hell of a day to call off sick." Agent Marin pushed the office chair across the room.

It caromed off a bank of servers and rolled to a stop, its back still spinning in mad circles over its stationary base. "I suggested doing it by phone, but from what Queasy just told me, the guy's already running a fever and is borderline delirious. Having him try to talk us through the technical motions is not gonna be very helpful." Agent Marin stared at the massive electronic array in front of him, his eyes darting around the property map as if trying to burn it into his memory cells, while contemplating his next move.

"I'm not ready to call it 'game over' yet. Are you?" Seph asked.

"No." Pause. "I'm definitely going in. I have to do something. But first I need to better define the battle plan. What are we on now—Plan C? D, maybe?" He shook his head in disgust. "It doesn't matter. Either way, the devil is in the details. You know that. There are a lot more variables than those you mentioned, Doc: like the fact that they could have already been tipped off to our presence, which could in turn lead to some pretty nasty booby traps. Remember what we talked about before we went into Baine's apartment in New York? We were lucky back then, probably because Baines's more of a double-dome scientist than a true terrorist *and* because, at that point, he didn't have the guidance of two ex-KGB agents. We might not be so lucky this time, and we need to plan our moves accordingly. But you're right—I'm sure as hell not gonna just stand around here waitin' to see if they poke their heads up from underground like a couple of stinkin' prairie dogs!"

"If you're going in, then I'm going in with you! This is not a B action movie, and I hate to break it to you, but you are not John Rambo. We're a team. I understand Baine's mind better than anyone at this point, so unless you intend to just blow him away on sight, I need to be there."

To Seph's surprise, Marin responded with only a preoccupied nod. No argument, no discussion. Either he knew better than to argue with her by now, or he still harbored some vestige of suspicion about her relationship to Baine's escape. If the latter were true, he might consider her presence advantageous, a human shield of sorts. On the other hand, he could also be worried that, if he let her out of his sight, she'd be the one to try to tip Baine off to the team's presence. She prayed she was just being paranoid. She meant it when she said she and Marin were in this together until the very end. She still planned to get that tattoo.

"We'll take three or four soldiers with us to help take out the Russians. Too many, and we'll make too much noise. They'll hear us coming. Too few, and we won't have the ability to cut off all the passages if they should choose to split up." Agent Marin turned to face Seph. "You can come, Doc, but you need to bring up the rear and stay in the rear, like you did in New York. No 'ladies first' this time. And you need to do exactly as I say at all times, okay?" Seph nodded, still feeling a bit insecure and hoping it didn't show.

If it did, Marin was too busy making things happen to notice, firing off a series of texts and emails and then settling the final details with a few phone calls. Within the hour, they were bouncing across the CERN campus, huddled with the rest of his hand-picked team in an armored vehicle provided by the Swiss military. Agent Marin detailed the soldiers and other support personnel in both English and French while en route to the drop point. His confidence settled their nerves and offered some much-needed reassurance. For many of them, this mission represented the most difficult and important event of their young lives.

Seph surveyed them as they sat in a tight row in the back of the vehicle: spines rigid, uniforms neatly pressed and boots spit and polished. They were all so young, their faces devoid of all expression as per their military training. Still, her skills allowed her to feel their fear and tension. She saw it in the set of one soldier's jaw, the shift in another's eyes toward the comrade sitting next to him, tacitly seeking solace.

Surely they had all suffered the loss of loved ones from the deadly contagion—spouses, children, brothers and sisters in arms—and likely some of these losses occurred while they were deployed serving their country. Yet here they all sat, doing their jobs as if nothing else mattered more at this moment.

Seph felt the sudden need to offer them comfort, to help fortify their resolve for what might lie ahead. "This is your chance to end this." Her abrupt words, out of nowhere and directed at no one soldier in particular, sliced through the silence and bounced off the metal frame of the truck, making her voice sound odd and unfamiliar. She tried again, adjusting her tone to try and sound gentler, more soothing.

"This is your chance to bring to justice the one who caused this to be in the first place. By tomorrow, the manhunt will be over, and you will have helped save what is left of our world. You should all be proud of yourselves." She gave them a slight smile, embarrassed at her motherly outburst, and hoped that her impromptu speech didn't sound as corny to them as it did to her. She wasn't even sure if they spoke English. They gave her no verbal response, but she could feel a subtle change in their demeanor, and she was satisfied with that.

The truck heaved to a stop outside the service entrance, but before Seph could disembark, her cell phone vibrated a text alert. She glanced at the four word message, her finger positioned to click the phone off for the duration of the mission. It was from Grace. *I have a fever.*

Seph stood in the truck, frozen until Agent Marin nudged her from behind. "I have to make a phone call." She blurted out the words in a rush, her fingers fumbling with the keypad.

"We don't have time for that right now." Agent Marin made a gesture, and four soldiers jumped out the back, their boots landing with a thud on the hard ground.

Seph ignored him and kept fumbling. Her phone beeped as the call dropped. No service. She tried again. Same response. *Not now!* She gritted her teeth and threw her phone into her bag, tossing it under the nearest seat. It wouldn't work where they were going anyway. "Is your phone working?"

Agent Marin glanced at his screen. "No, why?"

"Grace has a fever."

"You can't do anything about that."

"But if the truck would take me back to town, I could catch a flight home and . . ."

"There are no flights, Seph. We need you here. Now pull yourself together."

"You *need* me here or you want to keep an eye on me? Make sure I'm not a traitor. Is that it?"

Agent Marin ignored her outburst and directed the driver to take the remaining soldiers to their check points. They needed to blanket all the other possible exits Baine could use if he ascended from the collider. They would rendezvous at the exit at Saint-Genis-Pouilly. Seph watched with dismay as the truck lurched onward, rumbling over the narrow dirt road and exhaling a swirling cloud of dust into which the tail lights faded and finally disappeared.

The six of them were left alone, standing in a field of high grass and in front of a small metal shed that appeared to be no more than twelve feet square. It was the only man-made object visible to the naked eye; otherwise, they were completely isolated by their rural surroundings.

In comparison to the barrage of the control room, the field was a sensory oasis. The dried grass rustled as it swayed in the breeze, patiently awaiting the autumn harvest. A flock of sheep grazed in the distance, their coats in full fluff to protect against the chill in the air. The sun was setting, casting an orange glow over the entire idyllic scene, giving it the artificial appearance of an early Technicolor movie. There was nothing to indicate that deep beneath their feet lay one of man's greatest technical achievements, a machine that gave rise to an understanding of the so-called "God particle." The Higgs boson, a particle predicted to exist in the 1970s, had its existence confirmed by the collider, and the discovery changed humanity's view of the physical universe forever.

Unimpressed by the natural beauty around them, the soldiers shuffled their feet, eager to get on with it but too well-trained to do anything but await orders. Agent Marin motioned for one of them to cut the thick metal chain locking the door to the shed. The severed padlock landed with a loud clank against the foot of the building, the noise echoing through the field and frightening a murder of crows into revealing their hidden location within the brush. They scattered into the air and circled the shed, raucously expressing their discontent at being disturbed.

Agent Marin gave the all-go, and the soldiers, brandishing their Sig 551-A1's, rushed in. One of them grunted an "all clear," and Agent Marin, eyes blazing, fixed Seph in his gaze. "You ready, Doc?"

"You didn't answer my question."

"If I thought you were a traitor, you'd be locked in Baine's old cell. Are you ready or not? 'Cause if not, you can stay here and guard the sheep."

"No way in hell." Like a diver getting ready to submerge, Persephone took in a deep breath of the crisp, sweet air, exhaling it slowly out her mouth. It would be the last clean air she would have for the next several hours, and it needed to sustain her. *Now pull yourself together.* She shook off her panic, wrapped herself in her anger, and stepped over the threshold into the darkness.

Chapter Twenty-Five

The Underworld

September 12th, 2016, 1900 hours
Large Hadron Collider, Geneva, Switzerland

It took a few minutes for Seph's eyes to adjust to the dim illumination, provided only by the tactical lights on the soldiers' weapons. Agent Marin flipped the wall switch inside the door, but the bare bulb hanging from the center of the ceiling refused to respond. Directly below the bulb, in the middle of the floor, was a closed manhole surrounded by an iron handrail. The soldiers swept their lights around the room, revealing only a sturdy wooden table with a jumbled assortment of electronic gadgetry scattered across it.

"Parts for repair," Agent Marin said. "The only reason this building is here is to provide an access point for repairs to this sector of the collider." He turned to address the soldiers who were pressed together, shoulder to shoulder, in the tight quarters.

"Once we descend, we need to keep all verbal communication to a minimum. We don't know what kind of surveillance equipment, if any, they might have, and we're depending on our element of surprise. I would prefer to take Baine alive, although it's not essential for the mission to be considered a success. We will not have cellular access due to the depth and the magnetism, so we'll have two rendezvous points in case we get separated—one here and one at Saint-Genis-Pouilly. We believe our targets to be between this entrance and that exit, with their intention being to escape by ascending into France and moving onward from there, but remember—this is a circular tunnel system. If they catch wind of us following them, they could choose to bypass that exit and go on to the next. Likewise, if you get lost and pass the intended exit, you could be wandering around in circles for a very long time. Stay sharp, and stay close." He then gave what Seph imagined was the same speech in French.

Agent Marin pulled on the manhole cover. It creaked and groaned on its hinges like the heaving lid of an old coffin in a horror movie, finally releasing a rush of cold, dank air as it fell open with a reverberating clang. Seph peered into the black portal, dubiously eyeing the decidedly low-tech entrance to what was supposed to be such a futuristic facility. Where were the retinal scanners, the motion-controlled sliding doors, and the fingerprint locks? All she saw was an ancient-appearing ladder of questionable structural integrity descending into the darkness, with no bottom in sight. It looked like the entrance to a well.

Agent Marin, unfazed, pointed to the largest of the soldiers, a huge man with shoulders so broad Seph wasn't sure he would fit through the manhole at all. "You, Pallas." He squinted at the name embroidered on the pocket patch of the soldier's fatigues. "You're first. Then you, Delacroix." He pointed to the smallest of the soldiers. "Then me, Doc, and you two will bring up the rear. Down the hatch."

Pallas nonchalantly adjusted his rifle's tactical light, aimed it toward the abyss and began his descent, moving at a sure-footed clip Seph knew she would not be able to match. The iron ladder screamed and sagged under the soldier's considerable weight, and she held her breath waiting for it to give up entirely and send him plummeting to his death. It did not, and it also hung on for Delacroix's, then Agent Marin's subsequent descent.

When it was her turn, Seph positioned one foot on the first rung, gripping the handrails until her fingers turned numb. She took in another jittery breath and started her downward climb, jerking and freezing in place every time the ladder decided to fitfully utter a noise. Her descent seemed to take forever, and by the time she saw the dim light below, her feet and calves were cramping in protest. Pallas, Delacroix and Marin were waiting for her at the bottom.

Pallas extended a gentlemanly hand to help her hop off the bottom rung of the ladder, which ended a few feet above the cement floor. Agent Marin raised one eyebrow in amusement at the suave gesture. Seph aimed a scowl in his general direction before smiling sweetly at Pallas. She opened her mouth to thank him, but Agent Marin shushed her by putting a finger to his lips. Right. No talking. She massaged the spasms out of her calves and surveyed the area while waiting for the last two soldiers to reach the bottom.

They stood on a concrete floor in a narrow passageway that bore at least a superficial resemblance to a subway platform. To their right was a solid concrete wall. To their left, instead of a drop-off leading to train rails, stood another concrete wall, the upper portion replaced by a suspended

track enclosed in some kind of glass or clear plastic mate-
rial. The overhead lighting was dim at best, and the ceiling
was claustrophobically low. That combination made the passageway appear to extend to infinity, with the area behind
them looking identical to that in front. No wonder Marin
was worried they'd get turned around. The only identifying object in their immediate vicinity was the ladder upon
which they'd just descended.

Delacroix swung the backpack off his shoulders and
removed a set of headphones and a dish-shaped object. The
team stood in absolute silence while he used the parabolic
microphone to listen for evidence of Baine's presence—
footsteps, conversation, anything. After a few moments, he
removed the headphones and shook his head back and forth.
Nothing. Agent Marin pointed at Pallas and Delacroix to
take the lead, and weapons pointing forward, they strode
down the narrow corridor.

They had only gone about fifty yards when a sudden, ear-
splitting boom emanated from somewhere far behind them.
The shocking noise reverberated throughout their close
quarters and gained in intensity as the sonic wave rushed to
their location. Terrified, Seph crouched down and put both
hands over her head, suppressing a scream only by biting
down on her tongue so hard that she brought tears to her
eyes.

The soldiers dropped to one knee and swept their weapons around the perimeter, seeking a moving target but finding nothing. They inched back to their upright positions,
still on full alert. Wary, but not willing to abort the mission
over a little noise, Agent Marin signaled for them to resume

moving forward. The soldiers obeyed, but this time their pace was more deliberate than brisk.

They experienced similar clangs and bangs of various intensities every fifty-to-one hundred yards or so, each time dropping into their defensive positions until they finally realized that whatever was making the noise was mechanical and not a threat. Even so, the clamor remained unnerving; especially since with each sonic boom, the pathetically dim lights would flicker, hiss and pop, causing Seph to cower in fear and anticipation of either being showered by hot, shattering glass or plunged into total darkness.

She knew it was irrational, but she kept flashing back to last night's dream—or, in retrospect, maybe it was a premonition—where she was being hunted in a dark and sinister house of horrors. Today that house was the Large Hadron Collider, a living, growling creature, a Minotaur stalking its prey through its labyrinthine concrete innards. It was watching their every move, keeping their nerves on edge just because it could, and playing with them like a cat plays with a mouse before going in for the final, merciful kill. This mission was not turning out to be the grab-and-go scenario she'd envisioned in the safety of the control room, and she was starting to regret not staying aboveground.

They'd been walking for twenty minutes or so when Seph noticed an anomaly in the concrete wall roughly twenty feet ahead to their right. A large metal protrusion ran from floor to ceiling on the wall and jutted out far enough into the walkway to narrow it down to single file. At first blush it resembled a giant breaker box, and even from her current distance Seph spied a red light flashing rhythmically near the top right corner. They slowed their approach, and Pallas scoped it out first. He positioned himself in front of the object, poked at it a few times with one finger, and then gestured for the others to line up next to him.

From the front Seph could see it was an electronic map of sorts, a computer touch screen with squares, circles and other assorted shapes that seemed to represent the various important control areas of this section of the collider. The red circle, however, was the only thing flashing. She leaned in for closer inspection and discovered a linear smudge where someone had previously dragged a finger across the screen, tracing a line from the circle down the left side of the monitor. She assumed the "someone" in question was Baine or one of the Russians. They either thought the light was important, or they were as confused as she.

Seph, palms to the ceiling and eyebrows raised, looked at Agent Marin and Pallas, begging their input. Pallas shrugged his shoulders as if to say, *That's your job. I'm just the brawn here,* and stepped aside to allow Marin and Seph an unobstructed look at the screen. He and Delacroix shuffled a little farther down the passageway, peering around the corner of the object to make sure they encountered no surprises.

Agent Marin pointed to a lighted but not flashing green circle on the left side of the map. Above it was a rectangle with horizontal bars of red, white and blue lights—an obvious representation of the French flag and a clear indication of the exit into Saint-Genis-Pouilly. The logical assumption, then, was that the circles signified all the exits from the collider in this particular sector. *But why were some red and others green?* Seph was mulling the significance of the disparate colors when Agent Marin abruptly began flapping his hands at Guerin, the last soldier to enter the collider.

Puzzled, she watched as they attempted to nonverbally communicate by gesticulating back and forth in a complex game of charades. Piece by piece, Seph assembled the question Agent Marin was so desperately trying to ask. Her stomach lurched as she also realized, in a nauseating wave of horror, not only the answer to Marin's pantomimed question but just what that flashing red light meant. For their team it was an accusation of carelessness, an inexcusable lack of attention to detail. For the Russians it was an intruder alert warning them of a security breach.

Their team had literally and figuratively left the door open. Except in this case the door was a manhole cover. That rusty, old relic had been wired like a Mafia mole and had ratted on them the minute Pallas's boots hit the first rung. Their element of surprise was gone and had been gone for an extended period of time. Their silence was now moot, but before she could share her newfound knowledge with the others, the world exploded around them.

She saw it as if in slow motion. Agent Marin, standing in front of her, was still gesticulating madly at Guerin, who was behind her and to her left. Over Marin's shoulder, she saw Pallas and Delacroix, who having gotten bored with the mystery of the map, had moved a few feet ahead on their own. Then, in a flash of white light and a deafening roar, Pallas was gone, and Seph was flying backward.

She didn't remember landing but there she was, flat on her back on the cold concrete floor. She felt someone on top of her, and when she dared to open her eyes, she saw Marin, face covered in dust, streaks of blood, and bits of flesh, with his arms stretched overhead in an attempt to protect her face and head from the flying debris. She was disoriented by a loud hum in both ears, and everything happening around her sounded muffled and distant. A trickle of blood ran from her ear down her left cheek, and she moved a tremulous hand to her face to wipe it away. The explosion must have ruptured both her eardrums.

"Stay sharp and stay close." She again heard Agent Marin's succinct command, spoken just before their team had entered the hatch to the collider. The words bounced around in her skull, jumbling with the tinnitus in her ears until the combined cacophony made her feel nauseated with a severe threat of vomiting. She pushed desperately against Agent Marin's chest, and when he yielded she rolled onto her side, propped herself up on one elbow, and started to heave.

She stayed in that position for a few minutes, willing the vertigo to resolve. She was vaguely aware of Agent Marin rising to his feet and heard him shouting urgent orders to the others, who, after being frozen from the initial shock, were now scrambling to assess the situation and secure their positions. Marin returned to Seph, hovering over her, his face grim.

"Doc, you need to get up. Now."

Seph wobbled to her feet, swaying back and forth like a drunken vagrant. "I'm just fine, thank you very much." She responded to his brusque command with a scowl. "And, how are you?"

"Better than Pallas and Delacroix," he said. Seph was immediately conscience-stricken at her flippant remarks. Throughout her career she'd never expected to be coddled, no matter how bad the circumstances, and now was not the time for Marin to have to deal with her defensive posturing. She steeled herself to inspect the carnage in front of her, telling herself it was just another crime scene, not unlike a hundred others she had seen in the past decade.

There was nothing left of Pallas except for his helmet and his gun. The giant hulk of a man had been reduced to hunks of pulpy gore which were scattered over everything in the vicinity of the blast. Strands of flesh and coagulating blood dripped off the gouges in the grey concrete walls, making the collider itself appear to be hemorrhaging from its wounds. Delacroix's torso was intact, thanks to his body armor, but he was missing all four of his extremities and much of his face. He had bled out instantly.

Guerin, who appeared unharmed save a few minor lacerations, focused on inspecting the debris. The other remaining soldier, Bravard, stood stone-faced with his weapon at the ready and pointed into the distance, as if he expected the Russians to return to survey the damage and finish off any survivors. After Guerin completed his investigation, he and Agent Marin had a brief but intense huddle on the findings, which Marin presented to the surviving members of the team.

"Tripwire attached to the pin of a grenade. Old-school, but portable and highly effective. I'm sure they placed it, and God knows what other nasty surprises, as soon as they realized we were on to them. We're gonna have to turn back. They have the jump on us now, and we'll never catch up with them as carefully as we'd need to move in order to avoid walking into another booby trap. Once we're above ground, we'll divert all troops to the subsequent exits. That's the best we can do. Baine and the Russians will have to surface sometime."

Seph nodded in agreement. Despite how she yearned to see Baine back behind bars, one look at Delacroix's mutilated body was enough for her to appreciate the wisdom of Agent Marin's plan.

Bravard turned to lead the retreat, and Guerin took the rear. Seph didn't envy either of them, especially when Bravard matter-of-factly suggested they stagger themselves farther apart to reduce the potential death toll should there be any subsequent explosions. He began their slow but steady march back toward the escape hatch, his jaw clenched in concentration and fingers glued to his weapon as he cleared their path of any tripwires or other potentially deadly aberrancies.

They were ten minutes into their retreat when a siren began to wail. It was the same as those used during World War II to signify an air raid; the kind that sent panic-stricken Englishmen scrambling to take shelter underground before terror rained from the sky above. *But we're already underground.* Seph's mind reeled with panic and confusion. Then, in an instant, Bravard too was gone.

This time there was no explosion, just Bravard's scream and a strange, tingling sensation around her waist. Her lower body lurched forward against her will, as if she were caught in a tractor beam. Seph crouched and planted her feet and hands on the floor, curling her fingers in a futile attempt to claw a better hold on the smooth concrete surface.

A red strobe light flashed overhead, adding to the chaos, and in between its rhythmic bursts of crimson light she could see that Agent Marin, who had been walking several paces in front of her, was having an even harder time maintaining his position. His feet were sliding, and his back was swayed, as if his torso was being yanked forward by an invisible tether. He fought like a marlin on a hook, pulling for dear life against being reeled in.

He appeared to be losing his battle against the unknown force until, instead of continuing to resist by pushing backward, Marin did the unexpected. He dove forward, planting himself flat on his abdomen, cheek to the cement, arms splayed wide in front. He used his palms to push himself in a backward shuffle of sorts, all the while screaming for Seph and Guerin to do the same. The force lessened as they inched farther and farther away from the light and the siren, and they kept moving until they were almost back to their original positions at the electronic map, where they were finally able to stand.

"What the hell just happened?" Guerin asked as he struggled to his feet. Half-deaf from the blaring siren, he shouted so loudly that his voice echoed off the walls. He swung around in circles, wild-eyed and sweating, all semblance of a professional demeanor lost in the noise and confusion.

Seph looked up at the electronic array, which now had several additional alerts flashing, including one shaped like a red horseshoe followed by an exclamation point.

"I'm guessing that Baine and the Russians somehow activated the magnets in that sector, and we were caught in a strong magnetic field. You guys with your weapons and all your metallic gear would have been especially attracted by it," Seph said. "I remember Eric saying something about the collider having over a thousand magnets in it. That's how they move the particles along, I think."

She was shocked at how steady her voice sounded. She leaned forward from the waist and put her hands on her bent knees under the pretense of needing to catch her breath. Instead, she was just trying to hide her trembling hands. Still hunched over, she turned her face toward Agent Marin, who appeared to be genuinely short of breath from the effort of extracting himself from the pull of the magnetic field. "Did you see what happened to Bravard? Is he dead?"

"Yes. Impaled. You don't need to know the details," Marin replied.

Seph didn't really want him to tell her. She could imagine it on her own. Bravard, at the front of their line and thus closest to the magnets, would have experienced the full effect of the force field. She pictured him flailing helplessly as he careened forward, smashing into whatever objects happened to lie at the end of his path. She hoped he died quickly. They weren't going to be able to go back and check.

"They fucking cut us off from the exit," Guerin said, waving his gun in the air for emphasis. He had stopped spinning around in circles like a dog chasing its tail and was now pacing back and forth instead, his agitation building as he realized exactly how bad their situation had become.

Despite their dire set of circumstances, Seph could have laughed out loud at Guerin's very French pronunciation of the word "fucking," an inappropriate response given that Guerin was losing it fast. She forced back her chuckle, not wanting to be the one to push him over the brink. He continued his manic rambling, speaking in a nearly unintelligible combination of French and heavily accented English.

"They've trapped us between here . . ." He tapped the map

with the barrel of his gun. "... and wherever they are, the way we were supposed to be trapping them. We're like sitting..." His voice sputtered out as his command of English colloquialisms abandoned him.

"Steady, soldier." Agent Marin's voice was calm. "We have two options. We can sit tight and wait for a rescue team, or we can go back to the original plan and keep moving toward the exit at Saint-Genis-Pouilly."

"Couldn't we turn the magnetic field off and try again to go back out the same way we came in?" Seph asked. "I mean, they figured out how to turn it on, so maybe we can figure out how to turn it back off again." Three sets of eyes turned toward the screen and its multitude of flashing lights.

"I don't think they could have activated the magnetic field from this particular panel," she said. "They must have done it from the next one, probably after they heard the grenade explode. The blast would've not only given them unequivocal confirmation that they were being followed but also would have revealed our exact location. I'm sure they figured that anyone who survived would try to retreat."

Seph tapped the red magnet icon, and the map enlarged to a more detailed view of the sector affected by the field. She poked at it a few more times, trying to pull up something that resembled a control panel but was unsuccessful. She looked at Agent Marin for assistance, but he just shook his head helplessly.

"Got me, Doc. Not my area of expertise. Not by a long shot."

The French soldier let out a hiss of frustration and rammed the butt end of his gun into the touch screen, which shattered to the floor.

Seph jumped backward in surprise and dismay. "That did *not* help," she said.

Guerin muttered something guttural in French and resumed his pacing. Agent Marin, unruffled, responded as if nothing unusual had happened. "If the Russians activated the magnetic field from the next map, they must be pretty far ahead of us; far enough, in fact, to be approaching the exit at the French border. If we follow behind them at a slow pace, we shouldn't be in any danger of catching up to them. We can surface at Saint-Genis-Pouilly as well—*after* the troops we have stationed there take them in."

"Why wouldn't we want to catch up to them? We still have a chance at capturing them ourselves," Seph said.

"It's two against three now, Doc. Safer to let the rest of our team do it."

"It's three against three. Don't I count for something?"

"*You* are not armed."

"Baine probably isn't either."

"Baine has killed at least two people already. What's your body count?"

Guerin repeatedly rapped the butt of his gun on the concrete floor, trying to refocus their attention. He swept his hand around the narrow corridor, pockmarked by damage from the exploding grenade, and then pointed at the twisted metal and piles of debris. "So let's say we do as you recommend and keep moving forward. What makes you think we won't hit another trap?" he said.

Agent Marin turned away from Seph's glare long enough to answer Guerin's question. "If they're smart, and they obviously are, they realize they're going to meet some resistance at the exit. They wouldn't want to block the path of their own possibly hasty retreat, in case they need to use it. Remember, unlike us, they know how to turn off the magnetic field. I think they'll leave their options open."

Seph wished she had Marin's confidence, but the truth of the matter remained that both of their options sucked. Still, she was all for forging ahead and getting out of this hellhole, even if they died trying.

"I agree," she said, aligning herself with Marin. "Are you coming with us?" she asked Guerin. He stared at the concrete floor.

She pretended to look around. "It's not so bad here, you know. No fleas, no plague. You can stay here by yourself if you want. If none of us surface, I'm sure someone will come looking for you eventually."

Guerin again muttered something in French that Seph suspected was an unflattering expletive. He took a few deep breaths, readied his weapon and assumed the point. Agent Marin motioned for Seph to take up the middle position, and they once again started forward, crawling toward the exit at Saint-Genis-Pouilly.

The tension built with each passing yard, the echo of their tentative footsteps mocking their fears of another calamity yet to come. They traveled a good distance; long enough for Seph to convince herself that Agent Marin was right about the Russians's escape plan. She expected to see the next electronic map around the upcoming curve. What she didn't expect was to see Baine standing in front of it.

He was surrounded by a red and green aura from the glowing array, the flashing lights casting a strange pattern of symbols over the blank canvas of his face. He appeared inhuman; an android they had interrupted as he was conversing with a fellow machine.

He turned to face them as they halted in their tracks, still several feet away from his position. His movements were stiff and deliberate. He held his arms by his sides, palms open as if to signify that he was not a threat; and he had his eyes fixed, as his typically were, on Seph's face. Guerin aimed the red laser site of his gun squarely at Baine's forehead, his finger standing by on the trigger, awaiting Agent Marin's command.

"This stinks of a set-up," Marin said in a voice low enough so as to be audible only to Guerin and Seph. "Any idea what he's thinking, Doc?"

Seph shook her head. "No." A perfectly appropriate question asked in what sounded like a perfectly innocent tone, but she knew better. She both heard and felt the subtle edge in his voice. It was the same tone he had used this morning in the hotel lobby when he questioned her about Baine's escape. *What else did Baine say to you, and what did you say to him? Did you make any other kind of deals or promises I should know about?*

This nightmare scenario was exactly what Marin had been worried about. She imagined the accusations running through his head. *Will she betray me and escape with him, in exchange for protection from his virus? Is this part of the plan? Has she been manipulating me the whole time, leading me to this situation?* Marin was right—this was a set-up. Only she was the one being set up.

"Well then, whatever is gonna go down here is liable to go down badly. When it hits, you crouch down as low as you can and stay as close to the wall as you can, and don't get up until I say so. Got it?"

Seph nodded, afraid to speak lest her words inadvertently sounded incriminating. She hated how Baine, more so than any criminal she had faced in the past, was able to keep catching her off guard with his unpredictable actions, and worse yet, was able to weave her into his web of deceit. Did he know her motives would be suspect? He might have predicted that after his escape and was using it to his advantage. So, what was the trap?

What she found most unexpected was Baine's direct presence. He was the prize, the thing to be protected. It should have been the Russian assassins standing in front of them, not him. He was using himself as live bait, luring her toward him. Over the last few weeks, she'd allowed herself to become convinced that Baine wouldn't harm her; that he wanted her left alive. However, she doubted the Russians would grant her the same courtesy. Baine should know that, so what was his angle here? What was he expecting to happen?

Marin took one step forward, placing himself between Baine and Seph, and shouted toward Baine. "Where are your comrades?" Silence. "They have three seconds to show themselves with their hands in the air or else we blow your face off."

Baine smiled. "The fidelity of the answer depends on the quality of the question," he replied.

"What the hell is that supposed to mean?"

"It means they are not my comrades."

At that instant, the lights went out, and they were plunged into absolute darkness. Guerin didn't even have time to pull the trigger. Seph heard a swoosh and then a sickening thud, and she knew he was gone.

"Get down!" Marin said as he pulled his handgun out of its holster. Seph dodged to the right until she hit the concrete wall, then crouched low to the ground as instructed, covering her ears against the deafening bursts of gunfire. Agent Marin managed to get off a few rounds, shooting blindly into the total darkness before Seph heard him give a low grunt and fall to the ground. The return fire also stopped, and she heard someone running away—followed, strangely, by a delayed single gunshot and then more footsteps moving further and further into the distance.

For the longest second of Seph's life, she heard nothing at all. She stayed crouched down, alone in the blackness and the silence, unsure what to do next; unsure whether she could even make herself move. Then she heard Marin rustle on the floor. The noise broke her inertia, and she propelled forward, crawling on all fours, fingers splayed wide on the concrete floor as she attempted to listen and feel her way toward his last position.

"Paul!"

"Here." She was startled to hear his voice directly in front of her, and she lurched forward, touching the back of his shoulder. "Can you get Guerin's gun?" he asked. "He was behind us and to the left."

"Screw the gun. Are you hurt?"

"I took one or two in the leg, but we'll be dead if they come back and we don't have a gun. I'm almost out of rounds." He pulled his cell phone from his pocket and tried to shine its dim flashlight in the direction she needed to go, but the illumination was too faint to be of much help.

Seph felt around in the darkness until she bumped into Guerin's leg. From there, she patted her way up his body. He was flat on his back, his right arm stretched overhead, the rifle still in his hand. She had to roll him on his side to remove the gun's strap from around his left shoulder before she could extract the weapon from his grip.

"Make sure you're pointing that thing the other way, okay? I've got enough holes in me for one day," Marin said.

"Very funny." Still crouching at Guerin's side, Seph ran her hand over the barrel of the weapon, finding the tactical light and switching it on. She gasped as the powerful beam reflected off Guerin's dilated, glassy eyes, frozen wide open in shock. He had a knife imbedded into his forehead, perfectly placed in the narrow space between the edge of his helmet and his brow line. A single trickle of blood traced a path down the bridge of his nose and then veered off to the right of his gaping mouth before dripping off his chin.

Marin's voice, disembodied due to the darkness, floated her way. "Hell of a shot," he said.

Seph swung the light in Marin's direction and saw more blood, only this time it was streaming from his right thigh. "Jesus!" She got up and stumbled toward him. She handed him the gun so he could shine the light on his leg and better illuminate the wound for her inspection.

She didn't like what she saw. "It's all the way through. We need to get you out of here."

"What we need to do first is slow down the bleeding, or I won't live long enough to make it out of here." Marin struggled to remove his belt from around his waist. He wrapped the belt around his upper thigh and cinched it as tightly as he could, grimacing with both pain and the effort of doing so. "It must have missed the femoral artery, or I'd be dead already."

"Great. Great news. Best news I've heard all day." Seph's fingers flew back and forth as she shredded Marin's blood-soaked pant leg into long strips. "Still think I aided and abetted Baine's escape?"

"I never seriously thought you did, Doc. What are you doing?"

"Liar." She ignored his question. "Remember what I do for a living."

"Okay, maybe. Remember, it's *my* job to look at things from all possible angles. We get outta this hole alive, and I'll buy you a shot of Patrón. Then we'll drink until we both forget about the whole thing. Deal?"

"You're on." Seph wadded a bunch of the strips against the gaping wound, hoping it would promote clotting, then tied them fast to apply pressure. She was glad he couldn't see her face in the dark. She could control her voice, but she was sure her face would show her growing sense of desperation. They had at least a fifteen minute walk to the exit at Saint-Genis-Pouilly on the French-Swiss border and that was fifteen minutes with two good legs and overhead lighting. She didn't even want to consider the possibility of them needing to climb a ladder in order to reach the actual exit. After all, they'd had to climb down one in order to get into this mess in the first place.

Her mind raced as her fingers finished knotting the improvised bandage. Maybe if she could get him even anywhere close to the exit, she could run ahead and get help. At least a half a dozen soldiers should be standing by at that exit.

Seph tightened the last strip into place. "Nice job, Doc," Marin said. He was trying to sound jovial, but his voice was thick with pain.

"I spent a lot of time in disaster shelters, back in the day. You learn a trick or two in those places." She took the gun out of Marin's hands and slung it over her shoulder so that the tactical light shone more or less directly ahead of them.

"Okay. On your feet. Let's see how this holds." She wrapped her free arm around Marin's waist. He struggled to stand, and she strained against his weight, finally managing through sheer determination to heave him upright. They limped forward together, stopping every few dozen feet, ostensibly for Seph to check the integrity of his bandage but really to allow Marin to catch his breath. She admired his grit. He was a true Marine, grunting through clenched teeth but not once complaining, and they made better progress than Seph had dared to hope for. They stalled only once, when the light illuminated a dark mass stretched across their path.

"I need to check it out," Seph said. "It could be rigged—another trap. I'm gonna have to lean you against the wall for a minute."

"No way." Seph looked up at Marin's face, surprised by his adamant refusal.

"Seriously, what's the point, Doc? We don't have any other options except straight ahead, and I don't want you getting blown to bits on my behalf. Besides, I wouldn't be able to make it out on my own at this point anyway. May as well go together."

Seph couldn't argue with his logic, so they held their breath and sidled past what turned out to be one of the

Russian agents, dead from a gunshot wound to the back of the head. Another unexpected twist. His presence explained the solitary gunshot she had heard, but it raised several new questions. Who had shot him and why? She presumed the answer to the former question was Baine, but what happened to the other assassin? She doubted he would've just stood by and allowed his partner to be killed, unless he, too, was already dead. Or maybe the three of them had split up? Seph would have loved to mull the situation over more carefully, but Marin seemed to be getting heavier and heavier, and keeping him moving was requiring all her effort and concentration.

They rounded what she hoped was the last curve, and she heard him sigh with relief when a faint light manifested not far ahead. That light signified the next sector, and the next sector meant the next exit. As they got closer, leaving the darkness behind, she saw it—a life-saving gift, shimmering like a mirage in their concrete desert. She wouldn't have been at all surprised to hear the "Hallelujah Chorus" blaring from the overhead speakers. An elevator. The exit had both a ladder *and* an elevator. Two elevators, in fact. One appeared to be a freight elevator, a large and undoubtedly slow box with a massive door. The other looked like the typical version. Marin saw it too, and she felt him sag a little bit as the ebb in his stress level weakened him.

"Not yet. Not until you're in an ambulance," she said.

Marin nodded. They took a few more steps forward, and then he stopped completely.

"C'mon. We're almost there! You've made it this far. Just a few more feet." Seph pleaded with him to keep going.

"Look over there," he said. "At the wall next to the ladder."

The ladder looked the same as the one upon which they had descended what seemed like an eternity ago. The same except for the large quantity of blood and grey matter smeared on the wall beside it.

"Looks like someone else took a bullet to the brain," Marin said, "and if I had to guess, it *wasn't* Baine."

"You said before that he only needed the Russians to help him get out of Switzerland and disappear."

"Humph." Marin grunted a response and then fell silent, considering the situation. "The hatch is open at the top. I can see the light," he said. He took his cell phone out of his pocket and checked for a signal, then put it back in his pocket in disgust. "Dead from using the flashlight app. Drained the battery. You left yours in the truck, didn't you?"

Seph nodded, mentally berating herself for the error in judgement. At the time, it didn't seem practical to drag her bag around when she knew her cell phone wouldn't work down there anyway. Grace's text flashed through her mind, and she pushed it away. She had Marin's life to contend with first.

Marin cupped his hands to his mouth. "Mayday, mayday, mayday! Anyone copy up there? Please respond." Nothing. "Cover your ears." He pulled out his handgun and fired his last round, aiming upward toward the hatch. The bullet ricocheted its way off the walls and metal rungs, making enough of a din that Seph could hear it even with her perforated eardrums. Still no response.

"Something's wrong," Marin said.

"What could be wrong?" Seph said. "They probably just captured Baine and left to transport him somewhere." Marin's doubtful expression indicated he believed otherwise.

"I mean, we had a whole squadron of soldiers waiting. I refuse to believe . . ." Her voice rose in volume as she became increasingly nervous that she was, in fact, wrong. "I *refuse* to believe Baine is capable of taking out a whole squadron of soldiers single-handedly. He's a mutant scientist, for Christ's sake, not a Jedi master!"

"Hit both elevator buttons," Marin said, ignoring her growing hysteria. Seph punched both up buttons. The passenger elevated dinged in response and began to descend. The freight elevator did nothing. "Now give me the gun." Seph followed his command. He took it in his right hand, his left arm still resting on Seph's shoulders. They shuffled off to the side of the passenger elevator door and waited. It opened, and Marin, using Seph as a fulcrum, swung around, gun pointed. Nothing. The interior was pristine. Seph half-expected to hear a crappy Musak version of "Girl from Ipanema" burbling from its tinny speakers. Marin lowered his gun and peered through the door, inspecting the walls and ceiling.

"Come on. We need to get in," Seph said. She was on a different mission now, a mission to save Marin's life. Baine didn't matter at this point. She knew deep in her core that Marin was correct. Something *was* wrong. Exactly what happened they might never know, but they had failed, and Baine was long gone. Of that, she was certain.

She was less certain about the function of the elevator, fearing if the doors closed without them inside they might not get a second chance; and Marin, at least, was running out of time. She half-dragged him through the doors before he could utter a word of protest and hit the up button. "We'll deal with whatever is waiting for us when we get there," she told him with as much bravado as she could muster. *I just need to get aboveground.*

The ascent was much quicker than the descent, which was a good thing. The suspense was killing her.

Chapter Twenty-Six

Ascension

Marin and Seph huddled in the back left corner of the elevator to buy themselves a few extra precious seconds should it all hit the fan when the doors opened onto the ground floor. They might as well not have bothered. With a perky *ding,* the doors slid open to reveal a brightly lit but unattended room strewn with carnage.

The Customs and Border Security building straddling the French-Swiss border consisted of one large space separated into sections by simple room dividers and cubicles. Opposite the elevators was what had been a wall of windows, now shattered into blood-tipped glass shards that stuck up at crazy angles from the linoleum floor like stalagmites in a cavern.

They stepped out of the elevator, treading delicately to avoid the glass and the gore. The freight elevator to their right appeared to have been ground zero, based on the density of the body parts scattered around its buckled doors. A few feet from the elevators lay a cluster of three soldiers who were comparatively intact, with simple gunshot wounds to the head and chest. The other soldiers were in largely unidentifiable pieces.

"Check for cell phones or radios," Marin said to Seph. He leaned against the wall, balancing on one foot while she did a brief sweep.

"They're all gone."

"I'm not surprised. I guess it's too much to expect there to be a working vehicle outside, too, huh? Do me a favor and check the computers and desk phones first, though. Maybe we'll get lucky, but I doubt it. They're all probably on the same T1 line, which is easy to disable. You cut one, and the whole system goes down."

Seph picked up the nearest handset. As Marin had suspected, there was no dial tone. "What do you think happened here?" she asked as she helped him limp across the room and out the front of the building.

"I'm guessing Baine killed the Russian agent down below, dragged him into the freight elevator, propped a grenade under his arm, pulled the pin and sent him upstairs to say hello. A couple of the soldiers crowded into the freight elevator, one of them rolled the guy over or kicked him with his foot, and pop-goes-the-weasel. That would have taken most of them out in one fell swoop. The freight elevator would have moved slowly enough for Baine to climb the ladder to the manhole at the surface, allowing him to be ready and waiting to pick off any survivors. Then Baine took off, either in our truck or in whatever transportation the Russians had arranged to be on standby."

By this time, Seph and Marin were standing outdoors in the building's tiny parking lot. The lot was surrounded on all sides by fields tilled into tidy rows of a plant she could not identify in the dark. The sun had long-since set while they were underground, and the only visible light came from a solitary pole lamp and the blood red Hunter's Moon overhead. The parking lot was vacant except for a humungous military convoy truck, much larger than the one they were in earlier today. Their vehicle was nowhere to be seen.

"Do you have any idea how to drive one of these things?" Marin asked.

"No." Seph looked at Marin's face, which glowed a ghastly grey color in the dim light. "But I'll learn. Let's go." She helped him up the step and into the passenger seat, then grabbed the handle bar and pulled herself into the driver's position. Mercifully, the keys were in the ignition and she gave them a crank, pushing in the clutch as far as it would go. The truck shuddered to life. She pressed the gas pedal, and it lurched forward like a racehorse at the starting gate, only to promptly stall out. She glanced over at Marin, expecting a smart-assed comment, but he had his head back and his eyes closed. His chest rose and fell in a slow, deliberate pattern, as if the act of breathing required a great deal of effort.

Seph cranked the keys again. This time she managed to coax the truck forward, grinding the gears as it picked up speed, its headlights reflecting off the flat, paved surface of the rural road. They passed a sign indicating they were ten kilometers from town, and Seph pushed the gas pedal all the way to the floor, crossing her fingers that the town was big enough to have a hospital.

In the distance, Seph could see a farmhouse: surprisingly well-lit despite the late hour, with a wrap-around porch and smoke curling out of the chimney. They were three quarters of the way to the farmhouse when an alarm started dinging, accompanied by a flashing dashboard light. Marin opened his eyes and smiled slightly.

"I expected that to happen," he said. "The tires are losing air. Baine probably knifed them to slow us down. Wasn't sure if he was going to siphon the gas tank or flatten the tires, but I knew he'd do something."

The truck started to decelerate and began bouncing up and down as the tires lost pressure. Seph clung to the large steering wheel, trying to maintain control of the vehicle, which had begun veering from side to side.

"We're not going to make it to town," she said. "Not in this vehicle, anyway." She turned hard right on the wheel, aiming the truck for the narrow dirt lane that led to the farmhouse. They skirted past a crooked mailbox bearing the name "Moirai," and the truck chugged to a rest about fifteen feet from the front door. Seph jumped out and ran over to the passenger side. "Come on. We're going in." She pulled him out, nearly falling as his weight collapsed out of the seat and onto her shoulders.

The yard had no sidewalk, so she dragged him down the dark garden path leading to the front porch. The path was lined on both sides by the same plant as in the surrounding fields, and the foliage's shrubby bark scratched and tore at her ankles in protest as she trampled the blossoms without mercy. Their scent was sickeningly sweet and clung to her pant legs. Lavender. They were surrounded by fields of lavender. *You smell like purple flowers.* She heard Baine's voice mocking her desperation.

Seph jogged up the porch steps to the front door and pounded on it with her fist. "Please, open up. We need help! Please!" She grabbed the door knob to give it a jiggle and was surprised when it turned in her hand. The door swung open, but there was no one on the other side. She hoisted Marin up the steps, over the threshold and into the foyer, where she helped him lie down on the old oak floors. "Hello?" She smelled a fire burning and saw its light flickering through the doorway on her right. She tentatively stepped into the room.

The farmhouse was old, as evidenced by the exposed beams, wide plank floors and crumbling stone hearth; but its occupants appeared absolutely ancient, wrinkled and shriveled up like fallen autumn leaves ready to be blown away by the upcoming winter winds. The women sat on a threadbare velvet sofa in front of the warm fire, one right next to the other, and their facial similarities suggested they were sisters.

The woman seated on the end closest to Seph was rolling a ball of yarn as if her life depended on it, weaving the strings back and forth in intricate patterns. The one seated in the middle was doing embroidery, her arthritic fingers still able to deftly manipulate the fine needle and silk threads with ease. The third sat scrutinizing the orange flames, occasionally nodding her head as if she were mystically communicating with the dancing embers in a language only she understood.

The middle woman, who appeared to be the youngest of the three, glanced up from her needlepoint as Seph entered the room. Despite the fact that it was nearly three a.m., she didn't seem at all surprised to see a bloodied and frantic stranger walk into her living room, and she offered Seph a toothless smile.

Seph raised her blood-covered hands for emphasis and pointed toward the hallway where she'd left Marin. "We need help." She stepped forward and gestured for them to get up and follow her. Seph's movement jostled the fire whisperer out of her reverie. The old woman turned to fix her intense gaze on Seph's face, her eyes unexpectedly alert for her advanced age. As she rose from the sofa, a pair of antique silver scissors fell out of her lap, landing on the hardwood floor with a clatter that she either ignored or did not hear. Her two sisters followed her lead, and Seph guided them to the foyer, where Marin lay prostrate and bleeding. Their faces did not change at the scene before them.

"Do you have a phone?" Seph mimed holding a phone to her ear. The youngest shook her head, her expression solemn. Marin repeated the question in French but received the same negative response. He asked a few more questions, projecting his voice with as much force as he could muster in an attempt to overcome their deafness. Finally he hit the jackpot, receiving both a "oui" and a smile. The spinster tugged on Seph's elbow, pulling her toward the back of the house.

Seph resisted, not wanting to leave Marin alone with the strange old women. But the spinster was insistent, so Seph followed her through the house, out the back door and through the yard until they reached a barn. The weatherbeaten building listed precariously to the left, its fissured glass windows cloudy with age and exposure. Moonlight shone through gaping holes in the roof, illuminating a large, black mass parked in the middle of the barn's first floor.

The spinster unbarred the sliding door and pushed it wide open, then groped around in the dark for the cord to the overhead light. The bulb clicked on, revealing a tarp-covered vehicle, its tires peeking modestly out from beneath its black skirt. Like a magician uncovering a dove, she pulled the tarp away with a flourish and released a heavy plume of dust, feathers, and hay in the process. Seph coughed and blinked a few times to clear her vision before focusing on the vehicle that would become Marin's ambulance.

The vintage Renault was a beauty, its French-blue finish unblemished despite years of cohabitating with pigeons in the decrepit barn. It had to be at least sixty years old, but Seph doubted it had been driven more than a thousand miles in its lifetime. The old woman pointed Seph in the direction of a nearby gas can and picked up an antique milk bottle nestled in the corner of the barn. She turned it upside down, and out spilled the keys, landing on a heap of hay.

"*Merci*," Seph said, as she grabbed the keys and the gas can. She slid into the driver's seat and jammed the key into the ignition. *C'mon, baby, c'mon.* The motor turned over several times but would not start. Seph had a bleak vision of the cobwebs and nesting mice living side by side under the hood. *C'mon, baby, please!* She'd just about given up hope when the Renault decided to stop playing coy and purred back to life.

The old woman clasped her hands together and beamed as Seph eased the car out of the garage and around to the front of the house. After driving the clunky military vehicle, the Renault felt positively posh. She left the motor running and hurried back to the foyer to retrieve Marin. What she saw stopped her dead in her tracks.

Seph wasn't sure how two feeble, elderly women accomplished such a feat, but Marin had been moved. He was now lying on a moth-eaten, army green wool blanket positioned atop a makeshift cot of cobbled together suitcases and milk crates. His legs were propped at a forty-five degree angle on a stack of pillows, and his pants and the pressure dressing had been stripped off and were lying in a bloody heap of shredded fabric interspersed with some discarded silk threads.

The sisters were hunched over Marin's wounded leg, and on the floor next to them sat a glass apothecary jar containing a fine, white powder. One woman's fingertips were caked with the mysterious substance, which she'd packed into Marin's wound. Her sister held an old-fashioned, plunger style needle and glass syringe containing several ccs of a cloudy liquid, and she plunged it into Marin's thigh before Seph could scream in protest.

"What are you doing?" Seph ran to Marin's side and placed a restraining hand on the old woman's right arm. Whatever was in the syringe worked fast, because Marin began mumbling incoherently as his consciousness slipped away. With her job completed the woman stood, straightening her back as much as her kyphosis would allow. She nodded to her sisters. They joined her in moving single file toward the top edge of the blanket above Marin's head. They all three grabbed the hem and motioned for Seph to do the same at the bottom. Much to Seph's surprise, the four of them were able to easily lift and carry Marin to the Renault, where they cradled him on the back seat.

The sisters backed away as Seph jumped behind the wheel and slammed the car into gear, churning up a cloud of dust and lavender. She sped as fast as the Renault would carry them down the dirt lane and toward the main road. Only after she'd safely made the turn onto the asphalt did she dare peek into her rear view mirror. The three strange women still stood outside the dilapidated farmhouse, their gnarled figures nothing but dark silhouettes against the light of the moon.

Seph realized she hadn't even thanked them, but she wasn't sure if thanks were in order. She couldn't shake the image of them leaning over Marin's limp body, and she was consumed by a mounting wave of panic at the thought of what might have been in that syringe. She pushed the Renault even harder, flogging it until the needle hit upward of 128 kph, and she forced her mind to concentrate only on the dark road ahead and not on the what ifs.

Seph and Marin arrived at the outskirts of town around four a.m. Marin had long since stopped mumbling, but Seph was too afraid to call out his name lest she get no response. She slowed down only when she maneuvered the Renault onto the empty streets of the tiny French town, ignoring the stop lights as she followed the blue signs that led her to the hospital.

She screeched to a halt at the emergency entrance, honking her horn like a mad woman to get some attention. Seph had her hand on the Renault's handle, ready to roll out the driver's door, when Marin surprised her by speaking.

"Doc, I need you to pray with me."

Seph stopped mid-motion and gripped the door handle until her fingers hurt. "We don't have time for that right now. We need to get you inside. Besides, you know I can't do that." Her voice was barely a whisper. "I don't remember how."

"Yes, you do." The strength of his conviction belied his fragile state. "Please."

Please. That one word was nearly her undoing, and she blinked hard to keep the tears from falling. *Not yet. Just a few minutes more, and you will have done everything you could have possibly done for him.* Everything, that is, except pray. Would it be so bad, too hypocritical for her to say words she did not believe, and had not believed in a very long time, if they gave him comfort?

Seph could hear her mother, whose religious convictions were matched only by her pragmatism. *For heaven's sake, just pray for the man, Persephone! He's dying!* Seph pushed on the door handle and got out, opening the back door so she could lean into Marin's line of sight.

"Okay, Paul." Seph tried to keep her voice light but ruined it with a sniffle. "I will pray *for* you, but not *with* you, because . . ." She motioned toward the triage team running in their direction, gurney in tow. ". . . right now, these fine people are coming to save your life. Don't give them any trouble, okay? And you still owe me a shot of tequila. Don't think you're wiggling out of it so easily." She faked a smile and squeezed his hand before stepping out of the way.

The next few minutes were a flurry of activity as the hospital staff transferred Marin out of the vehicle and onto the litter. They whisked him away through the sliding double doors into the emergency room, leaving a stunned Persephone standing alone next to the idling Renault. Moving on autopilot, she got back into the car and eased it into a legitimate parking space in the visitors' lot. Seph turned off the ignition, and, as she felt the final bit of energy sputter out of the engine, she lowered her head to the steering wheel and began to sob.

Chapter Twenty-Seven

The Resurrection

Marin fluctuated in and out of consciousness for the better part of two weeks following his emergency surgery. The hospital staff had been decimated by the virus, and the facility had no untainted blood available for transfusion, so his recovery was slow and never assumed. Thankfully, there was no shortage of morphine, so Marin was able to remain blissfully unaware of his situation. Seph, on the other hand, fretted endlessly.

When she wasn't at the hospital, Seph holed up in a local hotel, and she occupied her time by talking to Grace and Eric, now back at the Centers for Disease Control's headquarters in Atlanta, on a regular basis.

"The inoculation program has been a success, and I'm optimistic we've halted the virus in its tracks," Eric said during their last conversation. "We've had no new cases in a week, which is a fantastic sign. Even more importantly, the populace has faith in the cure, hastening the recovery efforts. People are returning to work, businesses are reopening, and even air traffic has resumed—as long as you can prove you've gotten the vaccination. The cities were hardest hit and will take the longest to recover, but a lot of the smaller, more self-reliant communities are doing just fine."

Eric paused and lowered his voice. "Some of my peers are even touting the benefits of such a drastic reduction in the population. They've already documented an improvement in the ozone layer, for example. The environment's crawling toward a new state of equilibrium."

"Great. I'm sure Baine would be happy to hear that. Maybe your peers would like to join him in his super-secret research lab and help him churn out the next catastrophe."

"I wouldn't go that far." Eric chuckled. "I know you're upset you didn't catch him . . ."

"Ya think?"

"But the truth is, you convinced him to give up the cure to his virus, and that's all we needed. You saved the world, Seph."

"That's embarrassing and untrue." Seph cringed at his statement.

"It *is* true! Now go relax on an island somewhere."

"I will, but not until after Marin's discharged."

Homeland Security dispatched Marin's partner, Special Agent Craig Patterson, whom she'd met briefly in New York, to join her in Saint-Genis-Pouilly. He was young and formal—in short, everything Marin was not—and his primary assignments were to investigate the details of Baine's escape and to assist the local authorities with analyzing the Customs and Border Security Building crime scene. However, he also offered, in his overly polite way, to relieve Seph of her duties and allow her to return home "if she so desired." She did so desire, but she stayed anyway, mostly because Peggy was dead.

Later that night—the night of the grenade and the force field, the lavender and the old hags—after Seph had exhausted herself crying and snotting all over the Renault's refined, leather-clad steering wheel, she'd gathered herself together and walked into the hospital's main waiting room. She needed a phone. She had to call Grace. Her search for Peggy started with an innocent question asked via a translator. *Êtes-vous sa femme?* Are you his wife?

In that instant, Seph realized that not once, *not once* had she asked Marin if he had any family. And she was a psychologist, for Christ's sake! Marin knew about her Grace, but Seph had no clue if Marin had anyone she should notify if the worst should happen, anyone he'd been worrying about back home, anyone who might have died from Baine's virus. All she had to go on was her recollection of Marin's wedding ring and the tattoo on his right bicep, the crucifix adorned with "Peggy." Her first call was to Grace. She almost sobbed with relief when her sister answered the phone.

"Well, it took you long enough!"

"I'm sorry. I was underground, and then I lost my phone . . . it's a long story. How *are* you?"

"I'm fine. False alarm, praise the Lord. Ellie had that ear infection, and I guess I caught a cold from her. I shouldn't have worried you, but I was a little freaked out at the time."

"Yeah, I know what you mean . . ."

Seph's second call was to Homeland Security. She'd pumped them for information, explaining that Marin was near death and asking if he had an emergency contact, but the apathetic voice at the other end simply turfed her to his partner, Special Agent Patterson.

When Agent Patterson arrived in France, Seph had pounced on him before he cleared the hospital's lobby, ushering him to a seat and grilling him until he broke.

"I need info on Marin's personal contacts. And don't tell me to call central office, 'cause I already did that."

"Agent Marin likes to keep his personal life personal."

"Yeah, well, he might die. And if so, his personal life dies with him. He has to have somebody to notify. You may as well cough it up, kiddo, if you want to get any sleep over the new few days. I'll wear you down eventually."

"Kiddo?" Agent Patterson frowned, creasing his baby face. "I'm not much younger than you."

"It's not the age; it's the experience. You're outclassed." Seph stretched back in her chair and pulled an old fashioned Dictaphone she'd borrowed from the hospital out of her pocket. She held it in front of his face. "Just speak into the device, and we both get to have a nice day."

Agent Patterson hesitated, but only for a moment. "I can see why he likes you."

"He said that?" Seph leaned forward again, ruining her tough act with her overzealous response.

"Not in those words. I think what he actually said was that you have moxie. For him, that's a compliment."

Seph chuckled at the old fashioned term. So very Marin. "Well, then, Agent Patterson, you'd better start talking lest you be at the receiving end of my moxie. You wouldn't want that, now would you?"

"No, ma'am."

"So let's start with his wife. Peggy, right?"

Peggy, Marin's wife of forty years, died of breast cancer a year before William Baine became public enemy number one. Marin briefly retired to become her caretaker but, not content to sit and mourn, returned to duty after her death.

"Anyone else?"

"He has an older brother. Charlie, I think. He lives in a VA nursing home. Marin says Charlie's so demented, he doesn't even remember his own name. Not a good candidate for an emergency contact."

"What about kids?"

"One." Agent Patterson squirmed in his seat, and Seph's radar blipped.

"Son or daughter?"

"Daughter. Karen. Went to the Naval Academy."

"What year did she graduate?" Seph asked.

"Why?"

"Because my sister went to the Naval Academy."

"Oh." Silence.

"Where is she now?" Seph kept prodding, refusing to let Patterson off the hook despite his obvious discomfort.

"How would I know where your sister is?"

"*Karen,* you smart ass!"

"I don't know."

"Yes, you do!" By now, Seph was wishing she had Marin's cigar cutter handy.

"Honestly, I don't. She . . . she disappeared. I know that much. Right after graduation. He never talked about it. If the subject of family ever came up, he would just say 'let it be.' He never seemed broken up about it, though. I assumed . . ." Agent Patterson lowered his voice, as if the rural French hospital had spies hiding under every gurney, "I assumed she went into Naval intelligence, Dark Ops-type stuff. Either way, you're not going to find her. I don't think Marin even knows where she is."

Seph had tried, digging deep into the cesspool of dirty contacts she'd made over the last ten years, but to no avail. So with no family to contact, Seph did what came hardest to her. She sat and waited.

Seph didn't want Marin, after all he had been through, opening his eyes to anything but a familiar face; since Agent Patterson was spending most of his days at the Customs building, that familiar face would have to be hers. So she sat by his side and did crossword puzzles and watched TV and did all those other banal things people do while they wait for their loved ones to awaken from their narcotic-induced comas.

She left town only once, on a beautifully crisp and sunny autumn day. She had persuaded Agent Patterson into following her back to the farmhouse so she could return the freshly detailed Renault, with a fruit basket strapped in its passenger seat as a long overdue thank you gift, to its rightful owners.

The drive back was surreal; both unfamiliar and shorter than it had seemed a few weeks ago, even though she was driving at a much more leisurely pace. No one answered the door at the farmhouse, which was still and quiet except for the hushed murmur of the surrounding lavender as its branches brushed together and trembled in the breeze.

Seph left the fruit basket on the porch and pulled the Renault around back, parking it in the barn, the doors of which still stood wide open. She patted the hood, covered it with the tarp, and dropped the keys back into the milk bottle before sliding the barn doors shut again. Agent Patterson waited for her around front, and they drove back to the hospital in silence, allowing themselves to enjoy the pacific French countryside after the frenzy of the last two months.

Marin was awake and sitting upright in his bed when Seph entered his room. If she hadn't been so relieved, she would have been pissed off. She had waited around for two whole weeks, sitting at the foot of Marin's bed like a faithful mutt, just to be there when he woke up, and he ruined it.

Seph found it tough to stay angry when he looked so rough, his face wan and wasted from not eating. Marin appeared fragile in the paper-thin hospital gown, with IV lines and tubing sticking out from every angle, but his mood was upbeat, and his broad smile told her everything she needed to know. He was going to be okay.

"Doc, how the hell are ya?" His voice shook, but his attitude was intact.

"I should be the one asking you that question. Welcome back to the land of the living," Seph said as she moved to stand next to his hospital bed, her hands resting on the side rails.

"How about it! Craig taking good care of you?" He nodded in the direction of the door, where Agent Patterson was discretely hovering.

"Of course. He even offered to arrange for my flight home, but I wanted to make sure you were all tucked in before I left. You know, that sense of closure thing."

Marin's face clouded over. "I don't think either of us is going to have much closure knowing Baine is still out there. Any guesses as to where he went?"

"Agent Patterson hasn't found any clues at the Customs building, but I'm guessing Baine was pre-paid, at least in part, by the Russians and had a new home base set up and ready to go for after the second wave of the virus. They're probably searching for him, too. Maybe you two could join forces..."

Marin snorted and shook his head in disgust. "I just hope we never hear from the bastard again."

"We did everything we could. At least, that's what I keep telling myself. Baine's virus is all but beaten, and even though he's still a free man, he's going to have to hide under some really slimy rocks for the rest of his natural life instead of being the worshipful master of some new world order like he had envisioned."

Seph changed the subject. She would hear from Baine again. He had her wallet and cell phone from the truck. If he didn't know everything about her before, he did now. She wasn't ready to think about that in detail yet. "Did you get your vaccine today?"

"Not yet. Before discharge, they said. I've got a week or so left to go. They told me I need to walk around a bit, get some strength back in my legs before they'll let me out. When are you heading home?"

"I'm not sure yet. I was thinking of taking the train to Paris, enjoying the fall scenery en route, and then spending a week in the city. I'm planning on taking a really long vacation with my sister next year, but there's no reason I can't start now. Live for the moment and all that crap. Figured I'd hang around here until I'm sure you can survive without me!"

"I think I can handle it from here. You've done enough already. I really need to thank you..."

"You don't need to thank me for anything," Seph said, interrupting him out of guilt and embarrassment. She flashed back to that night a few weeks ago when she'd brought him to the emergency room. *I need you to pray with me.* Seph had promised to pray for him, but she never did. At first, she'd been so distracted with checking on Grace and hunting down his next of kin that her promise slipped her mind. She only remembered it when Marin had received a visit from the hospital chaplain.

One afternoon, while she was sitting at his bedside as usual, l'Abbé Henri had arrived to pray over Marin's unconscious body, reciting scripture in French and making the Sign of the Cross so many times Seph lost count. She'd stared at the portly, rosy-cheeked priest as he conducted his business, clinically fascinated by his religious fervor and the absolute conviction on his face, until he turned that attention to her.

Henri had clasped both her hands in his own and, fixing his gaze up toward the heavens, prayed with all his Catholic might. Seph had squirmed and attempted to demur with a gentle tug of her hands, but the priest didn't seem to notice, so intent was he on saving her unconverted soul. He spoke no English; Seph, face flushed with irritation, had gritted her teeth and tolerated his unwanted attention as best she could.

When Henri finally left, Seph remembered thinking that Marin had received all the prayer he could possibly ever need, and from an expert at that. He didn't need her feeble and disingenuous attempts. So Seph had *not* prayed for him as requested, and she had to say: so far, so good. He was still alive. Didn't stop her from feeling a wee bit guilty, though.

"Yes, I do need to thank you." Marin, unaware of the thoughts racing through Seph's mind, forged onward. "You never gave up on me, Doc, and I appreciate it, especially given my, uh, *concerns* about your relationship with Baine. Back in the day, I knew some Marines who would've wet their pants if they were caught in some of the situations we were in, but you stuck it out." Marin paused to fidget with one of his IV lines before continuing.

"I should thank those women, too, before I leave France. Whatever they did saved my life. The surgeon said he knew of them. Two of them had been nurses in World War II, and the third sister was rumored to have worked for the French underground. He said they managed to stop my bleeding with a clotting powder intended for horse hooves, and if they hadn't, I would have never made it to the hospital!"

"That makes a lot of sense," Seph said, thinking back to the army blanket, the apothecary jars and the glass syringe. "I tried to thank them today when I returned their car, but no one was home. I left them a fruit basket."

Marin's face turned serious, and he lowered his voice so Agent Patterson could not hear what he was about to say. He fixed his gaze on the strings of his hospital gown and plucked at them nervously. "The surgeon said he thought all three sisters had died from the virus."

"Really? That's strange. They didn't seem at all sick that night."

Marin looked up to meet her eyes. "With the first outbreak. The first wave."

It took a second for his meaning to register. "That's not possible."

"That's what I said, but I was pretty out of it that night. I thought maybe I was hallucinating . . ."

"But I wasn't," Seph said, interrupting Marin yet again. "You must have misunderstood him." She shook her head for emphasis. "I know what I saw." Her voice was firm and final.

"Mmm. Maybe so." Marin was smart enough to realize that the subject was hereby closed. "Anyway, I expect you to be on a train to Paris within the next forty-eight hours, you hear me? I don't need you to hold my hand while I do my physical therapy. Agent Patterson?"

Agent Patterson detached himself from the doorway and moved to stand next to Seph. "Yes, sir."

"See to it that Dr. Smith gets home safe and sound."

"Right away, sir."

"I'll see you around, Doc. You work out of Washington, right? I'm there from time to time, whenever I need to make a pilgrimage to the 'Big House.' Next time I'm in town, I'll give you a holler and we'll do lunch, as they say. Until then, you stay out of trouble, okay?"

"If I stayed out of trouble, I wouldn't have a job," Seph replied, extending her hand to give his a quick squeeze, "and neither would you. See you back in the States." She turned to leave but spun back around as one final thought ran through her mind.

"One more thing before I go. I want you to know in case you get any phone calls about it. I tried to find Karen for you. I thought you might've wanted her here with you."

Marin's eyebrows shot up in surprise, and he twisted in his bed to glower at his partner. Agent Patterson suddenly seemed to find the dripping IV line an utterly fascinating object at which to stare.

"Any luck with that?" Marin asked.

"No," Seph replied.

"Didn't think so."

Seph waited for a moment to see if he was going to add anything more, but Marin remained silent. Seph gave him a slight nod and another smile and then, accompanied by Agent Patterson, she turned and walked out the door.

Chapter Twenty-Eight

All Souls

October 14th, 2016
Paris, France

Seph was ensconced in a luxe Paris hotel within the week. The train ride was long and uncomfortable, but the rhythmic swaying of her passenger car was hypnotic, and the gentle movement gave her brain some long overdue downtime in which to process the events of the past few months. The cadence of the wheels on the tracks broke her thoughts into little sound bites. *Clickety-clack.* The world was different now. *Clickety-clack.* She was different now, too, with an uneasy empathetic connection to a master criminal-at-large which was hopefully counterbalanced by a healthy relationship with her new colleague and—dare she say the word—friend in Agent Paul Marin. *Clickety-clack.* Seph smiled at the thought of him. Their paths would cross again someday in the future. He was on her list. And despite her vow to take more time to enjoy life, she couldn't afford to stay on vacation forever. *Clickety-clack.*

Seph spent two weeks in the City of Light, reveling in the "new her" by doing things she would have previously considered unthinkably frivolous. She got a manicure and had her long hair, untouched since grad school, cut into a chic bob. She ignored an apologetic text from Dan by flirting with a much-younger waiter at the café where she ate her daily *pain au chocolat*.

Unfortunately, Baine stayed in Paris with her, lurking in the back of her mind no matter how hard she tried to distract herself. He threatened to assert himself only once, when she walked into a *parfumerie* and was assaulted by the overwhelming scent of lavender and roses. At that moment, if Seph had closed her eyes, she would've felt certain Baine was standing right next to her, his intense stare boring into her soul.

She hurried out of the boutique and threw herself into Christmas shopping for Grace and her nieces, sampling chocolates and wines until she could eat and drink no more. Then, and only then, was it finally time for the new Persephone Smith to return home.

Seph touched down in Washington D.C. on November 2nd and, determined to continue her newfound spontaneity, she opted against returning home to her apartment. She spent most of her time on the road anyway, so, as much as she hated to admit it, her apartment was nearly as barren as Baine's. Instead, she rented a car and started her drive up the East Coast to visit Grace and her family in Maine. She would surprise them by being there not just for Christmas, but for Thanksgiving as well.

Seph clicked on the radio's frequency scanner, and the first thing it settled on was a Catholic station airing a liturgy

for "The Commemoration of All the Faithful Departed"—
All Soul's Day. The Holy Day held a special significance this
year, given the estimated two billion who had died worldwide. *That's a lot of souls for whom to pray.* Seph couldn't help
but think of Cecilia, and she changed the channel as her eyes
misted over. She would mourn for all of them, but not today.

All things considered, Seph knew she'd been lucky.
Whether by accident or by her own subconscious design, she
had less to lose than most from this plague: no friends to
speak of, no God to renounce and no family except her sister.
Unlike countless others, Grace and her family had survived
unscathed, and for that Seph was grateful. She still had a lot
of celebrating to do, a lot of making up for lost time spent
fumbling in the dark, and she decided it would be a long
while before she accepted her next criminal case.

She took two days to drive to Maine. She didn't call
Grace until she was a half hour away, and when she pulled
up to the front porch, Seph was met with a flurry of kids
and dogs; hugs and kisses, exactly the way she'd envisioned it.
Gracie oohed and aahed over Seph's new hairdo, proclaim-
ing she looked "wicked good," which she was assured was a
compliment.

It wasn't until later that evening, after the kids had finally
settled down enough to occupy themselves by playing outdoors in the newly fallen snow, that Seph realized something
was amiss. She was helping Grace get dinner ready, chatting
about the usual nothing in particular, when Tom excused
himself and went to the den to watch football. Once Grace
heard the door click shut behind him, her whole affect
changed. She lowered her voice as she spoke.

"Did you mail me something from France?" Grace asked, ferociously plucking the feathers off a recently decapitated chicken.

"No."

"Well, then, were you *expecting* a package from France?"

"No. Why?" Seph felt the bile rising in her throat, and it wasn't from the mass of bloody feathers in the sink.

Grace stopped her plucking and wiped her hands, then turned to face Seph. "It's in the barn. I was afraid to bring it in the house after what happened the last time. Tom and the kids don't know about it."

"Do you have any idea what it is?"

"No. The box is fairly good-sized, but it was delivered through the post office, so I doubt it contains another pot of fresh flowers. I have to feed the animals after dinner. Thought maybe you could come with me, take a look."

Seph nodded, her mind racing through various scenarios as to what could be in the box, and more importantly, what Baine was trying to tell her. It had to be from Baine. *Didn't it?*

She faked her way through dinner with Tom and the kids. After the dishes were cleared, she and Grace casually announced they were heading over to the barn to take care of the animals. The moon glinted off the icy surface of the snow, illuminating their path through the dark. Duncan joined them on their trek, seemingly much happier than Seph to be outside on a November evening in Maine. The air was so bitterly cold Seph swore she could feel the inside of her nose freeze the minute she stepped off the porch.

"How can you live here?" she asked Grace.

"You get used to it."

Seph doubted that very much. At least the barn was heated. Grace's mare, Hope, nickered a gentle greeting when they entered, and Seph rubbed the horse's nose with her gloved hands. She helped Grace with her chores, and then Grace directed her to the stall next to Hope's. Sitting on the hay was a standard, brown, corrugated cardboard shipping box, two feet square with an international shipping label.

Seph moved in to take a closer look. The box had no other identifying marks and no return address label.

"At least it's not ticking," she said. Her sister did not appear amused. "Is it heavy?"

"Not particularly. I had no trouble carrying it myself. Has some weight, though. I don't think it's empty."

Seph picked it up and gave it a gentle shake. It made no noise beyond the slight rustle of what sounded like packing materials, but when she put it up to her ear and repeated the motion, she thought she detected the subtle smell of laven-der. *You're imaging things.* Seph scolded herself.

"Do you think it's from him?" Grace asked, whispering again although there was no one nearby to hear.

"Probably."

"What do you think we should do? Should we ask the police to open it?"

"No." Seph quickly nixed that idea. She had a mental image of the local bomb squad, all decked out in full regalia, opening the box behind a blast screen only to find a pair of lacy French panties from someone besides Baine. Like Dan, for instance.

"I'll take it back to FBI headquarters when I leave. They'll be able to analyze it more in depth before deciding what to do. You know, x-ray, chemical swabs, the whole shebang. In the meantime, we leave it here and forget about it until after the holidays. At least, unless it starts to smell like rotten flesh or something. Or unless Hope drops over dead."

"That's not funny." Grace looked close to tears.

"I know. You're right. That wasn't funny. I'm sorry." Seph put her arm around Gracie's shoulder and gave her a squeeze.

They walked arm in arm back to the farmhouse, neither speaking. Before they went in, Seph put her hands on Grace's shoulders. "You gonna be okay?"

"Yes. You don't really think something bad is going to happen if we leave the package there, do you?"

"No, I absolutely do not," Seph said, mentally kicking herself in the ass for being so cavalier. It was okay for her to talk like that with callous detectives, but she should've known better than to say something like that around her more fragile sister. "Now, come on, we need to get the kids ready for bed."

They never discussed the package again, although every time Grace went out to the barn to do her chores, Seph went with her. She'd pet Hope and eyeball the box for any apparent changes. Thankfully, none occurred. The box sat on its haystack, as static and mysterious as the Sphinx, begging for attention that Seph was not yet willing to give.

She stayed with Grace and her nieces through the New Year's holiday before renting another car to drive back to her apartment in Washington, D.C. Seph started out with the package on the back seat but found herself staring at it in the rear view mirror often enough that she almost ran herself off the road. Twice.

After the second event, Seph pulled over and got out of the car, cursing as she sank ankle deep in the January snow.

She removed the package from the back seat and shoved it in the trunk where it belonged. Out of sight, out of mind. Right. If only it worked that way.

Maybe that was Baine's ultimate plan, to drive her mad from fretting over what was in that goddamned box. Fuck 'im. When she got back to D.C., she was turning the box over to the FBI and making a courtesy phone call to her old friend Agent Marin at Homeland Security to fill him in on the situation. Marin would want to know. Besides, he still owed her a shot of tequila. Then she was done, out, finished with Dr. William Baine. *Until he resurfaces.* A little voice in Seph's head whispered the truth. Baine's ego all but guaranteed that he would. She would deal with that eventuality when it occurred.

Seph had just hit Upstate New York when her cell phone rang. Her stomach twisted as she considered who might be calling. She touched the on button to activate her Bluetooth and answered the call.

"Dr. Persephone Smith." She kept her eyes fixed on the road ahead. Her jaw clenched despite her efforts to remain cool and professional.

"Doc," said a familiar voice on the other end. "Have I got a case for you!"

Acknowledgements

To the Freemasons, for making a good man better.
    To Paul, who helped me start
    To Holly, who kept me going
    And to Angela, Annie, and Mom, who helped me finish
    My thanks and everlasting love.

About the Author

Dr. J. L. Delozier submitted her first story, handwritten in pencil on lined school paper, to Isaac Asimov's magazine while still in junior high school. Several years later, she took a creative writing elective at Penn State University and was hooked. She received her BS and MD degrees in a compact six years, which was followed by the blur of internship, residency and the launch of her medical career. But she never forgot her first love. When she sat down to write her debut thriller, she spent some time rediscovering her favorite physician writers. From the deductive reasoning of Sir Arthur Conan Doyle to the cutting edge science of Michael Crichton, she remains inspired by facts that lie on the edge of reality: bizarre medical anomalies, new genetic discoveries and so on. These are the backbone of *Type and Cross*.

Dr. Delozier spent the early part of her career as a rural family doctor and then later as a government physician, caring for America's veterans and deploying to disasters such as Hurricanes Katrina, Ike and Gustav. She continues to practice medicine and lives in Pennsylvania with her husband and four rescue cats.

FIC DEL
DeLozier, J. L.,
  Type and Cross

CPSIA information can be obtained
at www.ICGtesting.com
Printed in the USA
LVOW10s1417291017
554201LV00010B/253/P

Jan 2018